A TOUCH AWAY

Dearest Nzinga,
Tonight has been . . . shall I say . . . hectic? Something has happened. Something I'm not proud of, but I feel as though I've come one giant step closer to you. Please don't ask me how. All I know is that I made a decision this evening. And whatever happens between us, know that I am committed to you—to us. All of this rambling must sound strange at best, but I know what I feel. And what I feel is beholden to you. And now that I've gone on and on about me, tell me, what keeps you busy these days? What makes you smile?

A TOUCH AWAY

Kim Louise

BET Publications, LLC
www.bet.com
www.arabesquebooks.com

ARABESQUE BOOKS are published by

BET Publications, LLC
c/o BET BOOKS
One BET Plaza
1900 W Place NE
Washington, D.C. 20018-1211

ISBN 0-7394-2013-5

Printed in the United States of America

For my grandmothers, Goldie and Josephine.
For my aunts, Louise and Francis.
Now I know . . .

ACKNOWLEDGMENTS

I wouldn't have been able to write this book without my support system: my critique group (I'll beat those passives yet!), Cameo Writers (I promise to improve my attendance), Deanne Adams (for catching my mistakes and liking me anyway), Steve (the coolest son on the planet!), and the employees at Woodmen of the World (for making me feel like a celebrity). Thank you all!

Prologue

To: *Nzinga@blackluv.net*
From: *Osiris@blackluv.net*

Dearest Nzinga,
I know we've discussed this before, but things are different now. It's been months, and I feel so much closer to you—close enough to touch. My dearest Nzinga, warrior woman with soft breath, I believe it's time for us to meet.
Do you still have the amulet I sent you? I pray it remains in your care. Wear it, so I'll know who you are. Will you meet me at Carrie's Café tomorrow night? 7 P.M. Please say yes. My heart has waited so long for you. This separation is like a knife twisting in my soul. And I can't stand it any longer.
Yours forever,
Osiris

To: *Osiris@blackluv.net*
From: *Nzinga@blackluv.net*

My Dearest Osiris,
We have discussed this before. And before I was fearful of opening myself to a stranger. But during these months, I have come to expect your presence in my life as surely as my own heartbeat. My beloved Osiris, Nubian man of the bright sun, I will meet with you.

I have kept your amulet close to my breast where it reminds me of you. I will wear it tomorrow, so that you will recognize me at Carrie's Café. To your first step, I will add my own. Soon our long wait will be over.

Forever yours,

Nzinga

One

The trash bag was almost full. In it Sonji Stephens had placed all of the items that Chad Lovelace had left in her town house. As she filled the bag, she remembered his last words to her before he walked out of her life: "I don't want anything that will remind me of you."

And so all of the things she had bought for him, all of the things he had purchased for himself when they were together, and all of the things he had brought from home to keep at her place were left behind.

During the six months since the breakup, Sonji had been reluctant to do a thorough search for Chad's belongings. She knew she would find them in every nook and cranny of her home. Even though her relationship with Chad had lasted only two years, she had let him into every aspect of her life. Removing these leftovers would confirm that the relationship was over.

But today, after realizing that her life had almost come to a standstill since Chad had left, Sonji took the garbage bag from the kitchen cabinet and started rummaging through her home in search of every remnant of Chad she could find.

As she stuffed the bag with memories, Sonji replayed the details of the worst day of her life. She had been upstairs dressing for the opera. Chad was taking her to see *Porgy and Bess*. She was applying the finishing touches to her makeup when the doorbell rang.

Sonji glanced at the clock. *Chad's early,* she thought, slipping her feet into a pair of eggshell sling-back pumps and rushing downstairs. When she opened the door, a woman with striking features and expensive clothing stood on the stairs looking regal and slightly annoyed.

"Yes?" Sonji said, assuming she was about to be asked for directions.

"You know who I am?" The slight lift in the woman's voice turned the statement into a question. Sonji also detected a hint of authority sliding around in the woman's tone. But she had never seen the woman before.

"No, I don't," Sonji replied, frowning.

The woman flashed a ring the size of Texas at Sonji. "I'm Mrs. Lovelace. Mrs. *Chad* Lovelace."

Sonji's face fell, and her heart went into a slow crash and burn right there in her doorway. She stared at the woman in disbelief and blinked back the tears beginning to sting her eyes.

"We need to talk," the woman said, ushering herself past Sonji and into the house. Her floral perfume trailed behind her in a strong and thick backwash.

"Wait a minute," Sonji said, trying to prevent her from just walking in, but it was too late. The woman was already in the middle of her living room, standing like a statue with her arms folded in front of her. Sonji closed the door and stepped closer to her, taking in the sight of the woman who had barged into her home.

She was quite tall. Sonji figured the woman to be about three inches taller than her own five-feet, seven inches. The trench coat had to be a Don Carmello original, and the collar was definitely mink. The coat was wrapped well, but the woman was obviously trying to bulk up her size, which couldn't have been larger than a size four.

"They always want to compare themselves to me," the woman said, stretching her arms out to her sides. "And that's precisely why I'm here."

"You are Chad's *wife?*"

"Is that so hard to believe?" the woman asked, propping her hands on her hips. She walked around the living room examining Sonji's things. "Of course it is. He never mentioned me, isn't that right?" the woman asked. And then as if talking to herself, she answered. "Why certainly I'm right. He never does mention me, you know. Never."

Mrs. Chad Lovelace admired her reflection in a brass-framed mirror on Sonji's wall and continued talking. "Don't worry, you're not the only fool. Sometimes Chad's little excursions have gone on for more years than yours." The woman spun around on her heel and peered at Sonji like a wolf in charge of a clever secret. "But they all come to an end."

Sonji felt her resolve crumbling. "But . . . but . . ."

"I know dear, I know. You've been to his home, you've called him at home, etcetera, etcetera." The woman made a dismissive motion with her hands. "The place he takes you to belongs to me. I bought it for Chad during our first year of marriage when I caught him in our bed with another woman. I told him if he was going to sleep with trash, he should at least have the decency to keep it in the street where it belongs."

Sonji slumped down in her chair and put her head in her hands. There was no stopping the tears now. The shock had overwhelmed her, and they came in great waves. But along with the tears came anger. Before she realized what was happening, she was shouting at the top of her lungs, "Get out! Get out of here!"

The woman shook her head slowly. "They always cry, too."

Sonji rose to her feet and spoke through clinched teeth. "I said, get out of here."

"I've never seen one get this angry before, though," the woman said, walking toward the door.

Sonji watched as Mrs. Chad Lovelace strode triumphantly away. She was about to shut the door when the woman spun around. One eyebrow was raised and the corners of her lips were drawn up into a wide smile. "I'll send *my* Chad by later this evening for his things."

Sonji, who couldn't wait for the opportunity to confront Chad, put on a smile of her own. "You do that," she sneered, and slammed the door closed.

As the woman had proclaimed, Chad came calling that evening. When he knocked on the door instead of using his key, Sonji was furious, because that made it all true. She snatched the door open and stood there, fuming. Then her anger exploded in a slap across Chad's face.

"You son of a bitch!"

"Look," Chad said unmoved by her outburst. "I just want to get my things and be out."

"You can be out!" Sonji shouted as he walked past her. "And quickly. I've got all your crap in a pile waiting for you!"

Sonji pointed to the mound of clothes, after-shave, pictures, business files, shoes, and jewelry. Quickly, Chad began to sift through the heap.

Sonji folded her arms. "You don't have to check. It's all there, you grade-A asshole!"

After packing most of the items in the pile, Chad turned to leave.

"W-w-wait," Sonji said, following behind him. "Take all of it!"

"I don't want that other stuff."

"What!"

"I don't want anything that will remind me of you."

And with that, he was gone. Sonji walked over to the pile, picked up a picture of the two of them together, and threw it out the window at him. The picture fell short of its mark, and instead of smacking the back of Chad's head as she would have liked, it landed on the sidewalk and shattered.

"I hate you, Chad Lovelace," Sonji screamed. "I hate you!"

When Chad sped away in his black Porsche, Sonji went inside her house, closed the door, and slumped to the floor. She lay there crying for the rest of the evening and into the night.

Now the items Chad had refused to take with him were all stuffed into a thirty-gallon garbage bag. Sonji finally realized that to get on with her life, she had to get her past relationship out of her life. It still saddened her to think that she had wasted the last two years with a man who was never really hers.

Sonji decided that she couldn't waste another minute of her life wallowing in pity. In order to put the past behind her, she needed a change in her present—a dramatic change. And that's why, at the age of thirty-three, Sonji Stephens decided to go back to college and fulfill her dream of getting an education.

She knew she wouldn't be able to concentrate and focus on her classes if she was constantly reminded of the great sadness she'd felt when she was confronted by Mrs. Lovelace. So Sonji took a day off from her job as a supervisor at Wentworth Teleservices and dredged her house from top to bottom. Every one of Chad's leftover belongings went into the garbage. She even threw away the things that didn't belong to Chad but reminded her of him.

When she finally finished, she set the garbage out in the front yard for the next day's pickup. Immediately, she felt as if a great negative energy had been purged from her house. She pulled out the information she had recently received from Barnett University and poured through it with vigor.

Because she had decided to go back to school at the last minute, she had almost missed registration. There was only one day left. Sonji sat back in her rocking chair and smiled. For the first time since Chad, her mind was perfectly clear about what she wanted to do, and tomorrow was her big day. She clutched the university catalog to her chest and sighed, eager to begin her new journey.

After driving around campus for twenty minutes, Sonji finally found a place to park. Unfortunately, the place she found was in the faculty lot. She pulled into the parking space and looked around. There were people walking in the area, but no one seemed to notice her indiscretion.

Sonji hopped out of the car and grabbed the campus map. She found her location on the map and traced her route to the administration building. As she headed toward the building, Sonji felt the excitement rising within her. She glanced around the campus in awe of all she was about to undertake.

There were people everywhere, all walking intently across the campus. Sonji assumed they were students. They were dressed very casually and all of them had backpacks. It had been fifteen years since she had been to college. As Sonji took in her surroundings more closely, she got the feeling that she was overdressed and a little underconfident.

By the time she reached the administration building, she had counted nearly one hundred students, none of whom were her age. Sonji had known that her age would put her in the minority, but she wasn't sure to what extent. She was starting to get a bad feeling about her decision to return to school.

The administration building was a hive of activity, and there were lines everywhere. Sonji wasn't sure where to start. She headed for what appeared to be the shortest line and took her place behind a student who looked half her age. Her uneasiness was increasing. She took her registration papers out of her purse. She had completed them ahead of time, hoping it would speed up the process. Judging by the size of the line she was in, it wouldn't.

Sonji double-checked the information on the forms. She had filled out her requested classes, which were algebra, world civilizations, sociology, and English. She had completed her forms for a parking permit, library card, and student ID. As Sonji reviewed her forms a couple of loud and overzealous students came bounding around the corner. One of them bumped into Sonji, knocking the papers out of her hand.

"Whoa! I'm like, so sorry." As the young woman bent down and helped Sonji collect the papers, her long hair fell against the sides of her face.

"Do you see what you made me do?" she said to the young man accompanying her. She was still bent over and speaking to him through her legs. Sonji and the young woman straightened up together.

"Don't try to blame your clumsiness on me," the young man replied, bumping into the young woman and smiling.

"I am really sorry about this, ma'am." The young woman handed Sonji her papers. Sonji was undone.

"Ma'am!" Sonji thundered. She hated being called ma'am. She remembered calling old women that when she was a kid. And since she didn't consider herself anywhere near old age, she resented the label whenever it was applied to her.

"Oh, God, I've, like, done it again, professor, professor . . ." The young woman stared at Sonji in earnest.

"I'm not an instructor. I'm a student. And a new student at that."

The young woman's eyes widened brightly. "No kidding!" She stuck out her hand. "I'm Andromeda Simmonsis," she said, nudging her body against the young man with her. "This is Dr. Feelgood." Andromeda's eyes twinkled innocently. The young man extended his hand.

"You'll have to appreciate my shorty here. She's on a special journey. Actually, my name is Sebastian Dupree."

Andromeda looked confused. "But you just said to start calling you . . ."

"In private, baby. In private."

Andromeda frowned and nodded her head. Then her eyes lit up with understanding. "Oh!" she cooed.

The line moved up a few feet. Sonji moved with it, slightly amused by the two. "Pleased to meet you, Andromeda and Sebastian. I'm Sonji."

Sonji knew immediately that the young woman in front of her was the kind who would always have a youthful face. Even now she looked to be a mere teenager, though Sonji guessed she was in her mid-twenties. Her honey-hued complexion was flawless. She had wave upon wave of thick, brown hair that seemed to have a mind of its own. It was whimsically unsettled, and sur-

rounded her face extravagantly as if in the midst of
dancing some ancient African dance.

Sonji felt that the turquoise outfit Andromeda was
wearing was perhaps inappropriate for college. But
something in the girl's manner said that it was right
for her. The pants were long and flowing. She wore
a loosely crocheted tunic over it. Both the pants and
the tunic shimmered like a turquoise sea in the fluo-
rescent light of the building.

The young man with Andromeda was another story
entirely. His clean-cut appearance was almost annoy-
ingly perfect. His deep bronze skin made the ideal
contrast for his ink-black hair, which was close-cut and
expertly lined.

His eyebrows looked as though they had been
brushed into place. His mustache and goatee were
trimmed with precision. He wore a light blue denim
jacket and pants with a simple black T-shirt underneath. Sonji glanced at his fingernails and was not
surprised to discover that they were manicured. She
thought to herself that this young brother had the
kind of immaculate grooming only old money could
buy.

Andromeda studied the papers in Sonji's hand.
"Are you going through late registration?"

Sebastian frowned disapprovingly. "Baby, stay outta
grown folks' business."

There it is, Sonji thought. *Another crack about my age.*
Pretty soon she would really be annoyed. "As a matter
of fact, I am," Sonji replied, moving up in line again.
She noticed that Andromeda's eyes were the color of
Brach's caramel and her round, strawberry lips were
so warmly red they probably never needed lipstick.

"Let's see," Andromeda said, reaching for Sonji's
class registration form.

"Andi!"

"Honey, I would have killed to have someone look over my classes during my freshman year."

Sonji wasn't sure what to make of Andromeda, but something told her that she was genuinely trying to be helpful. Sonji handed over the form.

"You know," Andromeda said, waving the form. "Nowadays, most people register by computer or over the phone."

"Yes," Sonji said, grateful that she seemed to be getting closer to the front of the line.

"World civ. Looks like you've got Professor Carlson for that. He's old, but he's fair as long as you turn in all of your assignments on time. And you've got Dr. Billings for algebra. She's got a self-esteem problem. She likes class participation and plenty of compliments. Make sure you tell her how wonderful her lizard pin is. She wears it the first day of every semester."

Sebastian just stood with a wide smile on his face.

"Oh, *coo-l!* You're in my sociology class. That's Professor Lyman. He's new. We'll both be on our own with that one." Andromeda whipped her thick, wavy hair around to one side and frowned.

"Uh-oh. You have *got* to change this class."

"What?" Sonji asked concerned.

"This English class with PG. He is like, the *worst* instructor on the planet."

"PG?"

"Yeah. That's Professor Gilmore, but we call him PG."

"As in pretty God-awful," Sebastian added.

A woman standing in line just ahead of Sonji stepped into their conversation. "Positively gross!"

Sonji felt her earlier feeling of resignation returning. "What should I do?"

"When you get to the registration assistant, ask them to fill out a new form for you."

Sebastian shook his head. "You're supposed to fill one out yourself."

"They always do it for me. Anyway, they can do a computer search for another English class for you."

"Make sure you ask who's teaching it. Instead of having Gilmore at ten o'clock, you may end up in his three o'clock class. And you don't want his class at all." Sebastian looked reassuringly at Sonji.

Andromeda didn't miss a beat. "I heard that last semester he started his classes by saying, 'Welcome to English 101. Most of you will end up taking this class again.' "

"Damn."

"She's right," Sebastian agreed.

Andromeda handed Sonji's registration form back to her. "I just noticed something else. Our sociology class is in the Williams science building on the east side of campus. PG's English class is on the west side of campus. It's takes about fifteen minutes to walk from one end of campus to the other."

"So?"

"We only get ten minutes to pass."

The pit of Sonji's stomach sank into an abysmal spiral.

Sebastian checked his watch. "Andi, we need to get going if we are going to get to the bookstore before it closes."

Sonji was more confused than ever. Even though Andromeda had provided her with some interesting information, she wondered if she wouldn't have been better off not knowing it.

"I don't know what I would do without Sebastian," Andromeda said, walking toward the exit. "It was nice bumping into you." Sebastian took Andromeda's hand and pulled her along. Andromeda smiled, pushed her disorderly hair back from her face, and waved good-bye.

When Sonji finally reached the registration assistant, she was sure of one thing: She wanted out of Professor Gilmore's class. It was her first semester back to college in years, and she wasn't about to spend it sweating over some instructor on a power trip.

"Are you adding or dropping?" the man behind the counter asked.

"Neither. I'm enrolling." Sonji handed her enrollment form to the man.

The man began entering Sonji's information into the computer. "Your form shows you've enrolled for twelve credit hours. Is that correct?"

"Yes."

"That will be nine hundred dollars. You can pay at the cashier's window in the next line."

Sonji looked over at the line for the cashier. It was almost as long as the one she was in. Sonji let out a deep sigh.

"Do you need a printout of your classes?"

"Yes," Sonji replied. "And I'd like to change my English class. Can you look that up for me?"

"Sure." The man said checking her form. "You want freshman English?"

"Yes."

The man quickly typed some keystrokes into the computer. "There are only two freshman English classes open and they're almost full."

"Great!"

"One is a Tuesday-Thursday class from three P.M. to four-thirty."

"Perfect. Who's the instructor?"

"Gilmore."

Sonji's hopes faded. "What's the other open class?"

"The one that you're in. Monday, Wednesday, and Friday from ten to ten-fifty A.M.."

"Damn!"

"What's it gonna be, miss? There are lots of people behind you."

Sonji closed her eyes and shook her head. She couldn't believe her bad luck. She couldn't get out of the class, and she had waited too long to have the luxury of finding another class to replace it. *Oh well,* she thought. *I'll just have to tough it out.*

She thought that perhaps three short sessions with PG might be better than two long ones. So she opted to keep the Monday-Wednesday-Friday class.

The cashier's line went more quickly, and before she knew it, Sonji was headed toward the bookstore. Like the administration building, the bookstore was packed with people. Even with ten cashiers, the lines were long. Sonji studied her class printout and made quick work of finding her books, which were listed according to course number. In most cases, Sonji was able to find decent used ones.

The only book she didn't get was the one for her English class. That's because the store was sold out of both new and used. When Sonji asked a stocker, she was told that several people had asked already and the store expected to have some in within three weeks.

It took almost thirty minutes for Sonji to check out with her purchases. In addition to her textbooks, she bought school supplies and a backpack to carry everything in. She was beginning to feel like an actual student. She could envision herself walking across campus, recording notes in class, and even taking tests.

Despite the long wait in line, Sonji's mood was turning around. She knew in her heart she had made the right decision to go back to school. As she walked across campus the smile on her face got broader and broader—until she got to her car. Stuck under the blade of her left windshield wiper was a parking ticket. Sonji stared at it in disbelief.

She snatched the ticket from the windshield and got into her car. She was determined not to let it spoil her day. Deep down she knew that attending Barnett University was the key to her future. And nothing—not long lines, not a ticket, not even a crabby professor—was going to keep her from realizing her dream.

Two

It was the day before school, and instead of spending it relaxing as she'd planned, Sonji was headed back to campus to pay the parking ticket. For the second time in as many days, she decided that it was important for her to start school with a clean slate. She also thought that while her computer was in the shop, she would use one of the school's computers to see if she could order the English book she needed online.

When Sonji arrived on campus, she circled the lots until she found a spot with a parking meter. She put in a quarter, which gave her an hour's time to pay her parking ticket and search the web for an online bookstore.

There weren't as many students on campus because it was Sunday. Only a few offices were open: Campus Security, the library, and Campus Computing. Sonji went to Campus Security first to pay her parking ticket and purchase a student parking sticker. Next, it was on to Campus Computing. Although the semester hadn't started, every terminal was taken. Sonji scanned the room and stood dejected until she heard a familiar voice.

"Miss Sonji."

Sonji turned to see Andromeda in the back corner of the room smiling and waving energetically.

"I'll be finished in a minute. You can use this one!" she said just a little too loudly for Sonji's comfort.

Sonji strode over to where the young woman sat. Today Andromeda was dressed a bit more conservatively. But her style reminded Sonji of something a soothsayer would wear: a long orange skirt with broomstick pleats topped off with a purple short-sleeved cardigan embroidered with colorful passion fruits along the neck and sleeves. Andromeda's unusual and bold attire made Sonji's blue slacks and navy pullover seem boring and ordinary by comparison.

"What are you doing here?" Andromeda asked as Sonji pulled up an empty chair. Her bright eyes captured Sonji's heart. Whatever else this young woman was, Sonji thought, she was most definitely the epitome of curiosity and innocence. She was almost too much.

"I need the book for my English class. They were out of it at the bookstore, and I was hoping that I could order it through the Internet."

Sonji glanced at the computer screen. In large red, black, and green letters, it read *Blackluv.net*. The subheading said *Romantique Noir.* Sonji read the information on the first page aloud.

"Trying to find the perfect partner can be a series of trials and errors, of breakups, heartaches, and setbacks. At Blackluv.net we believe in soul mates. We believe in magic. We believe in true love. And we believe we can help you find it. If you are tired of disappointments and lonely nights, try BlackLuv. BlackLuv is True Love."

"Isn't this like ultra, mega cool?"

Sonji thought Andromeda was going to bubble out of her seat.

"And Miss Sonji . . ."

"Just Sonji."

"And Sonji, they've got pictures and everything."

Sonji had heard of personals on Web sites, but never accessed any. She used the Internet infrequently, and when she did, it was always for research. This was her first attempt at buying something over the Net.

A couple of clicks and a few minutes later, Andromeda was viewing pictures and descriptions of black men. Some of the men were handsome, some were not. Some didn't include pictures, just information. Sonji was amazed at all the people on the site who were looking for love.

"What are *you* doing, Andromeda? Aren't you and Sebastian a couple?"

"Just Andi. And of course we're a couple." Andromeda continued scrolling and smiling. "And *this* is how we met."

"What!" Sonji took off her windbreaker and stared at Andi in astonishment.

"I joined the BlackLuv network and added my profile to the site. A couple of guys emailed me. But Dr.—I mean Sebastian's reply was so perfect. I knew he was the one."

"I would be scared to take a chance like that. There are lots of weirdos on the Net."

"I know. That's why I did it the BlackLuv way. They have rules and regulations about what they call Making the Connection. That plus common sense will, like, take care of the perverts." Andi spoke with her hands punctuating her sentences and her eyes sparkling like stars.

She glanced quickly at Sonji's left hand.

"No ring," she said. "Are you attached to someone?"

Sonji pictured the trash collectors removing her garbage yesterday. "No," she replied.

"Then let's get you on the network!"

"No! No!" Sonji protested as Andi clicked away. In

seconds the screen read *BlackLuv Network Member Application.*

"First, you need a name," Andi said, sizing up Sonji. "The first contact rule is never use your real name. If there is a sicko out there, he may try to track you down, ya know?"

"Andi, I'm really not interested."

"Well then do it for the free e-mail account. Every registered network user gets free e-mail."

Now that sounded tempting. Sonji's old computer was on the fritz again for the third time in as many months. She really needed to get a new one, but couldn't afford it right now. With e-mail becoming a more essential form of communication for students, Sonji would need something. And *free* sounded good.

"I thought all students get a free e-mail account."

"We do, but that e-mail is yucky. It doesn't have cool features like stationery, animated signatures, and mood stamps."

"Alright," Sonji conceded. "What do I do?"

Andromeda led Sonji through a series of basic personal questions on the site. As Andi asked the questions, Sonji realized that the young woman's innocence was not only in her eyes, but in her voice as well. She sounded as if she truly wanted to know Sonji's answers to the questions herself.

As Sonji talked, Andi typed and clicked. After a few minutes, Sonji had completed a profile and was signing up for e-mail. Andi walked her through the process.

"When I chose my e-mail name, I thought of the woman that I admire most, and I called myself that."

"What name did you choose?" Sonji asked staring at the blank line on the screen before the address @blackluv.net.

"Sethe."

Sonji shook her head. "From *Beloved?*"

"Uh-huh." Andi's eyes looked far away then. As if she were staring at something so distant, even squinting wouldn't bring it into focus. "I've never met anyone like Sethe. I would like to be strong, smart, and courageous like her."

Sonji smiled, feeling a little sad for her young friend. "I'm sure you are all those things," Sonji said. Andi's eyes lit up like the fourth of July.

"You think so?"

Sonji didn't have to think long to come up with the name of the person she most admired. It was Nzinga, her grandmother. Her great-grandmother had heard of great warriors in Africa. Among the greatest was Nzinga, who had fought the Portuguese in defiance of the slave trade. And Gola wanted those in her lineage to be strong fighters. So she named her first and only child Nzinga.

True to her name, Nzinga had been a fighter all her life. And when her own daughter died during childbirth, she had raised her grandchild like her own. And like Zulu Nzinga, she had done everything in her power to provide for her progeny.

Sonji typed in the name herself, and pressed the Enter key.

"Now the Network will tell you if this address has already been chosen. If it has, you will be prompted to choose another address. If not, then welcome to the world of BlackLuv!" she read.

The hourglass disappeared and the message on the screen read, *Welcome to Blackluv.net! Your Soul Mate awaits . . .*

"From here you can review your profile, send e-mail, or exit. Which would you like to do?"

"Review my profile."

"No sweat," Andi said, clicking feverishly. Miraculously, Sonji's network profile appeared on the screen.

I am Nzinga—fighter, thinker, believer, dreamer. If you have ever marveled at the beauty of a poem, if you think jazz is the most exquisite music ever born, if you believe that life is short and each moment is precious, if you've ever dreamed of a sunset and wept—then you know my soul. My warrior woman soul . . . named Nzinga. Her will is strong, but her breath is soft. The door to her heart is open. Enter . . . if you dare.

That will keep them away, Sonji mused. *No one would dare respond to that.* "Thanks, Andi."

Andi shook her head and grinned. "This is beautiful, Sonji. You'll find your soul mate in no time with this profile."

Don't bet on it, Sonji thought. She had used the highbrow language to deter a response, not to attract one.

Andi gathered her books and papers. "I guess I'm finished here. I just wanted to kill some time while Sebastian picked up some books from the library."

The two women switched places.

"What are you doing again?"

"Getting the book for English class. *Gilmore's* English class."

"Didn't you drop that class?"

"I tried to, but his was the only class that was open."

"Darn it!"

"And the bookstore was out of the textbook."

"Yikes!"

"Tell me about it. So I was hoping to find an online bookstore that could get it to me quicker than three weeks."

"Wow. Good luck."

"Thanks," Sonji replied typing in the address for her favorite search engine.

"Miss Sonji—uh, Sonji. I didn't get the chance to tell you yesterday, but there is one good thing about PG."

"Really, what's that?"

"He is, like, way hand—"

"I'm back, baby."

The sound of Sebastian's voice pulled Andi's attention completely away from her conversation with Sonji. The two embraced and kissed as if they hadn't seen each other in days instead of hours.

"Miss Sonji, good to see you again." Sebastian greeted her with a room-warming smile.

"Please, just call me Sonji."

"Okay," the happy couple said in unison, and then kissed acknowledging their sync.

"Are you ready, Special?"

"Yes, Sebastian."

Sonji watched, fascinated, as the two separate beings operated as one whole. They gathered Andi's things and turned toward Sonji. They were arm in arm. There was a rhythm about their togetherness. And they were as perfect for each other as black-eyed peas and corn bread. In all of Sonji's relationships, and she hadn't had that many, she could not remember ever feeling as in harmony with someone as the couple standing before her obviously felt. Maybe there was something to this BlackLuv after all.

"We're outta here, Sonji."

"See you tomorrow in sociology class."

"Take care, you two," Sonji said, thinking that her earlier sadness for Andi was unjustified. Andi had the consummate companion. He was the zig for her zag. *Maybe I should have felt sorry for myself,* Sonji thought and typed in the words *online bookstore.* To Sonji's dismay the search engine returned 21,717 hits.

As Sonji started the beginning of her tedious search, she wondered what Andi was going to tell her about Professor Gilmore. *Oh well,* she thought. *I guess I'll find out tomorrow.*

Three

"Mr. Gilmore, the doctor would like to see you."

Grayson Gilmore rose from the leather seat and followed the nurse out of the waiting area and back into the patient-care facility.

The corridor was long and narrow. Everything about it was sterile. The carpet looked as though it had been recently cleaned, the walls looked freshly washed, and the ceiling was spotless—not a cobweb or spec of dirt anywhere. Grayson was relieved of some of his concern.

He and the nurse continued to walk single file down the corridor. They passed many closed doors along the way. They walked around one corner and then another. Soon Grayson noticed that the window on each closed door was blackened from the inside with paint. He felt his unease returning.

The nurse rounded another bend and took a metal staircase down to a lower level. The staircase was long and narrow, just like the corridor. There was something different, though. Not as much care had been taken with this area. There was silt on the stairs and on the railing. A silver, gelatinous substance was seeping through the walls, and large cordlike cobwebs sagged from the ceiling.

Grayson felt panic twisting in his chest. This couldn't be the way to the doctor. He was about to ask the nurse to stop when she turned to look at him. What was once a beautiful nurse with short, cropped hair and long silky legs was now a decaying skeleton that talked.

"The doctor is waiting for you, Mr. Gilmore. Please follow me." The skeleton-nurse crooked a skinless finger at him and Grayson Gilmore was compelled to follow.

They reached the bottom of the stairs and walked into a large open area with padded walls. Even the ceiling and floor were covered with the thick, taupe padding. The skeleton-nurse pointed to a large door. The window in the door was painted black just like the others. Grayson walked hesitantly toward the door and opened it.

The inside opened into an arena, and he was on the ground floor. In the center of the arena was a long table with a body lying covered on top of it. Tears streamed down Grayson's face as he walked toward the body. He tried to speak but could only move his mouth silently open and closed. When he reached the table, he knew what he had to do. He threw the sheet off the body, and there lying on the table was his wife, Veranda.

"No!" Grayson screamed, sitting up in bed. His heart was beating a hard rhythm in his chest and pellets of sweat slid down his neck and arms. Grayson placed his head in his hands and took short breaths to steady his nerves. Regaining his composure, he glanced at the clock. It read 3:00 A.M.

"Damn!" he said, swinging long muscular legs out of the bed. He went to the bathroom and splashed cold water on his face. He stared at his reflection in the mirror. His brows were furrowed into one, his lips were drawn and tight, and worry lines were starting to form under his eyes.

I used to be such a handsome man. At least Veranda thought so. His life with Veranda seemed to have occurred a hundred lifetimes ago. He pulled a towel from the rack and patted his face dry. In one of those other lifetimes, he would have heard the words, "Come back to bed, Gray. Everything will be fine."

But for years, there had been no other words in his life. Only those that haunted his dreams. He returned to bed knowing it was no use, but he had to try to sleep anyway. Tomorrow was the first day of school, and Grayson wanted to be fresh and well rested for his students. He already had a reputation for being a hard-ass. Lack of sleep on the first day would only support the students' theories of him.

For an hour he turned from one side of the bed to the other. He tried lying on his back and then on his stomach. Nothing helped. Eventually Grayson gave in and got up. He went into his den and turned on his computer. *Maybe I'll do some research on the Internet.* He clicked and hyperlinked his way across the information superhighway for about an hour. When Web browsing no longer interested him, he went for his morning run. With the extra time, he ran six miles instead of his usual five.

Grayson returned home from his run feeling invigorated. He took a shower and began preparations for his workday at Barnett University.

Andi was absolutely right, and Sonji was late. Not only was she late, but she was lost. Annex Seven? Annex Seven? Where in the hell was Annex Seven? All of the other buildings had names posted on big signs. College of Science and Technology. College of Nurs-

ing. The Law Library. Kiewit/Durham Student Center.
Williamson Dormitory. It was easy to find her algebra,
world civilizations, and sociology classes. But English
had to be located in a building called Annex Seven.

Sonji hadn't even seen Annexes One through Six.
If she had, she could have followed them to seven.
When she asked directions, she had been pointed to
the end of campus. She assumed it would be easy to
find. Unfortunately, her assumption was wrong.

Talking for those few minutes with Andi after sociology class wasn't a good thing to do. And now she
was paying for it. Sonji looked at her watch. It read
10:10. She decided to accost the next person she saw
and demand to be escorted to Annex Seven. Sonji
walked a little farther. All she could see was the library, a church, and the law school. When an older
gentleman came out of the library Sonji jogged up
to him.

"Excuse me, sir. Do you know where Annex Seven
is?"

"Yes," the man said, pointing toward the library. Go
through the library. Annex Seven is right behind it."

"Thank you," Sonji said, relieved.

When she entered the library, Sonji saw a large
sign that she hadn't seen from the outside: CREIGN-
TON LIBRARY/ANNEXES. *Damn,* she thought and trotted off to class. By the time she arrived, it was almost
twenty after the hour. When she walked in, The large
room was packed. There must have been fifty in the
class, and everyone watched her come in and scan
the room nervously for a seat. Sonji sighed because
the only empty seats were in the front row. She took
one of them and looked up apologetically at the professor. Sonji's racing heart settled into an easy rhythm
when she saw him. From Andi's description of his demeanor, she had expected an ogre, a crotchety old

man with deep wrinkles, warts, a fraying polyester suit, and bad breath. Nothing would have prepared her for the truth.

The man in front of the class was neither crotchety nor old. He had the beginnings of crows feet near his temples, but no deep wrinkles to speak of. His Earth-brown complexion was smooth, showing no sign of warts. The olive-green suit he wore had to be tailored. It fit his body as if he had been born in it. And as for his breath, Sonji could only imagine that it smelled as wonderful as he looked.

By the time she realized that she was staring at him, she also realized that he was staring at her.

"And you are?" he asked in a voice sultry enough to melt steel. His dark eyes looked out above wire-framed glasses.

"Sonji Stephens." Sonji felt as though the breakfast she ate was doing a slow churn in her stomach. "Sorry, I'm late. I got lo—"

"Just don't let it happen again." Grayson inter-rupted. "Your grade depends on it." The instructor made notes in an assignment book and returned his attention to the class.

Sonji slumped in her seat, dejected. *He is just too rude. Perhaps he is an ogre after all.* Sonji took a notebook from her backpack. Grayson handed her a class syllabus.

"Speak to me after class about the first assign-ment," he said with that velvet voice.

Sonji nodded.

Grayson walked to the other side of the classroom and leaned against the wall. He didn't look like any professor Sonji had ever seen. His hair was so thick and curly, Sonji could see her fingers running through it— all the way to where it tapered to a V in the back.

"Miss Stephens?"

"Yes," Sonji replied, snapping out of her fantasy.

"I asked you to read page one of the Preface."

When I found out about PG, I should have forgotten about taking English all together, Sonji thought.

"I don't have a book, Professor Gilmore. The bookstore was sold out."

"I see," Grayson said, returning to the desk. He opened the assignment book again and began writing.

"Who else is waiting for a book?" he asked.

Five other students raised their hands.

"I see."

Grayson entered more notes into the assignment book and closed it again.

"Those of you without books will have to find a partner—someone to share the text with until your book arrives." Grayson cleared his throat and looked sternly at the students who had raised their hands.

"Don't think that not having a book is an excuse to turn in late assignments or assignments that aren't thorough. You will still be responsible for the readings and for your work. Do you all understand that?"

The six students without books nodded.

"Then, Miss Stephens, I ask you again. Please read page one of the Preface."

Sonji looked around to ask to borrow someone's book. But the man sitting beside her was already offering his.

"Thanks," she said, taking his book and smiling with relief.

She was not beautiful. The same way that Jada Pinkett Smith and Janet Jackson were not beautiful. But they were so overwhelmingly cute that the mind was overcome and fascinated by their allure. Grayson was convinced that Sonji Stephens could hold a thousand men hostage with just her eyes.

He had wished that their first words to each other had been more pleasant. But her entrance to his class caught him on the tail end of a rotten morning. First, he had narrowly escaped a car accident when someone who wasn't paying attention tried to merge into the space where he was driving. Then when he got to his office, he discovered that the instructor for 20th Century American Literature was offered another job, so he was asked to take on the class until a replacement was found. And waking up at three A.M. hadn't helped. By the time Sonji came into his class late, and without a textbook, his mood was in a bad place.

Now, he was feeling guilty about his attraction to Sonji. And it had nothing to do with teacher-student ethics and everything to do with a woman who hadn't been in his life for years. "Veranda," he said out loud.

Grayson reached across his desk and picked up the only picture in his house. A small pewter frame enclosed a closeup of a boy who was the mirror image of his father. Grayson ran his hand down the picture as if trying to touch the child framed inside. A tear slid down his face, and he returned the picture to where it had rested for five years.

Grayson turned his attention to the blank lesson plan before him. The only thing he had managed to do was write the name of the class at the top of his legal pad. Then an idea occurred to him that brushed his murky mood aside.

He strode over to the large, mahogany bookcase and retrieved several titles. *I'm going to teach an American literature class that they'll never forget.* Methodically he wrote the names of authors on his pad—N. Scott Momaday, Dorothy West, Tomas Rivera, Maxine Hong Kingston, Norma Elia Cantú.

After selecting the multi-ethnic authors to feature

in the class, the lesson plan came easily. When he finished writing it, he felt better about teaching the class. *If we don't find a replacement, I won't feel put upon,* he thought. *I'm going to enjoy teaching this class.*

His excitement brought his mind back to English 101. There was something else to be excited about— and her name was Sonji Stephens.

Sonji went straight from school to work. She arrived early, but didn't mind. Her first day at school was exciting, but too much of a good thing could be bad. So Sonji left right after her English class.

She brought her backpack with her and sat in the break room. She was grateful that her employer was not only paying her tuition, but allowing her to participate in a job-sharing program. While Sonji was at school in the mornings, another woman, Phyllis Herndon, took on the supervisory responsibilities. Phyllis worked until noon. Then Sonji came on duty at one and stayed until five. It was a well-designed program, and several employees at her company were taking advantage of it.

Since it was only 11:30, Sonji decided to see how much of her homework she could get out of the way. She sat looking at her textbooks and notebooks wondering if anyone was ever really prepared for college. Since she considered herself a decent writer she took out her notes from PG's class. *This should be easy,* she thought.

She was grateful that the man whose textbook she read from in class was kind enough to let her photocopy the first chapter. She took out the photocopied pages and began reading and highlighting. Her assignment was to write a two-page essay speculating on why the title of the textbook was *The Art of Persuasion.*

After finishing reading Chapter One, Sonji set to

work writing about the book's title. The focus of her
paper was that the art of writing was in essence the art
of persuading—persuading the reader to read on.

Sonji felt good about her paper. She finished it in
enough time to grab a quick bite to eat before starting her shift.

At five P.M., Sonji left work and headed back to campus. In addition to her English assignment, she had
completed the sociology assignment during a break and
wanted to use the school computer to type her work.

When she arrived at Campus Computing, all the
computers were in use. She had to wait fifteen minutes before one became available. *I'll be glad when my
computer is fixed,* she thought. Sonji sat down and selected the word processor program from the Start
menu. A blank screen appeared and Sonji proceeded
to type both her English and sociology assignments.

Satisfied with her work, Sonji was ready to leave
when curiosity got the best of her. In a few quick
clicks of the mouse, Sonji was on the Blackluv.net Web
site. She entered her password into the special field
to access her e-mail. To her surprise, she had three
e-mail messages waiting.

The first message was from Andi, a.k.a. Sethe.

*Hail up, Nzinga! In case you were wondering if your
e-mail works, now you know. Have a happy day, and I'll
see you in class.*

The next message was from Byron Moore, the guy
from English class. Since he had agreed to be her study
partner—at least until her book came—they had exchanged e-mail addresses to keep in touch.

*Sonji, I find your e-mail address intriguing. Care to share
what it means? Anyway, I was just checking in to see if*

you needed help with today's assignment and also to say don't let Professor Gilmore get to you. He's tough, but I hear that he's also one of the best. So hang in there, and I'll see you in class.

The last e-mail was from an address Sonji didn't recognize. *Oh no, not SPAM already,* she thought. And then she read the subject line more carefully. It read *Obeisance to the Great Elephant.* Sonji felt a quick shudder sliding down her spine. She pointed the mouse to the message and opened it.

To Nzinga, Warrior Woman with Soft Breath, I greet you with joy. For your profile has placed a smile upon my heart. Although I feel that I am unworthy of responding to such a regal call, I am compelled to answer the trumpet of the great elephant.

I am Osiris—Griot, builder, protector, lover. If you relish the story of life, if your mission is to change the world, if you acknowledge our role as custodians of the earth, if you know that love truly conquers all—then you share my spirit. This Nubian man, born of the bright sun, presents himself to you and awaits your reply.

Sonji read and reread the e-mail message. She couldn't believe that anyone would respond to her profile. Not only did Osiris respond, but his response was pure and not to be improved upon. Sonji clicked the Reply button and began typing. Then she thought better of it. *What am I doing? My membership in the personals Network was merely for the convenience of getting free e-mail.* She clicked the Cancel button and sat back in her chair, unsure of what to do. One thing was for sure, she wasn't going to delete the message from Osiris. His words were so eloquent, she felt as though she could read them every day like a daily meditation.

Instead of sending an answer, Sonji signed off the computer, retrieved her assignments from the printer, and went home.

Day two of college was much less hectic than the first. Sonji had gotten her bearings now and passed from her algebra class to her world civilizations class without incident. After her last class, she decided to spend some time on campus instead of going straight to work.

Sonji headed to the student center. There she saw people of all races and ethnicities. Although most of them were much younger, she saw a few her own age there as well. She tried not to walk around like a tourist, but the sights and sounds were fascinating. The entire building was teeming with people moving past wall-to-wall signs, announcements, and posters. Sonji looked around and found a snack shop, study area, arcade, meeting rooms, and offices of student organizations. What really caught her attention was a bulletin board that took up an entire wall from floor to ceiling, along with overstuffed chairs and couches strategically placed throughout the center.

Sonji looked around with wonder. *The energy of this place is what will keep my sanity when ol' PG starts getting on my nerves,* she thought.

"Hey, Miss Sonji!"

She had only heard his voice a few times, but she recognized it instantly. She turned around to see Sebastian smiling like a million dollars beside her.

"You have the look of a true freshman on your face." Sebastian pursed his lips and nodded his head. "It takes me back. It takes me back."

"This is so exciting. If only I were ten years younger to enjoy it all."

"What's age got to do with it?"

Sonji couldn't come up with a reasonable answer to Sebastian's question. "Nothing, I guess," she said, smiling.

"Come on," he said, motioning to the student offices. "Let me show you around."

Their first stop was the big bulletin board.

"This is the Board. You'll find anything here, from roommate listings, to study partners needed, free cats, or drivers wanted." They paused for a moment and Sonji read a few of the postings.

"If you want to put something up, it has to be approved by student government."

A group of four students walked past. All were African-American males.

"Dupree!"

"Yo wassup, G?"

"Everything is everything," was Sebastian's response.

The two continued walking throughout the student center. Sebastian showed Sonji all the functional areas of the center. Places to get copies made, where to get stamps, cash checks, the automatic teller machine, and campus information. Then he showed her the recreational areas. Sonji couldn't believe how many people were there playing pool and videogames. She wondered how they had time with all the homework that was required.

"And now the pièce de résistance."

Sonji could tell by the look on his face that what he was going to show her next was very special.

"Saved the best for last, huh?"

"Of course," Sebastian said, strolling proudly.

On the east end of the student center, they approached an office encased in glass. The sign on the door read, MULTICULTURAL STUDENTS ORGANIZATION. They walked in to find a group of students of color gathered in the medium-sized office.

"Hey, Sebastian," several greetings rang out from the group.

"Everybody, this is Sonji."

Sebastian introduced Sonji to each person one by one. "Sonji this is Jesus, Wilma, Fan, Capiz, LaShay, Ricardo, Henry, and I think you know my right hand, Andi."

They all extended words and handshakes of welcome. Andi appeared pleased to see Sonji.

"I'm so glad you're here." Andi beamed. "Are you thinking about joining?"

"Joining what?"

Sebastian chimed in. "The MSO is a student organization that exists to ensure the success of students of color on campus."

Andi's eyes sparkled like small twinkling stars. "Sebastian is the president."

"Really?" Sonji was impressed. But she knew that it would be hard enough for her to get into the swing of things without adding additional responsibilities of being a member of a student organization.

"Sorry, guys. I think I'm going to have to pass on the membership. But thanks."

"Well the offer stands. You are welcome to join us at any time. And stop by for a visit whenever you like. There's always something going on."

"Yeah," Andi added. "You might want to go to a step show or a poetry slam. We plan those all the time."

Andi handed Sonji a bright orange brochure and a membership form. "We do all kinds of activities to raise money for our community service projects."

Ricardo added his two cents. "We help coordinate voter registration booths, citizen patrols, and literacy projects."

"But we also do a lot with the students on campus,

so let us know if we can help you in any way," Sebastian said.

Sonji thought about her college experience so far. Andi had been right about all of her teachers. She believed she had a handle on them all—all except for PG. Now there was an enigma. "Can you do anything about crude teachers?"

Sebastian shook his head and sat on the edge of what looked like the secretary's desk. "Andi told me you couldn't drop the class."

"What class?" asked Capiz, a beautiful Asian woman with long black hair.

"English," Sonji replied.

"She's got PG," Andi said.

From the disgusted sounds of the bunch, Sonji assessed their reaction.

Capiz just smiled. "He's not so bad."

Sebastian scooted back on the desk. "Your opinion doesn't have anything to do with that A you got in his class, now does it?"

"Of course," Capiz said, looking around slyly and then returning her gaze to Sonji. "He's an instructor that gives a hundred and ten percent. He expects the same from his students. If he feels that you aren't operating in that zone, then your grade will reflect that."

Andi, who was shuffling her feet during Capiz's explanation, spoke up quickly. "But that's not fair!"

"This is college, y'all," Wilma blurted.

"In other words," Jesus interrupted, "It's a microcosm of the real world."

LaShay gave Jesus a high-five. "I heard that."

Sebastian swung his legs back and forth as they dangled from the desk. He looked at both Sonji and Andi. "What is fair?"

"Not much," Andi said, hiking her backpack over her shoulder.

"The key to survival in college is to determine exactly what your instructors require of you and give it to them. The problem is that sometimes what they want is not written in the syllabus," Sebastian offered.

Now all the students in the room were gathering around, sort of huddling together.

"Let me give you an example," Henry said. "I took a photography class once from Dr. Clark. Even though I followed every technique he taught, I kept getting C's and D's in his class. Then one day Fan here saw me with my camera, and we started talking about the class. I told her that no matter what I did, I couldn't raise my grade past a C."

"And I told him that Clark likes dark pictures," Fan said.

"So from then on, I started turning in darker pictures and sure enough my grades improved. I ended up getting a B-plus out of the class."

Sebastian hopped down from the desk at that point. "That's what we're about here. We each have a piece of the puzzle for success. I'm just trying to make it easy for us to put all of our pieces together."

Sonji didn't know whether she was encouraged, but she knew she felt better just talking about it and hearing others talk about their struggles.

"For Professor Gilmore, you've just got to make sure you go that extra mile. I think it pains him somehow to feel that he's losing a student," Capiz said.

"Thanks for your insight," Sonji said, sighing. *Amazing,* she thought. In the space of ten minutes, she had been made to feel like part of a family. All of these students still came together for a common purpose, in spite of their different ethnicities and races. Sonji realized that she did feel encouraged after all.

She looked at her watch. If she hurried, she had

time to get to Campus Computing to type up her latest assignment and still get to work on time.

"I'd better go work on my assignment then."

"I'll go with you," Andi said, following behind her. Before she left, Andi kissed Sebastian on the cheek. Sonji had no difficulty reading the expression on his face. It said, "I adore you, Andi," loud and clear.

"Thanks for all of your help," Sonji said to the students as she exited the office with Andi, who was smiling broadly.

"Andi, I think you found the last good man on the planet."

"No way! There's one for you, too. I can, like, feel it, ya know?"

Andromeda swung her rambunctious hair around to the side. "As a matter of fact, let's go see what you got."

They arrived at the computer room early enough to get two computers next to each other. With Andi's coaxing, Sonji logged on to the BlackLuv.net Web site. Osiris' e-mail was still there. Andromeda's face lit up.

"Wow. You got one already."

"Actually, this came yesterday."

"What does it say?"

Andromeda leaned over closer to Sonji's screen.

"Obeisance to the Great Elephant? Oh, that's terrible! He's comparing you to a large mammal, and he hasn't even seen you. And I'm not even sure what obeisance means, but I don't like the look of it." Andromeda shook her head firmly. "He is definitely not the one."

Sonji began to chuckle. "No, No, Andi. In many African cultures, royalty is often referred to in animal terms—elephant being one of the most respected."

"Oh," Andi said, nodding her head in understanding.

"As for obeisance, that's a formal acknowledgement, like a bow."

"Oh, my gosh, Sonji. Do you know what this means? It means you got a response from a man who is saying, 'I bow before my queen.'"

There's no arguing with the truth, Sonji thought. "I guess so."

"Ooh, that's good. Now what did the e-mail say?"

Sonji felt a smile curling across her face. She clicked Open, presenting the words that had made her pulse beat a double rhythm.

"Bingo!" Andromeda said. "That's him."

"No, Andi. That's just an e-mail."

"But it's an e-mail from your soul mate."

Sonji looked around the computer room. In just the short time that they had arrived, it had begun to fill up. She thought about Andi's words. Too bad finding your soul mate, if there was such a thing, wasn't that simple.

"I wish I could share your optimism."

"Well I know what would help."

"What?" Sonji asked, really wanting to know.

"Write him back."

"What!"

"Sure."

"I'm not going to write back to some guy I don't even know. He could be a nutcase."

"And he could be your love and happiness. Just look at me and Sebastian."

Andromeda did have a point. She and Sebastian were simply created with each other in mind. It was a miracle that they'd found each other.

"You and Sebastian are lucky. You have a one-of-a-kind thing going. You know what they say about lightning striking the same place twice. It will never happen."

Andromeda reached over and made a few swift clicks of Sonji's mouse. "Statistically speaking, lightning has the same chance of striking the same place twice as it does any other place on Earth. Now," Andi said, turning the keyboard toward Sonji.

The screen read, Making the Connection. Sonji recognized it as the BlackLuv e-mailing rules and regulations that Andi mentioned earlier. Sonji read through them.

"The most important things to remember are not to give out any personal information right away, like your real name, where you live, where you work, or your phone number."

Sonji took a deep breath.

"What *I* did was create another persona altogether. I kept it real, because I talked about things that I was interested in—things that I like. But I didn't give anything specific away, so I felt, you know, safe."

Andromeda once again took over Sonji's mouse. She scrolled down to the end of the Web page.

"MatchMaker? What's that?" Sonji asked.

"When you feel like a relationship is getting serious, you can have a matchmaker come in to test your compatibility. It's like a moderator that sends questions to both of you. And they're, like, really neat because they make you think."

"What kind of questions?"

"Sometimes they're easy, like 'Toilet paper flap: over or under?' And sometimes they're more difficult, like 'Donate your body to science: yes or no?' "

"Hmmm. That might be interesting to discuss with someone."

"Then what are you waiting for?"

Sonji was convinced. She could e-mail Osiris and feel comfortable about it. And if for some reason they hit it off, they could take their discussions to the next level with a matchmaker.

"Okay," Sonji said, giving in.

She pulled the keyboard in close and clicked the Reply button on the screen. She decided to continue the poetically enchanted style she had begun since Osiris had responded in the same mode. *Maybe that will be my persona,* she thought. And now, how does a queen respond to her humble servant?

Osiris—Lord of New Beginnings
Thank you for your kind words. I, too, share your relish for life, your commitment to a better world, and your defer-ence for love. If you are so inclined, I will correspond with you. Nubian man of the bright sun, I await your response.

Grayson walked around the classroom handing back papers. The soft moans and groans from the students signaled that some were not too happy with their grades. Sonji, who was quite confident about her pa-per before, now felt a stiff tightening of her stomach muscles.

But some of that tightening had to do with her instructor. He was impeccably dressed again, this time in a navy blue suit and leather shoes shined so brightly, the light in the room seemed to be coming from them and not the fluorescents overhead. He was wearing a deep, musky-smelling cologne that aroused her senses and made her sit up straight in her seat. And then she remembered what her GrandmaZee told her. "If he's not beautiful on the inside, he's not beautiful." So far, the things that came out of PG were far from beautiful.

Sonji was the last to get her assignment back. She stared at the grade in disbelief. There at the top of her paper written in red was a large D. Sonji added her own moan to those of her classmates.

"I had Miss Stephens read the preface of your textbook for a reason," Grayson said, and despite her disappointment regarding her grade, Sonji felt his words sliding smoothly over her body like a caress and smiled.

"It is *Miss* Stephens, isn't it?" he asked, leaning over toward her.

"Yes, it is," Sonji offered as if there were no one else in the room. A young girl seated behind her snickered, and she realized her faux pas.

PG either didn't notice or didn't care about her syrupy-sounding reply. "Can someone in here summarize Miss Stephens' reading from last week?"

Byron, Sonji's study partner, raised his hand.

"Mr. Moore?"

"The text assumes that we have a basic understanding of grammar, punctuation, and sentence structure."

"Not just basic understanding, Mr. Moore, but a certain level of mastery. The kind of mastery befitting collegiate compositions." Grayson walked about the classroom with his hands clasped behind his back. The students watched him carefully.

"What I read in some of your papers wouldn't merit a decent grade in junior high school." He paused as if for effect.

"From the looks of these papers, most of you will inevitably repeat this class next semester."

There it is, Sonji thought. Just like Andi said.

Grayson stood at the head of the class. His large physique and regal features were strongly masculine. There was no doubt that he was very much in charge of the classroom. His posture and presence said it all.

"What I suggest," he offered, placing a hand to his chin, "is that you all buy yourselves a *Gregg Reference Manual* and study it. And I want you all, every one of you, to find a study partner, someone in this class that you can show your papers to before you hand them in to me. It's always good to get a second opinion."

His head was perfectly still, but his eyes glanced from one end of the classroom to the other, allowing him to take in the full room. "I want you to have purchased the *Gregg Reference Manual* by the next class."

"Save those essays. By the end of the semester, I hope you will be far better writers. And I will ask you, those of you who are left, to write another essay on what was wrong with the first essay you wrote. Perhaps by then you will have learned something."

"And now, on to today's lesson."

Sonji felt sick. It was hard for her to concentrate. Her first grade in college, and it was a D. Maybe she wasn't ready for this school stuff at all. Maybe she should drop all of her classes. Then she could go back to life as a full-time supervisor. She made a decent living, far from minimum wage. She had her own home, a car. Really . . . what more did she need?

As she asked herself that question, visions of Mrs. Chad Lovelace and her pitiful husband floated through her mind. *No!* she thought. *I'm going to stay on course. Professor Gilmore will not stop me. I'll take Capiz's advice and find out exactly what he wants. If it's 110 percent, I'll give him 130!*

Sonji took copious notes during her English class. She wrote down exact words, inferences of opinions, students' comments he agreed with, and made several comments herself. By the end of class, Sonji had been through a mental workout. She felt mentally exhausted and emotionally exhilarated at the same time. Their next assignment was to choose their favorite prose piece and write a five-page paper on their analysis of it.

While leaving class, Sonji ran into Byron. "Wow, he

really socks us with the assignments. Two papers in one week."

"Yeah," Sonji responded.

"Say," Byron said, walking down the hall with her. "What did you get on your paper?"

Sonji frowned. "A D."

"Same here," Byron admitted. "Look, I've gotta run to my next class, but I copied Chapter Two for you." He reached into his portfolio, withdrew several sheets of paper, and handed them to Sonji.

"Byron . . . thank you." Sonji took the photocopies. "How much do I owe you?"

"Nothing." Byron said, turning down an adjacent hallway. "I'll see you Friday."

A gleeful smile overtook Sonji's face. *I must have a guardian angel.* With the thought of so many people helping her, the multicultural students and now Byron, she walked toward her car feeling more confident than ever. "Look out, PG," she said. "Here comes Sonji Stephens."

It was all Sonji could do to get through work. Most of her supervisory duties involved making sure her people had what they needed to do their jobs as Lost/Stolen Specialists. Today was a little more demanding. She had just hired a new person to her team, bringing the total to eight team members. She spent most of her time at work acclimating the new person to her job. And the new person was about as sharp as a bowling ball.

She took her time explaining that it was her small department's job to place blocks on credit cards when they were lost or stolen. No matter how slowly Sonji went over the details of the Report Entry computer screens, the new person had a hard time catching on.

It wasn't like that when Jacquelyn Jackson worked in their Human Resources Department. When Jackie hired someone, you knew that someone came with skills. Too bad she had only lasted about six months. Now, Sonji was lucky if HR hired someone that could type. So instead of heading to school right after work, Sonji ended up spending extra time with the new hire.

By the time she returned to school, Campus Computing was packed again. Sonji, hoping for a break, searched for Andromeda and found her on the far side of the room.

"Hey, Sonji."

"Hi, Andi!"

Andromeda took a full look at her new friend. "You sound better," she said, combing her fingers through her long mane of hair.

Sonji smoothed her hands down the sides of her carmel-colored pantsuit. "I feel better, Andi." Sonji pulled a chair up next to Andromeda. "Thanks to Capiz, I'm going to write PG a paper that will make his head spin."

"I knew you could do it. Did you finish the assignment for Lyman?"

"Yes. I did that during my break at work."

"Geez. I've been struggling with that for more than an hour."

"Just use the United States as a contrasting example. That's what I did."

"Oh. Gosh. That's just so totally the right thing to do."

Andromeda pressed a few buttons on the keyboard and a blank page appeared in the word processing program. Then she clicked a button on the toolbar and was prompted for her name and class information. After she entered it, the system formatted it onto the page.

"Hey, I like that. I didn't know these computers could do that," Sonji said.

"Not all of them can. Only the ones I sit at. I always add macros like that so that I can save time on my assignments."

"Do you program them yourself?"

Andi smiled triumphantly. "Uh-huh."

"I'm impressed, Andi."

"Don't be. I do stuff like that all the time. It's fun."

"Andi, if I tried to do something like that, I would have a headache the size of Canada."

Then Sonji heard Andromeda let go a laugh that was so free and unencumbered, she was almost jealous. *To be that carefree,* Sonji thought.

Andromeda made a few swift clicks of the mouse. The screen changed quickly from a word processing program to BlackLuv.net.

"Oh Andi, I just came to do my assignment and go."

"We'll just take a peek to see what Osiris said next. You know he's the one."

"Yeah, sure," Sonji replied, flippantly.

Andromeda tossed her wayward hair once more and flashed a brilliant smile. "Let's see," she said.

Sonji entered her password and waited. After a few seconds a new screen appeared with a list of e-mails, all addressed to Nzinga.

"Oh, my gosh," Sonji said, looking at the list of would-be suitors.

Andromeda pressed the Page Down button on the keyboard to scroll through the list. Sonji felt her stomach lurch as she read the names and message lines.

GOOD Man Waiting to Be FOUND from Your G.

Hot and Ready to Be Cooled from SuperFreak.

Come See About Meeeeeee from Lonely Lad.

Happiness Is Bearing Me 10 Babies from BigBlkStud.

Can I Get A WHAT, WHAT! from JockRock.

The list went on. Sonji felt sick.

"Andi, what have you done?"

"Don't worry. If you don't write back, they leave you alone."

Andi reached the end of the list and sighed. "Sorry, Sonji. I thought for sure he would have written back by now."

Sonji wasn't ready to admit it, but she was hoping that Osiris would have returned her e-mail. Just from one e-mail, he seemed intriguing and engaging and intelligent and sensitive and . . .

"Well, I'll get out of your way here. But don't give up on him. He'll write back. I can feel it."

Sonji took a breath. "I'm not worried about Osiris. I just want to get my paper done and impress the hell out of PG."

"Good luck, then," Andi said and clicked back to the word processing program.

"There you go, Sonji. And if you want to use that macro, it's this button."

Andromeda pointed to a button with a picture of a document and an exclamation mark on it.

"Thanks, Andi."

Andromeda gathered her books and papers into her backpack. "See ya," she said, and walked to the exit.

For the next three and a half-hours, Sonji worked on the five-page paper. She reviewed and reread her notes. She reviewed and reread the chapter. She included quotes from discussions in class, the textbook, information on the Internet and even ol' PG himself.

By the time she finished, she had light perspiration on her brow and was exhausted. For one final quality check, she asked a student next to her to read her paper and give her some feedback. She had chosen wisely, because the young man found a couple of typos and an unclear paragraph.

Sonji made the changes and printed out her final draft. She was so satisfied with her work, she forgot how disappointed she was to find that Osiris hadn't written back. Sonji strolled from Campus Computing with renewed confidence. She couldn't wait to see the big red *A* on her paper.

Four

Grayson sat at the mahogany desk in his den, trying to work. He was surrounded by works by the greatest authors of the twentieth century, but he had writer's block. Every time he began a new lesson plan for his literature class, he was halted by visions of Sonji Stephens. This time it was her dimples.

Her dimples were set so deep, he kept imagining what it would be like to slowly circle them with his tongue and then . . .

"Confound it!" he said, rising from his chair. He pushed the thoughts of Sonji aside and tried to concentrate on his class. He had many books and many authors to draw from. What he needed was a staple. Something he could focus on, while allowing the list of works he'd already compiled to add the coloring and flavor the class deserved. He scanned his extensive library once more and found what he was looking for. He pulled the book from his shelf.

Breaking Ice: An Anthology of Contemporary African-American Fiction, edited by Terry McMillian.

That is it, he thought.

Grayson took the book and sat down at his desk. He flipped through the pages to refamiliarize himself with the work. Then he turned to his computer and began typing. After a few minutes, the lesson plan seemed to write itself.

It was the last day of the first week of classes, and Sonji was riding high. *I actually think I'm going to make it,* she thought. Her algebra class was a high-level review of what she had studied in high school. Thank goodness she still remembered most of it. The world civilizations class was boring, but Andi had been right. Those students that turned their assignments in on time got very good grades. Those that turned them in late got extremely poor grades. And sociology— that was a fascinating subject, and it was nice to have someone she knew in class. Although Andi was having a tough time grasping some of the concepts, Sonji was willing to help her.

English class with PG was going to be different, starting today. Sonji knew that this paper she was handing in was going to be a turning point. *No more D's,* she thought as she placed her paper on PG's desk at the end of class. And she had a method down pat now. Just as in the previous class, Sonji took thorough notes. She recorded what PG said, what others in the class said. She paid particular attention to those comments that seemed near and dear to his heart and put stars by them in her notebook.

The only difficulty she had taking notes was when she allowed her concentration to come undone by Professor Gilmore's dashing smile. And when he took off his jacket halfway into the class, and the honey-gold silk shirt he wore revealed outlines of his muscular arms, Sonji dropped her pen.

But those were only fleeting moments. By the end of class, Sonji felt confident about the next assignment. It was another five-page paper. This time, the class was instructed to write about the worst work of prose they'd ever read, what made it bad, and how they though it could be improved.

Sonji whisked herself out of the classroom and walked briskly down the hall.

"Sonji, wait."

Byron jogged up beside her. "What's up?"

Sonji smiled. "You know, Byron, I think I've got this college thing licked," she pronounced.

"So soon?" Byron asked, looking amused.

"Yeah. It's not nearly as bad as I thought it was going to be. After all, I've been out of school for a number of years now."

Byron nodded in agreement. "Me, too."

Sonji took a good look at Byron. He looked to be about thirty.

Byron stopped walking and pulled some papers from his portfolio. "I've got Chapter Three, if you want it."

"Thank you, Byron." Sonji took the papers and put them in her backpack. "You have been so helpful in what has got to be my toughest class. How can I repay you?"

"Well actually, I was hoping that we could get together over the weekend and study. I'm going to write my paper tonight. Maybe we can meet at the library on Saturday or Sunday to critique each other's work."

"I like the sound of that. It's probably exactly what ol' PG had in mind."

"Who?"

"Professor Gilmore. Some of the students on campus call him PG. Quite apropos, wouldn't you say?"

"Definitely."

Byron started off toward his next class. "When should we meet?"

"How about two o'clock on Sunday?"

"Perfect. I'll meet you on the main floor of the lobby—by the circulation desk."

"See you then," Sonji said as Byron disappeared around a corner.

Now Sonji felt better than ever. She felt so good that she decided to stop by a bakery on the way to work and bring her team some doughnuts and bagels as treats. And to top it off, she would stop by Grandma-Zee's house on the way home. *Today is a good day,* she said to herself.

Sonji's good thoughts carried her through her afternoon at work. She filled out forms, attended a meeting, and provided more training to her new team member. For once, there were no fires to put out, and Sonji left work still positive, and headed for her old neighborhood.

Her grandmother had lived in the same house for fifty years. Although some of the neighbors had changed, many of the families from Sonji's childhood still lived in the neighborhood. As she turned up Fulton Street to Thirty-third, she saw Mrs. Bratton in her yard raking leaves. Sonji knew Mrs. Bratton was well into her eighties, but she wouldn't dare let anyone do for her what she had been doing all her life.

"It just takes me a little longer, but I can do for myself," the feisty old woman often said.

Sonji waved as she drove by.

"Hi, Baby," was Mrs. Bratton's familiar greeting.

She drove into her grandmother's driveway and parked the car. Before she stepped out, she checked herself in the mirror. If she didn't look well put together, her grandmother would have a fit. After pushing her short curls into place and applying fresh lipstick, she got out of the car and walked toward the house.

It was funny how the house she grew up in got

smaller and smaller as the years went by. When she was
younger, she thought that her grandmother had the
largest house on the block. Looking at it now, she realized that it was about the same as all the others.

"I knew I heard my baby."

"Hey, GrandmaZee."

The two women embraced.

"Let me look at you."

The older woman stepped back and examined the
younger woman closely. "That's Momma's beauty,"
she said through a smile. "Come on inside."

Sonji and Nzinga walked into the house arm in arm.

"What can I get you?" Nzinga said, heading toward
the kitchen.

"Nothing, GrandmaZee. I'm fine."

Nzinga came back and sat in the living room with
her granddaughter. "You sho' are dear. You sho' are."

Her grandmother was wearing one of the many
housedresses that had become a staple of her ward-
robe these days. She wore an off-white apron over the
green-and-white dress, its deep pockets bulging with
who knew what.

Nzinga rocked back and forth in her chair, smiling.
"Just look at you. You got the glow about you, chile.
You gonna tell me his name, or you gonna make me
guess?"

"Ah, Grandma, you always think you know something about me."

"I'm the one what changed your diapers regular. I
should know a little somthin'."

"There's no man, Grandma."

"Pretty thing like you . . . they's always a man. It's
just that sometimes you don't know it."

Sonji felt her face flush. Maybe there was a man.
But how could she explain to her seventy-three-year-
old grandmother that for now, their courtship was

electronic? She decided right then and there that she wasn't going to tell anyone about her online experiment. There was no telling what people might think.

For the next hour, Sonji talked with her grandmother about all of the wonderful things that she had experienced since she started school. She talked about her new friends, the multicultural students organization, and even about PG. By the time she left, she was worn-out from her long day.

By noon Sunday, Sonji had finished her paper for English class. She fell into the rhythm of her previous paper and added all the details she thought Professor Gilmore would find to his liking. She even included a highlighted copy of the prose she was critiquing along with a rewrite of a section she found particularly bad.

Byron was at the library on time, and they found a place on the main floor to study. At first they made small talk, but after a few moments, they were ready to tackle their assignments. They switched papers and for the next ten minutes each was silent—occasionally writing a comment on the other's paper. When they were finished, Byron broke the silence first.

"This is outstanding. I would definitely give you an A."

"Really?" Sonji said, feeling a bit of that confidence from Friday.

"Oh, no doubt. It's good stuff. I can almost hear Gilmore using the same examples and making the same points."

"Thanks," Sonji said.

"What about mine?"

Sonji had to admit, Byron had a very original approach to bad prose. He had selected an essay from a well-known and respected author and pointed out why the piece was inappropriate for its purpose. She thought it would most assuredly raise an eyebrow. And it was genuinely well written.

"I liked your position. I thought it was unique and different. And you made your points very well."

"Well, we'll see. After that D, I decided that I've just got to write the best papers that I can write. To heck with Mr. . . . What do you call him?"

"PG."

"Yeah, PG. We've got three weeks until the last drop day. If I haven't improved my grade by then, bye-bye, PG."

Somehow, Sonji didn't think she would have that problem. Byron and Sonji spent the rest of their time in the library talking about their other classes and their jobs. When they left, they wished each other luck on their papers and promised to get together for lunch sometime.

Getting through sociology on Monday was torture. Sonji took notes, but her thoughts were on English class. She was eager to get her paper back to see what grade she had gotten. In the middle of class, Andromeda passed her a note asking her if she was alright. Sonji assured her that she was.

After class she filled Andromeda in.

"I'm just wondering what I got on my English paper, that's all. I took Capiz's advice, and now I'm ready to reap the results."

"Well, you'd better get to class," Andi said. "You know how long it takes to get there from here."

"I know," Sonji said, trotting off in the direction of the annexes.

For the fourth time in as many classes, Sonji was late.

That meant she was sitting up front again. *Darn,* she thought, and took a seat in the corner. PG glanced at her, and then wrote something in his assignment book. *What is he writing?* Sonji wondered as he walked by and handed her the assignment from last week. She was first to get her paper back this time.

Sonji took a look at the grade in the upper right corner of the paper and felt the hairs at the nape of her neck curl. There in red pen was a large *D+*. Sonji was livid. She spent the remainder of the class battling the thunderclouds of emotion she felt were threatening to erupt at any moment. When the end of the class period came, Sonji hadn't taken one note, and she had no idea what the next assignment was. She probably wouldn't have realized that class was over if everyone hadn't gotten up and left.

She rose slowly out of her seat and watched as PG erased the blackboard. When he finished, he turned around and brushed his hands together to remove the chalk dust. He looked surprised to see her still in the room.

"Yes?" he said, looking at her over the top of his glasses.

"PG . . . I mean Professor Gilmore, I need to talk to you about my grade."

Grayson packed up his papers and books into a leather briefcase and closed it. He started walking toward the door.

"That's just as well. I need to talk to you about your tardiness." He turned toward her and looked as though he was giving her a subtle once-over. Despite her anger, Sonji's goose bumps were immediate. "My office is this way."

Grayson walked slowly toward his office. Sonji seemed like the gutsy type. So many students took what they were given without ever questioning it, good or bad. And many of those who received less than satisfactory grades simply dropped out.

But Sonji was a fighter. He could tell that about her in the way she wrote—even in the way she walked into class and sat in her seat. Something about her manner said *look out, world.* And just as he had expected, she had called him on her grade. *Good,* he thought. *Very good.*

When they reached his office, Grayson took a seat behind his desk and waited for Sonji to speak.

"Professor Grayson, I don't believe I deserved a D on this paper."

"Miss Stephens, that's not a D. It's a D-plus. You've improved from your last assignment."

Sonji's jaw tightened slightly.

She holds her anger very well, Grayson thought.

"Professor, this is an outstanding paper."

"Indeed."

"You can't tell me you don't agree with what I've written here."

"You're right, Miss Stephens. I can't."

"Then I think you should change my grade. I deserve better than a D-plus."

Grayson got up from his desk and walked around to where Sonji was standing. He couldn't believe that in the middle of an important discussion like this, his mind was very much aware of the perfume she had on and how her dress seemed to be wearing her instead of vice versa.

"Do you deserve better than a D-plus Miss Stephens?"

"Yes," Sonji said, agitation raising her voice.

"Why?"

He could see Sonji's chest rise and fall with deep breaths. She had tightened her grip on her assignment and moved closer to him.

"Because I busted my ass writing this paper! I took

so many notes for this thing that I almost got a cramp in my hand. And I've got sources up the wazu! Just because you're a jerk doesn't mean you have to make other people suffer. I put too much into this!" Sonji waved her paper in front of Grayson's face, and he caught her wrist with his hand.

"Then where are you?" he asked, then released her hand.

Sonji backed up slightly. "What!"

He smiled. *Oh, no, you don't get away that easily,* he thought.

"Of all of the sources up your . . . wazu . . . where are you?"

Sonji started to speak, but Grayson interrupted. "No, you had your say. Now let me have mine."

Grayson moved closer to Sonji. "I could have written this paper myself. As a matter of fact, I did, didn't I? Let's see . . . me and about half of the class. You did a nice job of prettying it up. But I already know what I think. And as your instructor, I'm interested in what *you* think, Miss Stephens. So, before you come back into my office demanding that your grade be raised, be sure you've earned it. Because as of yet, you haven't."

He moved closer to her still, and even though his voice sounded gruff and forceful, he realized that it wasn't anger that he felt. It was desire. Strong and acute desire. He summoned all of his professional ethics to keep himself from sweeping Sonji into his arms and kissing her with the reckless abandon he felt at that very moment.

From what he could tell, Sonji looked startled and apprehensive. He decided he had better back away and give her some room. When he did, her words came out tentatively.

"I'm—I'm, sorry Professor Gilmore. I just thought that I would try to give you what you wanted."

Grayson sat on the edge of his desk. "Hmmm. That's not a bad approach actually. Shall I tell you what I want?"

"Please."

"I want to know what's in *your* head, Sonji. I want to present you with the kind of information that will allow you to come to your own conclusions. Not latch on to mine. I want . . . well, you get the picture."

"Yes, I think so."

Grayson raised an eyebrow. "Do you still think I'm a jerk?"

Sonji was silent for a few seconds then nodded. "Yes. I do."

"Well, at least you're honest." Grayson got up and took his seat behind the desk again. He listened as Sonji's disgruntled footsteps approached the door to his office. She took the jacket that was draped over her arm and wrapped it around her shoulders. As she reached for the doorknob, the motion dislodged something from the jacket pocket. A piece of folded paper wafted to the floor of Grayson's office.

"Just a moment," he said rising. "It seems you are in need of a tailor."

Sonji paused and turned as Grayson walked to where the paper lay on the floor. He picked it up and handed it to her.

"Oh," she said, seemingly relieved.

Grayson, for reasons he was unable to fathom, moved closer. "Something important?"

Sonji offered a reluctant smile. "Byron's phone number."

Grayson felt a slight stitch in his side—like the kind he got when he went running without warming up first. "I see," he said, trying to relax the facial muscles tightening against his jaw.

Sonji took the paper. "See you on Wednesday, professor," Sonji said, walking toward the door.

Grayson lowered his glasses and gave Sonji a stern look. "At what time, Miss Stephens?"

Sonji turned and smiled. "At ten A.M."

"I will hold you to that."

Sonji headed away from PG's office in a hurry. She was frazzled and a bit confused. Her bold attempt had backfired. Time to regroup for Plan B. *I could use a good dose of Osiris right about now,* she said to herself. Feeling slightly dejected but not defeated, Sonji walked over to Campus Computing.

I wonder if he wrote back, Sonji thought as she signed on to BlackLuv. She closed her eyes and chanted, *Please be there, please be there* like a magic mantra. When she opened her eyes, a message in her box read *New Mail: I Accept from Osiris.*

Sonji took a deep breath and slowly shook her head. Finally something was going right. Still feeling a little off-kilter from her confrontation with PG, Sonji was hesitant about opening the e-mail. *What if it's not good news? What if he accepts my offer of correspondence but under certain conditions?* After fussing with all manner of possibilities in her head, Sonji finally opened the e-mail.

At first she couldn't make out the contents, then as she scrolled down farther and farther, she discovered the e-mail message was a single yellow rose in the center of the screen. There was a message underneath it.

Nzinga, I believe it is customary to approach the door of friendship with a gift. Since our connection exists in cyberspace, I hope this virtual rose will do. Please accept it as a token of my intent to get to know and understand you.

If I'm being too forward, please say so. It's just that your profile touched something in me—awakened it actually. And although we have spoken to each other with a certain formality, I felt compelled to extend a gesture toward the familiar.

Grayson couldn't understand it, but for his morning run he had grabbed his Walkman and popped in a Lenny Kravitz tape. "I haven't run with a Walkman in years and listening to Lenny Kravitz, it's been even more years."

"You always revert to your original form when you're stressed or in love."

Grayson's younger brother Kyle sat in Grayson's kitchen, blowing on a hot cup of coffee.

"You will not disrespect me in my own home, Kyle."

"Why do you always accuse me of disrespecting you whenever I remind you of where you came from?"

"I'm well aware of the location of my upbringing."

"Look, Mr. Ph.D., I know you know what I mean."

Grayson decided to ignore his brother's comments. He was more concerned with getting to the root of his concerns. He had been doing things that were out of character lately, and he found that fact extremely unsettling. Although he and his brother had their differences, Grayson knew that when it came to working through issues, there was no better person suited to help him than Dr. Kyle Gilmore, psychologist.

Kyle sipped at his coffee. "All right, let's start over. You want to know why you're doing weird stuff. Is that right?"

"A crude interpretation, but accurate."

"Well . . . let's see. Do you find yourself getting bored easily? Sometimes boredom will cause people to unconsciously act in ways that add variety. In which case you would find yourself doing things out of the ordinary."

"No, I'm not bored. As a matter of fact, I just started teaching a new course, and I find designing the curriculum quite stimulating."

Grayson sat at his kitchen table and watched as his brother sipped at his coffee some more. He often wondered why his brother asked for fresh coffee, since he never started drinking it until it was cold.

"How are your finances? I know you like nice things and sometimes in providing ourselves with the things we like, we become overextended."

"No. My finances are in perfect order."

"Now you know when we were kids, you would always start doing weird stuff whenever a girl was around. Are you seeing someone?"

"No."

"Are you in love with someone?"

"I just told you I wasn't seeing anyone."

"That doesn't make any difference."

"In this case it does."

And then it came. The question he had been dreading and at the same time needing.

"Are you anxious or nervous about something?"

Now that was the million-dollar question, wasn't it? These last few years, he and his brother had a silent understanding about some things. And all of those things involved Veranda and Gray Jr. But in his own subtle way, Kyle had managed to mention the unmentionable.

"I take it from your silence that that's a yes."

Grayson could only sigh in response.

"How long has it been, Gray?"

"Seven years."

"I know it's not the kind of thing that you could

ever forget, but in these past few years I thought you had healed."

Grayson ran a hand down his face. "I have healed, mostly. My emotional baggage is empty, anyway."

"Then what's up?"

"Just the fact that it's been seven years."

Kyle finished off his cold coffee in large gulps. "I see." He got up from the table and set his coffee cup in the sink, then turned toward his brother.

"So, what are you going to do?"

"Well, there's no avoiding it now. I've got to go take care of things."

Kyle walked over to stand behind his brother's chair. He put his hands on Grayson's shoulders. "I'm glad you're finally in a place where you can do what needs to be done."

Grayson looked down at the Walkman on the kitchen counter and the empty cassette box with Lenny Kravitz's picture on it.

"Me too," he replied, remembering the lyrics *Baby, it ain't over till it's over.*

Five

The pile of papers in front of Grayson looked more formidable by the minute. He thought by introducing a multicultural element into an otherwise monocultural curriculum he would challenge the students and help them think outside the box. So far his effort was to no avail. Judging by the students' analysis projects, they needed more help than perhaps Grayson and a three credit-hour literature course could give them.

It was as if the more progress the world seemed to make, the more experience, exposure, and just plain understanding seemed to be lacking in people. And as cool as some of the kids in his literature class professed to be—with their sagging pants, urban speech, and multiracial friends—the sad truth was, they really had no concept of what they were emulating or, for that matter, why.

He had read and graded over half of the students' essays on their short-story assignment, and the same comments kept repeating themselves again and again. "The dialogue doesn't seem true." "The characters are too preoccupied with their differences." And his favorite, "Why are they so concerned with skin color?" One of the students even requested that he be able to write his report on another story, something that had more significance.

Grayson couldn't fathom their comments or the perspective from which they came. It was almost as if, to teach multicultural literature to people who are not multicultural, one must first teach racism and the effects it has on groups and individuals over a two-, three-, and four-hundred-year period.

Grayson continued to grade papers wondering how he could change the curriculum so that the students might gain some insight into themselves, others, and therefore the literature. He hoped an answer would come soon. Otherwise, he would be forced to grade the papers of students who were closed-minded and unreceptive to the unique circumstance that is America. Somehow he would find a way. He refused to lose this battle.

The life of a college student—copious note taking, late-night studying, last-minute research, rushing from class to class, innumerable student activities, hectic parking, confounding teacher personalities—were all becoming minor concerns to Sonji. She had returned to school at the right time in her life. That meant she had the focus, determination, and stamina she needed to devote herself to achieving her goal. But she wasn't prepared for the cyber relationship that gave her goose bumps whenever the thought of signing on to get her e-mail crossed her mind.

In every class, she found her mind wandering, drifting to the last letter she had received from Osiris and hoping that he had sent her another. Even in PG's class, as fine as he was, she found that looking at his face always made her wonder what Osiris looked like. Once, when she was supposed to be doing an in-class writing assignment, she looked down at her paper to discover that she had written the name Osiris over and over. Luckily she was able to put it away before PG caught her slacking in his class.

She and her electronic pen pal were following the BlackLuv connection protocol to the letter—hardly any personal disclosures. Because the risk of corresponding with a kook was so great on the Internet, they had only shared some of their interests, their philosophies of life, their goals and aspirations, and what they were looking for in a relationship. They didn't reveal their real names, where they lived, where they worked, or what their occupations were.

Sonji remembered Andi's story of a woman who mentioned to a guy online that she was a department-store clerk in the Bay Area. Two weeks later, he showed up at her job. Sonji wasn't about to take a chance like that. So she followed the network etiquette implicitly.

Osiris told her he was interested in a woman with drive, determination, intelligence, and compassion. She responded to his list by telling him the she was partial to someone with honesty, integrity, ambition, and a sense of personal vision. So far, Osiris seemed to have everything on her list.

The most tender moment of their relationship came on the one-month anniversary of their correspondence. Osiris sent her a poem by Etheridge Knight entitled, "Belly Song" and a file attachment addressed to Queen Nzinga. When she downloaded the file, it was a photo of a room full of roses in spectacular color and variety. The words *Happy One-Month Anniversary* appeared across the bottom of the picture.

Sonji couldn't think of anyone from her past relationships who had remembered their one-month anniversary. To thank him, she put on her reddest lipstick and pressed her lips to a piece of paper. Then she scanned the image and e-mailed it to him. Slowly, ever so slowly, she was beginning to think that perhaps Andi was right. Could it be? she asked herself. Had she found *the one?*

Her preoccupation with Osiris was driving her to do some unusual things. She was so intrigued by his code name that she looked up Egyptian mythology on the Encyclopedia Africana CD-ROM and discovered that Osiris was the Egyptian god of the afterlife. He was once ruler of Egypt, the Egyptians' means to eternal life, and the very first mummy. He was the one that decided who could cross over into the afterlife and who could not. Sonji wondered if Osiris's screen ame held some special significance for him.

She was also compelled to do more research on her chosen name. She didn't like arbitrary decisions. And she wanted to make sure that her screen name selection was appropriate and not a hasty choice. What she found surprised her. She had known that the name belonged to a strong and powerful warrior. But she didn't know that Nzinga was a primary military strategist, and led her own warriors into battle.

The other thing Sonji found herself doing was an inordinate amount of daydreaming. In class, her fantasies were never distracting enough for her to fall behind, but if she didn't get a handle on them, they would be. Twice while she was in her office at work, she daydreamed about being teleported back to one of the remarkable Egyptian dynasties and ruling the Two Lands with Osiris as her pharaoh. When she realized what she was doing, she felt guilty for neglecting her duties and worked overtime to make up for her transgression.

As Sonji sat at her kitchen table, she realized that she was doing it again. Although she was surrounded by research she'd collected for her world civilizations project, she was thinking about Osiris as if he were someone she could touch. She had to keep reminding herself that so far he was really just words on a screen. For all she knew they would probably never meet.

"He could be living in Tokyo," she said, rising from the table. She walked over to her butcher-block counter and made herself a French vanilla cappuccino. She poured the drink into an oversized ceramic cup that looked more like a bowl with handles, and walked out to her patio. Fall was coming on steadily now. The leaves on the trees were a multitude of oranges, reds, yellows, and fading greens, and the wind had begun blowing them gently from their place of residence on the branches.

A squirrel came traipsing across Sonji's lawn, carrying a large nut in its mouth. It paused when it saw her, and she remained perfectly still. After watching her for a moment, the squirrel continued on its way across the grass and up into the evergreen tree in her backyard.

It's funny, Sonji thought, *how nature knows instinctively when to make preparations for the changing seasons. But humans! Sometimes they never change.* Her thoughts brought a fleeting image of Chad into her mind. She quickly cast it aside and went back into her town house. She sat down at her kitchen table and returned her attention to her project, determined to concentrate on getting an A.

Grayson parked his car on the side of the gravel road and got out. He trudged down the familiar paths of the Prospect Hill Cemetery with fresh flowers in hand. He read the section signs, realizing for the first time how contrived they were. Serenity Sea, Tranquil Park, Hope Hill. These were all things to make those who were left behind feel better about their loved ones being gone. But nothing would ever make him feel better about his loss.

Grayson looked around. The cemetery was quiet and still except for a slight breeze that rustled the leaves on the trees and made him pull his black, ankle-length trench coat closer around him.

Everything always looks the same, he thought. *Has anything changed? I could find my way around here blindfolded.*

For a place so old, it was the final resting place for some of the youngest in the city. Some of the markers and headstones in the cemetery were more than a hundred years old. Grayson had heard his parents talking about their grandparents being buried at Prospect Hill but not having grave markers because they didn't provide them for "colored" people in those days. As he rounded the bend to where his son was buried, his footsteps became heavy and guilt-ridden.

The marker before him was a large concrete structure with a basketball, a baseball bat, a toy train, and an airplane carved into it. The inscription read GRAYSON BARTHOLOMEW GILMORE, JR., 1990–1994. BELOVED SON. NO MAN KNOWS THE HOUR.

After all these years, it never got easier. He knelt down and leaned against the marker. Just like always, there was anger, hot and unabashed. And then there was simmering regret. "Why couldn't I have been there to save him?" He placed the flowers on the gravesite and looked up into the sky. "Why?" he said as a single tear flowed from his eye and hit the ground below.

Grayson watched as the terrain transformed from pristinely landscaped lawns and rows of tightly clustered, similar-looking homes to old neighborhoods, large front yards, and older, more distinct homes with roomy front porches. His brother's home was one of the oldest in the neighborhood. He parked his car in the driveway and was reminded again of how different he and his brother were.

Kyle and his wife, Jerika, actually had a house with a white picket fence, a dog, Smedley—a collie, no less— and right now two-point-five children. Grayson hid the sack of goodies behind his back and pushed the doorbell.

He heard the familiar voice of his four-year-old niece, Klarice.

"I'll get it!"

The interior door swung open, and Klarice stood in the doorway with a broad smile. "Uncle Gray!" she exclaimed. She threw open the storm door and jumped into his arms.

"Hi, Crumbcake," he said, returning her big hug.

He walked into the house and hoisted her onto his shoulders.

"Did you bring me something, Uncle Gray?" Klarice asked, eyeing the Kay Bee Toys bag.

"Have you been a good girl?" he asked as a pregnant Jerika walked into the entryway.

"Yes, I've been a *real* good girl!"

"Now, Klarice, tell the truth," Jerika said, placing a hand on her hip.

Klarice's wide smile narrowed a bit. "Well . . . I was trying to be good," she said, looking at her mother.

"I think that counts for something," Grayson said, following Jerika into the kitchen. He set his niece down and reached into the bag. He pulled out a CD-ROM of mathematics and reading games.

"Ooh, thank you, Uncle Gray! Mommy, can I go play on the 'puter?"

"*Com*puter, baby. Say it with Mommy."

Klarice said the word *computer* with her mother and then waited.

"Only for a few minutes. We're about to eat dinner."

"Yay!" Klarice yelled, running off to the family room.

"Have your dad get you started!" Jerika called after her daughter.

Grayson smiled broadly, watching his niece skip away happily. "She's grown since the last time I saw her."

"You always say that, Bart. Even if you were just here yesterday. And what are you trying to do, turn her into a rocket scientist? That's what, the fifth CD-ROM?"

Grayson leaned against the counter and drummed his fingers on its smooth surface. "The sooner kids get acclimated to computers, the better." He smiled at Jerika's raised eyebrow. "Just wait until I introduce her to the Internet!"

Jerika stirred a pot filled to the brim with greens. "Don't you dare expose my child to that filth!"

"Jeri, the Internet is not a bad place. It's like the downtown area of a big city. There are wonderful places you can go. Good places. Places that will inspire, elate, even educate."

Grayson moved closer to the pot, inhaling the enticing aroma of his favorite food. "There are also places where I wouldn't take Smedley. Seedy, raunchy places that are best left alone."

"Make your point, Bart."

"The point is, the choice is yours. Where you go is up to you. What you do with the Internet is up to you. And you know I would never do anything to harm or allow harm to come to my niece."

Jerika covered the pot before Grayson could stick his nose in it. He looked slightly disappointed.

"I know, but I'm not convinced the Internet is as

great as you and Kyle seem to think it is. There's something not quite right about it. It's not human, but people interact with it like it is. It's . . . it's . . . wrong."

Jerika walked over to the pantry and retrieved some ceramic serving dishes. Just then Grayson dashed over to the simmering pot and lifted the lid. He inhaled the aroma deeply and sighed audibly.

"Sniffing the pot again, big brother?" Kyle entered the kitchen with his ten-month-old daughter, Kya, on his hip.

Grayson replaced the lid with a look of contented bliss shining on his face. "You know I have a weakness for greens, little brother."

"That's why he asked me to cook them," Jerika interjected, smiling. "Now all three of you, get out of my kitchen so I can finish dinner," she said, making shooing motions with her arms.

"Yes, ma'am!" Kyle said, saluting.

"Daa, baa!" Kya said, mimicking her father.

"That's makes three!" Grayson said, following his brother into the other room.

He reached out for his niece, and she came to him happily. She sat on his lap and played with the gold herringbone necklace lying against his skin.

"No, Kya," Kyle said, seeing the object of his daughter's attention. She turned and looked at her father, then back to Grayson.

"She's okay," Grayson said.

"Yeah well, if she breaks it, don't look at me to replace it!" Kyle said, laughing.

"It's just a necklace," Grayson replied. Then he reached into the Kay Bee Toys bag and took out the other gift. It was a large, clear rattle with multicolored numbers and letters that slid around and made noise on the inside. Kya's attentions quickly changed from the necklace to the rattle. She shook it and grinned.

"Gray, you buy more stuff for my kids than I do."

"Funny."

"No, Gray. It's true. Every time you come over here, you bring something for the kids. That's not necessary."

"I know. But I *want* to do it."

"Why, Gray?"

"Because I love them. They're my nieces, for goodness' sake."

"And that's the only reason?"

"Of course."

Kyle wanted to respond, but remained silent. He was hoping that his brother would realize that his behavior might stem from his loss of Gray Jr. But he wanted Grayson to say it. If it came from anywhere other than himself, he would probably dismiss it.

"I don't know, Kyle. Maybe I'm trying to make up for the things I'll never be able to do for Gray Jr." Grayson set Kya on the floor and she began crawling around with her new rattle.

"Even after all these years, I still feel like a part of me is missing."

"That's because it is. And it will always be. But I guess there are worse things you could do to help ease the pain of your loss than buying my kids toys. But any behavior that's not healthy, no matter how innocuous it seems, can eventually cause more harm than good."

A memory flashed through Grayson's mind. He could see a multitude of boy dolls in every room of his home. He remembered that at first there was only one doll. But soon one doll became ten, and ten became one hundred. And then Veranda—

"Gray?"

Grayson disengaged himself from the tragic image.

"Sorry, Kyle. I seemed to have fallen victim to an errant thought."

"Care to share it?"

"Not now."

"Then I will repeat what Jerika just said. Dinner is ready."

The Gilmore family ate their dinner leisurely, and woven throughout the helpings of smothered pork chops, greens, candied yams, potato salad, and corn bread, were conversations of politics, friends, acquaintances, the latest weather catastrophe, Klarice's new computer program, and the pros and cons of the Internet.

Jerika talked about her preparations to home-school Klarice. Grayson was impressed. When Kyle had first started going out with Jerika years ago, Grayson had his doubts about her. They were so different. Once Grayson had insinuated that Jerika might be from the wrong side of the tracks, and Kyle had given him a left hook that he could still feel if he thought about it long enough. That's when he knew his brother was in love.

It didn't take long for Grayson to see that Kyle and Jerika were the right blend of flavors for each other. They weren't water and oil; they were peanut butter and jelly. Or looking at his plate, greens and corn bread. They just went together. And after a full apology, his unkind remark was forgotten.

As he watched Jerika now feeding the baby a spoonful of greens, he realized that she was a wonderful wife and mother. Better, perhaps, than Veranda would have been. And after years of being a bachelor, Grayson was ready to try love again. He knew that somewhere there was a woman who he could build a life with. Like an emerging brilliance of light, the image of Sonji Stephens lit up his mind and made him smile and wonder.

Jerika nudged her husband. "Look at Bart," she whispered.

"I know that look," Kyle said. "You got a woman in there?"

Grayson finished off the last of the greens on his plate. "In where?"

Kyle spoke with a mouthful of corn bread. "In your head."

"Nonsense!"

"Now, Bart," Jerika said, rising from the table and walking into the kitchen. "You can't fool us," she called back.

Jerika returned with the pot of greens and ladled another large portion onto Grayson's plate.

"Thanks, Jeri," Grayson said, digging in.

Klarice scrunched up her face. "Mommy, why do you call Uncle Gray Bart?"

"Your mother is being mean to me," Grayson answered, grateful for the distraction. "She thinks my middle name is funny."

"That's because it is!" Jerika said, returning to her seat.

"What *is* your middle name, Uncle Gray?" Klarice asked, wide-eyed.

Kyle and Jerika tried to stifle their snickers but were unsuccessful.

"Bartholomew," Grayson said, his voice deep with exaggerated regality. He straightened in his chair and stuck his nose in the air.

This time Klarice squished her face together as if she smelled something weird in the air. "Mommy's right, Uncle Gray. Your middle name *is* funny."

The three adults erupted with laugher and after a few seconds, Klarice joined them. The baby looked around and added a drool-laden smile of her own.

After their meals, they all helped to clear the dining

room table, clean the kitchen, and put away the food. Then Jerika took the kids for a walk, and Kyle and Grayson went into the family room.

Sometimes reality hit Grayson and reminded him starkly that his little brother was a grown man, with a family and a home of his own. Grayson viewed his surroundings with fresh eyes. Kyle and Jerika had chosen a minimalist decor, which created the illusion that their three-bedroom home was much larger than its actual size. He recognized the paintings and artwork throughout the house: Bearden, Annie Lee, and even a couple of prints by Billy Dee Williams, Donna Summer, and Miles Davis. *Yep,* he thought. *My kid brother has definitely done all right for himself.*

Kyle walked over from the bar. "The usual?" he asked.

"What else?" Grayson responded, taking the bottle of Guinness from his brother.

Kyle sat across from Grayson in a rocking chair, looking quite comfortable in a tan T-shirt and faded blue jeans. His long, wavy hair was pulled back into a ponytail. People always remarked at how much alike they looked, and it was true. They always feigned disgust when anyone mentioned it, but every now and again, Grayson would catch a glimpse of himself in Kyle's face and become astonished by the resemblance.

"What ya thinkin', Gray?" Kyle asked and tipped his bottle to his lips.

"I'm thinking," Grayson said, rubbing his beard, "that you and I don't look *anything* alike." Then he chuckled warmly. "Actually, I was thinking the exact opposite. Sometimes we do look alike."

"Is that good or bad?"

"That's my brother—always the analyst."

"Not always. Only when it's necessary."

"Oh, I suppose you think it's necessary now."

"I do."

The pleasure of eating Jerika's cooking was fading into a distant memory for Grayson, and the concerns that had been pressing him for the last several weeks came bobbing to the surface.

"Damn, you're good."

Kyle was silent.

"No wonder they pay you the big bucks."

Kyle remained silent.

"All right! I feel like I'm being tortured here."

There was still no response from Kyle—only a stubborn expression of determination that meant he understood that his brother needed to talk and that he was simply going to shut up and listen.

Grayson felt as though he had been rebandaging an old war wound that refused to heal.

"It's been rough lately, Kyle. I feel like everything is happening all over again. The same confusing emotions, the same hesitation, the same doubts and reservations are coming up like a bad meal.

"When I get to a point in my life where I think I've moved on, I'm thrust back into it.

"It took me years to be able to deal with Veranda's condition. And now, it's like I'm abandoning her." Grayson took a long draught from the dark brown bottle, then continued.

"On the other hand, she doesn't need me. She hasn't for a long time now. And I was all right with that. I'd made my peace. And then this. It makes me wonder if I'm really ready to let go"

Kyle crossed one leg over the other and watched his brother intently. He had seen Grayson fret and anguish over some of the hardest challenges anyone could face, and ultimately come to the decisions that were right for him. Sometimes it just took a while for him to see the correct path, but he always found it.

"Only you can answer that, Gray," Kyle said, thinking this was a good time to interject. "And there's one thing I know about you and that is, when the time comes for you to make your decision, you will know exactly what to do. And you'll make the right one."

"But in the meantime . . ."

"In the meantime, you'll focus on taking care of yourself. When was the last time you did something just for you?"

Grayson was silent and reflective. He honestly couldn't remember. He was always so focused on university activities, he forgot sometimes that there was an entire world outside of the campus.

"That's what I thought," Kyle said. "Contrary to popular opinion, it's okay to be selfish once and a while. As long as it doesn't become a habit."

"Something just for me, huh?"

Grayson really couldn't think of anything he wanted to do specifically for himself. But there was something that he had been meaning to do but had never found the time for.

"Actually, I'd like to get more involved with the Midlands Literacy Council."

"That's not exactly what I had in mind. Besides, you already sit on the board. How much more involved do you need to be?"

"I miss the hands-on experience. I want to be back with the students again. I miss that."

"Teach during the day; teach at night. Don't burn yourself out."

"I won't. Teaching at night actually helps me relax and put what I do during the day into perspective."

"Really? How so?"

"The college students have been literate nearly all of their lives. They take for granted what a blessing it is that they can actually read and write. A lot of them put forth only enough effort to coax a C or C-minus out of my classes."

Grayson sat back and smiled. "But the people in the adult literacy classes—they want to learn so desperately. They understand the significance of language and communication. And they work hard at making sure that they get it right. It's a pure joy to see people genuinely enthusiastic about learning the language. And I would be willing to bet that they will never take their literacy for granted."

The house was quaint—ideal for a small family. It was set up high and had a narrow, glass-enclosed front porch that overlooked the busy street. Sonji and her GrandmaZee often sat out on the porch, especially on warm summer nights when the inside of the house was hotter than the temperature outside.

Sonji often worried about her grandmother in that tiny house in the summer. When she had asked her why she wouldn't get an air conditioner, GrandmaZee had just shrugged her shoulders and said that she had been living all these years without one. No sense in getting one now.

A community of knick-knacks, brickabrack, and whatnots lived inside GrandmaZee's house. They were everywhere—on tables, shelves, mantels, and even in their own cabinets and special stands. And then there were the photos of everyone in the family. If there was a space not taken up by a figurine, there was a photo in it. And all of her grandmother's furniture was almost as old as she was. Sonji recalled a recent conversation in which she had tried to persuade her grandmother to get new furniture and her grandmother's predictable reaction.

"What do I need new furniture for? This furniture is still good," she had said.

Now Sonji looked at the furniture and realized GrandmaZee was right. She had taken good care of it. For as far back as Sonji could remember, the furniture had been covered in some fashion by afghans, elaborate bed sheets, doilies, and even plastic. At times it was hard to remember what the actual piece underneath looked like. And GrandmaZee had each piece of furniture cleaned during the spring, so they were always fresh and spot-free. But Sonji thought that Nzinga Mae Stephens deserved so much more. And she was willing to give it to her, but her gifts and offers of gifts were almost always kindly rejected.

"Now, baby, you save your money. You buy *yourself* something nice. That's present enough for me."

Sonji couldn't remember how many times she had heard that. *One day,* she thought, *I'm just going to surprise GrandmaZee and buy something nice for her. She won't be able to say no if the furniture shows up here on a truck.*

"What's that look for, Sonji Kay? You hatching something in that cute little head of yours?"

"Aw, Grandma, you deserve so much more than this!"

"I deserve what the good Lord sees fit to provide for me. And I'm doing all right. This house and everything in it is paid for. Besides, it was good enough for you and your mama to grow up in."

Whenever her grandmother brought up that fact, Sonji knew she had been bested. Sonji decided simply to be quiet for a while and watch her grandmother cook.

"How come you don't never bring nobody with you on Sundays? You know I make enough for a whole gang of folks."

Every Sunday since Sonji moved out on her own, she

had gone over to her grandmother's for dinner. Sometimes she would cook, but most of the time GrandmaZee would cook. It sometimes took all of Sonji's willpower to wait until Sunday to get some of her grandmother's cooking. It was the best food Sonji had ever tasted. She made all the southern staples: catfish, hot-water corn bread, gumbo, jambalaya, red beans and rice. And according to the neighbors, Zinga Mae—as her friends called her—made the best black-eyed peas in four states!

But Sonji rarely had anyone to share her Sundays with. Sonji was an only child and kind of a loner. It wasn't that she didn't like people, but she was so used to being by herself growing up, she didn't seem to make friends easily. And the friends she did make, for one reason or another, had all moved away to other cities. So that just left Sonji.

Maybe one day she would invite Andi and Sebastian over for Sunday dinner. She was sure they would like her grandmother and she them. And then she entertained a thought that made her feel like her insides were glowing. What she would really like to do is invite Professor Gilmore to dinner.

"Woo, I know that look as sure as I know my own nose. What's his name, and when is he coming to visit?"

"Aw, GrandmaZee. Why do you always think you know me so well?"

"Because I raised you. And that gives me a special way to know things. Now, what's his name?"

Sonji sighed. There was no sense trying to hide her feelings.

"Grayson Gilmore."

Nzinga put down her spatula and put her hand on her hip. "Gilmore . . . Gilmore? I know some Gilmores. Grayson, you say?"

"Uh-huh. He's my . . . uh . . . English professor."

"I take it from the goo-goo in your eyes that he's a looker?"

"Mmm-hmmm," Sonji emitted a feline purr from her lips.

"Ha, ha, ha. Got your nose open I see." Nzinga went back to her catfish, which was frying in a cast-iron skillet. "Well, don't go too far off the deep end. You might fall and bump your head. You understand?"

"Yes, Grandma."

"Now, when can I meet him?"

"Never! We're not dating or anything."

The elderly yet spry woman checked on a roasting pan of spaghetti in the oven. "Not yet, baby. Not yet."

Suddenly, Sonji felt like doing something with herself instead of simply waiting for her grandmother to finish cooking.

"I'll make the garlic bread," she said hopping out of her seat.

"Okay," Nzinga said, and together the two women put the finishing touches on their Sunday meal.

Looking at her grandmother, Sonji remembered that oftentimes wise people come in unusual packages. Her grandmother had not changed much in all the years of Sonji's life. She still wore what she referred to as a housecoat, which always looked like a dress that was simply two sizes too big. Today, GrandmaZee's housecoat had an explosion of tiny red and blue flowers on it and zipped up the front. It had big pockets sewn on the front, and Sonji knew that in one there was a handkerchief embroidered with the initials *WCS*. The WCS stood for William Cleofis Stephens, Sonji's grandfather, who had died of cancer before Sonji was born.

A chain of four or five safety pins always hung down the front of the housecoat, pinned just below her left shoulder. Where most people carried a pocket knife for utility jobs, GrandmaZee claimed safety pins would do just about anything. She insisted they had one thousand uses, not the least of which was occasionally picking a tooth.

She was cooking on the same gas stove that Sonji remembered from her youth. Not only had the best catfish been cooked on that stove, but on Sunday mornings, when Sonji was a little girl, a hot comb was heated there just enough to catch up Sonji's kitchens and edges in between pressings and right before church.

Sonji had to admit that most people who met her grandmother didn't like her; they loved her.

"I swear sometimes you leave this earth in the space of a few seconds. Such deep thoughts for such a young woman."

Sonji just looked up and smiled. Nzinga joined her granddaughter at the kitchen table. "Umgh," she uttered, sitting down. Her dusky brown and life-worn hands patted the backs of Sonji's.

"Kids nowadays have so much on their minds. And most of it isn't too important. Only they don't know it. And they don't find out until it's too late. Until they've gone their entire lives and realize that instead of thinkin', they should have been doin'.

"What is it that *you're* supposed to be doin', honey? Don't wait until you get my age to figure it out."

Sonji took a deep breath and inhaled the faint traces of hair pomade, Listerine, and primrose perfume. These were her grandmother's smells. Their mingled fragrances were permanently imprinted in her heart. In a crowd of a thousand people, Sonji thought she would be able to find GrandmaZee by scent alone—the scent of the wise, old sage that she was.

"There you go again," GrandmaZee said, pushing herself up. "Umgh," came the sound of her hoisting herself up from the chair and back to the stove.

"Set the table, baby. Do you think your mighty mind can fix its big ol' self around that idea?"

"Yes, ma'am," Sonji said, walking toward the cabinet.

Six

Sonji sat at a desk in the corner of the Multicultural Students Organization office and poured over her notes. She had several tests coming up, and despite all her efforts, she felt she still hadn't gotten enough studying done. She was stressed and anxious—so much so that she had taken the day off from work to give herself more study time.

As she underlined, outlined, and highlighted important aspects of her sociology book, she was also aware of the students around her. They had been coming in and out in steady streams since she arrived. The office was the place to be if a student of color needed information about financial aid, scholarships, studying techniques, or jobs. And Sonji soon found out that it also provided a wealth of information when it came to recreational activities. Several members of Delta Sigma Theta sorority were busily talking about an upcoming step show, a fashion show, and a poetry slam.

Sonji was surprised to find that she could concentrate despite all the activity going on in the office. During a recent conversation with Andi, she had all but insisted that she couldn't possibly study effectively in an office as busy as MSO.

"Meet me in MSO after your class. You can study

until I get there." The innocence in Andi's voice came across loud and clear even over the telephone.

"Study in MSO? That's an oxymoron, isn't it?"

"There's a study table in the back of the room. People do homework there all the time. And everyone else knows not to bother you if you're sitting back there. Besides, you need to be around people more. I don't like the way you shut yourself off from everyone."

Sonji thought about that. What she was really trying to do was avoid encounters that might put her in close proximity to couples or people in relationships. The reminder of her fiasco with Chad was still smarting like a fresh bruise. An occasional exposure to that life, like Andi and Sebastian, was all right but more than that might prove way beyond what Sonji's tolerance level could withstand.

Her only solace was Osiris. He was like a great hand against her back, propping her up and urging her on. Beyond that, Sonji dared not contemplate relationships, or men in any broad sense.

"Sonji?" Andi's earth-laden voice nudged Sonji's psyche.

"I suppose you're right, Andi. I can't play the avoidance game forever, but I still don't see how I'm going to be able to get any studying done."

"I get out of lab a half hour after you get out of class. I'll bet in that time you will have done so much studying that even I'll be amazed."

Sonji doubted it then. But looking down at her notes now, she had actually made a pretty good dent in her work. Now, if she could just put a dent in her test anxiety, she would be fine.

"Miss Sonji!" Sebastian's voice bellowed out her name from the front of the office. He arrived with Andi in tow, and students parted like the Red Sea to let them pass.

"How are you, Sebastian? And are you ever going to just call me Sonji?"

"I don't mean to imply anything by the title other than respect. Old habits are tough to break, right Special?" Sebastian looked at Andromeda, his eyes turning into wells of admiration. Her whole demeanor softened in his glance.

"I love you, Sebastian," she said.

Andromeda kissed the object of her affection gingerly on his cheek and walked over to where Sonji sat silently observing their love-play.

"You two don't study too hard, now. Especially you, baby. You've got the literacy council orientation tomorrow."

"Oh, wow! I almost forgot. Gee, thanks, Sebastian."

Sebastian winked. "That's my job," he said and walked back to the front of the office where several students were gathered talking.

Sonji's curiosity was piqued. "I didn't know you were involved with the literacy council."

"Yeah," Andi said, taking books out of her book bag and setting them on the table. "Many of us in MSO are. For a while, we taught adults that just hadn't learned how to read. But now there's this big push for volunteers to, like, teach English as a Second Language."

"Really?"

"Yes. And MSO is heading up the council's program for the Sudanese. There are so many people from the Sudan moving here that the council wanted to have something special just for them. When Sebastian heard about it, he consulted MSO, and we all agreed that it was a project we could handle."

"That sounds like a tremendous undertaking."

"Well, now what we do is support the volunteers from the community. We orient them to the program, introduce them to the materials they will use to teach English, and then let them practice before they actually have to get up in front of a room full of people who don't understand much of what they're saying."

"Is that what you're doing tomorrow?"

"Yep. It's my first time flying solo. I've always done it with Sebastian or Capiz, but neither of them can make it tomorrow evening."

Sonji watched the birth of an idea gradually change the expression of Andi's face from one of uncertainty to excitement.

"Why don't you be my partner tomorrow?"

Sonji's eyes grew wide with surprise. "I don't know anything about how to teach an adult how to read, let alone an adult who doesn't speak much English."

Andi flipped the pages in her sociology book aimlessly. The intensity in her eyes told Sonji that she wasn't going to let her off that easily.

"Orientation is basically a teach-the-teacher session. The students won't be there—just the volunteers. And besides, as my assistant all you have to do is pass out materials, make copies of things, take attendance, make coffee, stuff like that."

"What about this test we have coming up?" Sonji asked, feeling herself weaken. Being a volunteer with the literacy council was just what Sonji needed to get some teaching experience under her belt. She hadn't imagined that an opportunity would come so quickly after she started school, but here it was. And after all, Andi was just asking her to assist. If she didn't like it after this one time, she didn't have to do it ever again.

Sonji could see the wheels turning in Andi's mind. Andi ran her hand through her mass of unruly hair. "We'll just study longer today. You said you had the afternoon off, right? So, what do you say?" Andi asked, but her perky eyes said it all.

Sonji drummed her fingers on the top of her sociology book. "Okay, I'll do it."

The Saint Augustine Community Center was tucked away in the grassy hillside of Pleasant View Park. The one-story brick building was long and unusually shaped—taking up the better portion of the flat part of the lush plateau. Inside the center were meeting rooms, a computer facility, a learning lab, a rec room and a day-care facility.

MSO made arrangements with the community center to use one of its meeting rooms under the stipulation that all set-up and clean-up was to be done by an MSO volunteer. As long as the room was returned to its original neat and clean condition, the MSO students could continue to use the room for their literacy project.

Sonji and Andi arrived one hour ahead of schedule so that they would have enough time to set up the room and materials. They started by arranging the tables and chairs into chevron-style seating with tables and chairs sequenced into a V-shaped configuration. Then they took one table and moved it to one side of the room, where they set out coffee, juice, and rolls. Next, they moved one of the tables outside the room entrance and placed preprinted name tags and information packets there.

The two women stood back and scrutinized their handiwork.

"It looks good," Sonji commented.

"Just like Sebastian taught me," Andi responded. Andi spied the lectern in the back of the room. "Will you give me a hand with that?" she asked, pointing to the large speaker's stand.

Together, they wheeled the lectern to the front of

the room and placed it strategically in the middle of the tables. Sonji looked around the room, satisfied. She glanced at the clock. It read 6:40.

"What else can I help with?" Sonji asked.

"Well," Andi began, and then swallowed hard. "When they arrive, will you make sure that everyone gets a packet and a n-name tag?"

Sonji noticed the slight quiver in Andi's voice. "Are you okay?"

"Maybe you could do the food table, and I could do the packets and name tags. No, that wouldn't be right because then we wouldn't have a speaker. Oh, we're gonna need three people!"

Sonji could see that Andi's nerves were dealing her a fit. She knew she had to do something to calm her friend or the meeting would be a disaster.

"Take it easy, Andi. I'll take care of the packets and name tags. I'm sure the people can help themselves to the food. And *you* will be just fine." Sonji placed a reassuring hand on Andi's forearm. "Why don't you study your notes until it's time to start?"

Andi gathered her notes and stood behind the lectern. Sonji watched as she paced back and forth. She reminded Sonji of an actor preparing for an important role. Sonji smiled and took a seat behind the welcome table.

Before long, volunteers trickled into the meeting room. They were greeted with a warm smile and a handshake as Sonji took her role as greeter very seriously. Meanwhile, Andi continued to rehearse at the front of the room, occasionally looking up to acknowledge a volunteer.

By 6:55 there was a small line of volunteers at the table waiting in turn for their materials. Sonji worked as fast as she could without making them feel rushed or hurried. As soon as she felt that she had gotten into a rhythm with her greeting procedures, she was nearly halted in midsentence by the sight of one particular person in line. Standing ravishingly in a slate-gray suit was Professor Gilmore. And he was staring intently at Sonji with electric, coal-black eyes.

Sonji wasn't sure how much of her admiration was showing, but one thing was for certain—the man definitely knew how to wear a suit. Between the movements of the people in front of him, Sonji could see that his wool jacket stretched tightly against broad shoulders that tapered at the waist, and his pin-pressed slacks were form-fitted against thighs as massive as tree trunks. The impeccable crease in the pants led Sonji's eye down along Grayson's muscle-bound legs until they reached the black leather shoes he wore.

"Is that all I need?"

"I'm sorry . . . what?" Sonji blinked, relieving her dry eyes.

"Do I need anything else?"

"No, just the packet."

The woman stepped aside and another woman moved up in line. Sonji curtailed the slight tremor in her hands as she handed the woman an information packet and a name tag. The woman signed her name on the sign-in sheet and stepped aside for the next person.

Another woman walked up to the table. She smiled brightly at Sonji.

"Sign in, please," Sonji said, suddenly concerned about the number of women who had registered as volunteers.

Five more, she thought. *Just five more volunteers, and Professor Gilmore will be standing right in front of me.* The thought made the trembling in Sonji's hands return, and she wished that she had a glass of ice water to cool her rising body heat.

The next five volunteers were processed in a blur of voices and actions. Sonji felt as if she were in a slow-motion machine and time was about to come to a sensuous and seductive halt. All she could remember was that the five people between herself and Professor Gilmore seemed to be together and all appeared to be from the Sudan. She only hoped that she had processed their registrations correctly.

Now, Sonji's palms were sweating. The pounding of her heart rumbled in her ears like an African drum song she had heard once. The drummer, Mane, had said the song was used to welcome home the warriors after a successful hunt. Grayson Gilmore approached her table with a warrior's confident stride. And Sonji felt as helpless as prey.

"S-sign in, please." Sonji's usual greeting was gone—forgotten to the smoldering glint she caught coming from Professor Gilmore's eyes. She reached over to hand him a packet, and her nose entered the path that his after-shave had cut through the air. The scent was a bold and courageous blend of amber, mosses, and spice. Sonji felt light as a feather.

"Miss Stephens," he said with a cursory nod. "How nice to see you."

Sonji struggled to regain her composure. She propped up her spirit on the deep strength resonating in his voice.

"It's nice to see you as well, professor."

The handsomely statuesque man took the folder from Sonji's hand and frowned.

"Are you all right, Miss Stephens? You look a bit peaked."

"I'm fine," she fibbed, feeling like she had just had what her grandmother often referred to as a flash.

Sonji would almost swear that she saw a glimmer of amusement twinkling in his eye as he walked into the room and began to mill around with those already present.

What is he doing here? she wondered. She quickly glanced into the room and saw Andi writing something on the whiteboard. Across from her stood the most exquisite specimen of manhood Sonji had ever known. It was taking all of her resolve to keep herself from ogling him during class, and now she was fighting the same battle here.

Some of the young women in her class either lost the same battle or simply did not struggle against the urge. Their facial expressions often reflected the attraction they so obviously felt for their teacher.

And now, Sonji was seeing that same look on the face of an attractive woman who was engaged in a lively conversation with the professor. Despite what appeared to be strong flirtatious gestures—a casual toss of the head, a feminine giggle, and almost unbroken eye contact—his response was something Sonji had seen again and again in class—cool and unaffected.

He must be involved with someone, Sonji reasoned, and returned her thoughts to the dwindling line of volunteers. It was almost time for Andi to start, and it looked as though nearly everyone who had signed up was there. There were only five packets unaccounted for and there were three people left in line.

Sonji made quick work of processing the last volunteers as she heard Andi's voice welcoming people and asking them to take their seats. When Sonji finished, she straightened the remaining items on the registration table and headed into the conference room. Surprisingly, all the seats in the front were taken. Sonji strolled over to the refreshment table and made sure everything was in order there before heading toward the back of the room.

She scanned the back of the room for a seat and

found herself under the intense scrutiny of Professor Gilmore. He was seated in the midst of the only open seats in the back. With unchecked attraction running amuck in her soul, Sonji took a seat next to her English teacher.

The next thing he knew, the woman would probably show up in his dreams. Grayson Gilmore opened his training packet along with the others and followed along as a Miss Andromeda Simmons took them through a guided tour of their materials and the agenda for the evening. But he was more aware of the woman seated next to him than the papers in his hands.

Since he had seen Sonji at the front table, he hadn't been able to take his eyes off her. He found her charm enthralling. And now that she was seated next to him, the need he had to stroke her cheek, her neck, her thigh, was more sensual desire than he had experienced in a long time. He had no idea that Sonji Stephens was part of MSO, but he was certainly glad she was here. It made his decision to return to volunteering that much sweeter.

For the next two hours, Andi provided them with an outline of the ESL program and process. She explained the teaching techniques, the manuals that were used, and gave the volunteers an opportunity to practice the process through role-playing exercises. She seemed to have gotten over her nervousness quite well. During this time, Sonji made several pots of coffee, replenished the cream and sugar, distributed pencils, and helped people get into groups for skill practice. Then Andi introduced Sahar and Zaina. They were two women from the Sudan who had been in the United States for five years and spoke English as if they had been born there.

The women taught the volunteers a few words in Su-

danese to help bridge the communication gap on both
ends. Sonji noticed that Zaina, who looked like she
could very easily be a model, was the same one who
had been putting the moves on Professor Gilmore earlier. Her lesson of basic Sudanese phrases included,
Nan nyanyar do, which to Sonji's chagrin meant *I love
you.*

Sonji noticed that Professor Gilmore sent a smile
of appreciation toward the bilingual beauty. Sonji suddenly felt uncomfortably self-conscious and wasn't
sure why.

Maybe it had to do with the intricate braiding of the
woman's hair. Maybe it had to do with the gold-brown
pantsuit that was cut against her body like a first skin.
Perhaps it was her eyes that looked wise and reflective.
Or just maybe it was the expression of admiration that
took over Professor Gilmore's face whenever she spoke
Dinka, her primary language.

As Andi gazed out into the faces of the crowd, Sonji
looked around as well. Even from her seat in the back,
she could make out the expressions of excitement,
eagerness, and uncertainty. Most seemed to be pleased
and content with what they'd heard and experienced.
Others weren't so sure.

"This is the part where I'm supposed to introduce
Barbara Steele, vice president of the Midlands Literacy
Council Board, but I see she's not here. So I'm sorry
that she's not here to wrap up tonight's session." Sonji
saw Professor Gilmore's hand rise into the air at the
same time as he loudly cleared his throat.

"Yes, professor," Andi acknowledged.

"Miss Simmons, I'm president of the board and if
you'd permit me, I would like to say a few words."

"Oh, sure," Andi said brightly, and stepped aside.

Many heads turned toward the professor as he
stood and walked to the front of the room.

"Good evening, everyone. I'm Grayson Gilmore, and I would like to publicly thank Andromeda Simmons for her efforts this evening. You did a wonderful job acclimating these volunteers to their new role as ESL teachers," he said, addressing Andi.

The volunteers joined Grayson in light applause.

"I would also like to thank Sonji Stephens, Miss Simmons's assistant, for making sure that everything was in order for us to have an informative and productive meeting."

More light applause. "Sahar, Zaina, what can I say about the importance of your presence. Not enough, I suspect. So I will simply say thank you. And," Grayson said, stepping from behind the lectern, "I want to thank *you* for being willing to make a difference in someone's life." Grayson scanned the room and clasped his hands behind his back.

"When I first got involved with the literacy council, I was as excited as some of you seem to be, but I was also apprehensive. A host of questions plagued my mind: How many people will be in the class? Will they understand me? How much time is it going to take? And did I *really* sign up to do this?"

Grayson walked a slow and steady path before the volunteers, from one side of the room to the other. Occasionally he would pause. But for the most part he was in motion.

Sonji's libido was also in motion. Professor Gilmore's commanding presence at the front of the room sent warmth radiating to all of Sonji's pulse points. For a brief moment, Sonji fantasized what it would be like to have him kiss her in the places where her body was now beating a soft throb.

She pushed the fantasy away from her thoughts, but not before she got an eyeful of Grayson Gilmore's intense gaze on her body. He folded his bottom lip inward the way some black men did when they were about to do something important, and returned his gaze to the rest of the people in the room.

"But after the first session, I felt I had done the right thing, because I could see the understanding forming on the faces of the students, and I knew that what I had done that night mattered."

Grayson stood next to the lectern and propped his arm on top of it. Sonji glanced around to see Andi standing with her hands clutched in front of her. Everyone else leaned forward in their seats, waiting for him to begin again. Zaina seemed especially keen with her fawnlike eyes batting innocently in his direction.

"Our mission at the literacy council is a simple one: to deliver the highest quality individualized basic reading and English language instruction to adults so that they may attain their literacy goals, develop self-confidence, and become independent learners. In order to achieve our mission, we rely on people like you who are committed to their communities and this country."

It was quiet enough in the room to hear a mouse's footsteps.

"Now, being an ESL teacher isn't for everyone. And if you discover that it isn't for you, that's all right. We have many other ways for you to volunteer, and they are all listed in your information packet."

Grayson stopped walking and positioned himself in the middle of the room.

"No matter what, I'm convinced that you've made the right choice. You will quickly discover that for those in this country who are deemed illiterate, attaining the American Dream can feel more like living a nightmare. But with your help, we can change that nightmare into a bright and shining dream."

After Grayson's impassioned speech, there was resounding applause from the volunteers. Then a brief question and answer period followed, after which the volunteers began trickling out of the center.

While Sonji and Andi started cleaning up, Sahar and Zaina lingered a while to talk to Professor Gilmore. Sonji, who couldn't bear to watch anymore of Zaina's overt flirtations, left the room to gather the remaining materials from the sign-in desk.

"Good night," the two women said to Sonji when they finally left the center.

"Good night," Sonji said pleasantly. She put all the remaining materials in a pile and then pulled the table back into the conference room.

"Here, let me help you with that," Grayson's deep, modular voice came at her from across the room. With moves as fleet as a cheetah, he was at her side and sliding the table away from her and back into position with the row of tables at the end of the room.

"Thank you," Sonji responded, willing the admiration of his swift movements to leave her face.

"You are most welcome, Miss Stephens."

Before Sonji realized what was happening, his unwavering gaze riveted her where she stood. She became acutely aware of everything around her. Her breathing and his breathing became synchronous. She could neither blink nor turn away.

"Well, how did I do?" Andi's bubbly voice came between them and broke the spell. They both turned in her direction.

"You were great, Andi."

"Andromeda Simmons, I commend you on an excellent presentation. You have represented Midlands Literacy Council most admirably."

"Really? I was so, so nervous."

Sonji gave Andi a reassuring hug. "Sebastian will be proud of you."

"Thanks, Sonji," Andi said. "I'm going to get Mr.

Rutherford. As soon as he inspects the room, we can go grab a bite to eat. My treat—for being the assistant."

Andi was so happy, it almost looked as though she were skipping toward the door. "Would you like to join us, professor?"

"No thank you, Andromeda. Some other time, perhaps."

"Okay. Sonji, you choose the restaurant. I'll be right back." Andromeda disappeared into the hallway, and Sonji was left alone with a man more handsome than words could describe. He didn't seem in a hurry to leave, so she felt compelled to make small talk.

"I'm glad we're going out to dinner. I'm hungry, but I'm too tired to cook anything."

"Too tired to cook? Nonsense! There is no such thing."

Sonji raised an eyebrow. "There is in my book."

"There's not in mine, but when you're a gourmet chef like me—"

"You're a gourmet chef?" Sonji tried not to let the disbelief come through in her tone, but was unsuccessful.

"Is that so difficult to believe?"

"As a matter of fact, professor, it is."

"Well, there's only one way to settle this little dispute of ours."

"And what's that, professor?"

"Have dinner with me Friday."

A clever smile positioned itself across Sonji's mouth. "Dinner, you say?"

"Yes, with me. Say around . . . seven thirty?"

Now they were aware of their lighthearted venery. But neither seemed to mind.

"And where would we have our dinner?"

"Why, my place, of course."

"But I don't know where you live."

Grayson paused and removed a gold business card

case and matching pen from a pocket inside his suit jacket. He wrote his address quickly on the back of a business card and handed it to Sonji.

She took the card with disbelief shining in her eyes. "You're serious."

"Very," he said, walking toward the door. "Oh, and Miss Stephens—"

"Yes," she replied softly.

"Try not to be late."

Sonji couldn't move. Even when Andi returned with Mr. Rutherford several seconds later, she was still standing in the same spot, holding Professor Grayson's card, and smiling royally like the Queen of Sheba.

I must be out of my mind, Grayson thought as he ran down the path through Bemis Park. He had started his daily run an hour earlier this morning, because dreams of Sonji kept interfering with his sleep.

He knew he was treading on dangerous ground now. Entertaining a student privately in his home had to run an ethical borderline on some oath he had taken as a professor. But something about Sonji's allure called out strongly to him. It made him forget his English lesson in mid sentence sometimes and made him always want to call on her in class. Her voice moved him like a symphony playing in his soul.

Ah, Sonji, he thought running through a thick grove of trees. Their leaves were turning the most delightful shades of crimson and mustard. Fall was a good word for both the weather and his heart. Despite himself, he was falling for Miss Sonji Stephens.

Grayson turned down the small bend in the path and ran past the statue of a woman nursing a child. As always when he came to this point in his running routine, images of Veranda and Gray Jr. filled his mind. But Gray Jr. had not been suckled by his mother. Veranda would have none of it.

"Breast feeding is for indolents and beasts," she'd said shortly after delivery. The doctor had unknowingly suggested that Veranda might want to nurse the child. Grayson was not surprised by his wife's response, but he was nonetheless disappointed and injured by it.

No, Veranda was not the nursing kind. Nor was she the nurturing kind. If she had been, perhaps Gray Jr.—

"No!" Grayson yelled, halting his run abruptly. He placed his hands at the sides of his head in an attempt to press away the headache he felt coming on. Panting, he walked over to a white iron bench and sat down. For having just started his run, Grayson was a bit more winded than normal. He sat still for a few moments to catch his breath.

When he felt better, Grayson continued his run. He let his mind drift back to thoughts of Sonji and all the wonderful foods he would prepare for their meal together. He soon picked up his pace and was back to running at his normal level. Before returning home he made a conscious decision to alter his running route away from the location of the mother and child statue. There were too many painful memories in that place.

"Would you like some tea?"

"Yes, Andi. Thank you." Sonji sat back in the director's chair and closed her eyes. If she never looked at another textbook, it would be too soon. She and Andi had been studying for hours. They helped each other review, quizzed each other, and read each other's papers on topics ranging from pi to single cell division to conjunctive adverbs. Sonji's brain was on information overload. She massaged her temples to relieve the growing tension.

"Here we are," Andi said, returning from the kitchen. She carried the tea on a silver tray laden with honey, cream, and freshly sliced lemons. Sonji removed a teacup from the tray and lifted it to her nose. Andi set the tray down on the table in front of them and took her seat.

"It smells heavenly. What kind is it?"

"Chamomile," Andi responded.

"Mmm," Sonji said, rubbing the teacup like a magic lamp between her hands.

"I thought that after all the hard studying we did, we could use some nice soothing tea."

"Amen to that," Sonji replied, taking a sip. The liquid warmed her insides. It felt good going down.

Andi took a sip of her tea as well. "I always drink a cup of chamomile when I need to let go or if I'm having trouble sleeping."

The two sat in silence for a few moments. Sonji added just a touch of honey and cream to her tea. Andi drank hers plain.

Sonji was grateful to get away from the confines of her town house. When Andi invited her over to study, she had jumped at the chance. And just as she'd thought, the new surroundings were just the stimulus she needed to attack her homework with renewed vigor. And they both had made good use of their time. Before they realized it, it was nearly midnight. But each had done what she had set out to do.

"Sonji, we've been at it practically all day. Do you want to check your e-mail while you're here?"

Sonji's heart leaped. Stewing in the back of her mind had been thoughts of Osiris. She wondered if he had sent her a message today. What started out as a ploy to get a free e-mail account had ended up being so much more. At first, they exchanged messages several times a month. Then it was several times a week, and now, they wrote each other every day. Even though Sonji enjoyed their correspondence, she was beginning to wonder if their relationship was getting out of hand.

"Thanks for the offer, but I'll pass."

"What? Why?" Andi took another sip of tea. "Don't you want to see if he sent you something?"

For the past two weeks, Osiris had been as regular as clockwork. Every night, between 9:30 and 10:30, he had sent her an e-mail, each one more charming than the last. Sonji was beginning to feel somewhat expectant now. And that was a feeling she couldn't afford to have. She had expected Chad always to be there for her too, and that had gotten her nowhere but deeper into a lie. And wasn't an online romance the ultimate lie? You could say anything, become anyone. And unless you met, no one would know. *No,* she thought. *It's better if I don't become too attached to this mystery man's letters.* Sonji felt it was the only way to safeguard her feelings.

"Look at you," Andi said, filling her cup and Sonji's with more tea. "You're thinking about him now. I can see it in the highlights of your face. Why not drop him a line or two?"

"Because, Andi, I feel like this whole online thing is going too far."

"Really? How come?"

Sonji stirred honey and cream into her tea. "For one, I don't have time to write him every day."

"Every day? Does he write you every day?"

"Yes and—"

"Wow! That's great."

"Actually, it isn't. It's too soon for us to be writing each other like this. I'm going to tell him we need to ease the pace."

Andi took a couple of deep sips from her teacup. She looked up dreamily and pushed back the hair threatening to take over the left side of her face. "I remember when Sebastian and I started writing to each other every day."

"Weren't you scared?"

"No. It just seemed like the most natural thing in the world. And you know what?"

"What?"

"We still write each other every day."

"You're kidding!"

"Nope," Andi said, looking over at the computer sitting on the small cedar hutch in the corner of the room. "I'll bet if I signed on now, there would be a message there waiting for me to read it."

Now it was Sonji's turn. "Wow. That's great . . . for you. Not so great for me."

"But Sonji, why not?"

Sonji had considered this very question ever since she and Osiris stared e-mailing each other on a daily basis. Perhaps a discussion with Andi would help her to sort out the conflicting perspectives wrestling in her head.

"It's like I'm always trying to transcend the technology. Every time I read one of Osiris' letters, I ask myself fifty million questions. Is he being truthful and sincere? Why does he seem so interested? What does he mean by that? Did he like my letter? What does he look like? What's his life like? Why did he choose to write to me?"

Andi slid down from the couch to the floor and folded her legs beneath her. "Here's another question for you. What was it like when you got the very first letter from Osiris?"

"Magic," she said. "It was like getting a present."

Then, Sonji thought better of her response. "No, it was better than that. It was like getting a promise."

"That's because you felt his words with your heart. You didn't try to rationalize it or scrutinize it or any other kind of -ize it. You knew that it was just like you said . . . magic. And that's all that matters."

Sonji thought back to Chad. "If only things were that simple, Andi."

"They are . . . when it's right."

"It doesn't make much sense for me to invest my heart and soul in a man who I may never meet."

"Why not?"

"Because, Andi, for all I know, this guy could live in Vancouver."

"Vancouver! That's ridiculous. BlackLuv is a student site."

Sonji was about to take a sip from her teacup but lowered it instead. "What do you mean?"

"Some of the members of MSO started it as a class project. They are about to list their site with all the major search engines. Most of the users are connected with the university in some way."

"What!"

"Yeah. Their only promotion is word of mouth and sometimes, like, an ad in the school paper."

Sonji sat up in the chair. "Andi, why didn't you tell me?"

"Whoa. Don't get upset. I didn't think it mattered."

Sonji was stunned. A minute ago, Osiris was a beautiful dream, a miracle just beyond her reach. And now, he was a living, breathing, person—someone she may have walked past on her way to class. For all she knew, he could be *in* one of her classes.

Andi stared at Sonji intently. "Does it make a difference?"

"Of course it does, Andi."

"Why?"

"Because it does."

"But why?"

Sonji placed her teacup on the table and crossed her arms in front of her. "Because it just does."

"Because now it's real, and you have to take it seriously, huh?"

Sonji swallowed hard and her heart thumped heavily in her chest.

"Sonji . . . what are you afraid of?"

So many words whirled around in Sonji's head that she was nearly dizzy. Deception. Fraud. Dishonesty. Deceit. Sabotage. Subterfuge. Lies. She had allowed herself to be duped before. And now, to have this revelation about the proximity of Osiris was more than slightly disturbing.

Sonji finished her tea and helped Andromeda clean up the cups and utensils they used. When the two said their good-byes, each held with them a silent reminder of how one discovery could alter the present so that it was barely recognizable. With Andromeda focusing on her triumph at the rec center and Sonji thinking of Osiris, the next day would be the beginning of a new stage in both of their lives.

Seven

Grayson checked the table setting again—sterling silver flatware, Tuscan Brio china set atop Ashanti mudcloth place mats, and crystal goblets trimmed in eighteen-karat gold. The arrangement was enhanced by a small pewter vase that held a silk rose, flanked by two long white candles in matching pewter holders. He couldn't remember his Victorian-styled dining room table looking more inviting.

Grayson checked the dinner again—tomatoes stuffed with salmon and pasta for starters, then thinly sliced strips of beef Dijon with a lemon-herb vegetable medley of carrots, zucchini, red peppers, and peas as a side. After cooking bachelor-style for seven years, Grayson wondered if he still retained his culinary skills. He tasted the sauce for the beef strips and smiled. The precise blend of seasonings told him he could still whip up a gourmet meal or two when the mood struck him.

And the mood had definitely struck him. So now, for the fifth time in half an hour, Grayson found himself checking to make sure that everything was perfect. He walked over to the stereo and sorted through the stack of CD's his brother had left for him. Rachelle Ferrell, Cassandra Wilson, Michael Franks, Will Downing, Lalah Hathaway. He had no idea who these people were, but his brother claimed that this was the kind of music he should play tonight.

Music. Just one of the many things he had shut himself off from over the years. Listening to music usually made him happy, but after the accident, there wasn't much to be happy about. Since he didn't know one artist from the other, Grayson opened the carousel of his fifty-disk CD changer and dropped them all in. Then he set the player for random play. Instantly the music came through the speakers and filled the room. Grayson was still for a moment and listened. He didn't know who was singing, but he liked what he heard. It was rich and full and sounded the way he had felt ever since the day Sonji had walked into his classroom.

He had checked on the meal. He had checked on the table setting. And he had checked on the music. But still, he had the feeling he was forgetting something. He walked to the long mirror in the hallway and checked his attire. *This will never do,* he thought, staring at his reflection. *I'm dressed like a black Don Johnson.* His casual gray suit jacket was open to reveal a simple white T-shirt tucked into gray pants. *I can't entertain Sonji looking like Crockett from Miami Vice,* he decided, and walked into his bedroom to change. Before he could take off his jacket, the doorbell rang.

Grayson looked down at the clock on the headboard of his waterbed. It read 7:30. *I can't believe it,* he thought, walking to the door. *She's on time.* Grayson reached the front door, stopped, took a deep breath, and opened the door. First, his eyes met hers, and he could have sworn he saw them twinkle, if only for half a second. His eyes traveled the length of her body, pausing briefly in those areas so curvy and round he had to swallow to keep from gaping.

Her usual business suit was gone, replaced with a

silk blouse and matching pants that changed gradi-
ently from yellow around the shoulders and neckline
to deep orange at the ankle. The outfit was accented
with a coordinating calf-length duster that flowed
about Sonji's body like a royal robe.

"Is something wrong?" she asked.

"Er, no," Grayson responded, thinking *not anymore*.
He stood at the doorway, drinking in the sight of her
as if his soul were parched and dehydrated.

Sonji smiled and raised an eyebrow. "May I come
in, professor?"

Grayson opened the door wider and then stepped
aside for Sonji to enter.

"You're going to have to call me Grayson," he said,
watching her ardently as she entered. He closed the
door and stood beside Sonji as she paused in the
foyer. She looked at the painting on the wall. When
she walked over and touched it slightly, Grayson was
struck by the intensity of her gaze.

"This is magnificent, prof— Grayson." Sonji
stretched her palm out in front of the wall. "May I?"
she asked.

"By all means."

Sonji ran her fingers across the thick lines, streaks,
and swatches of paint on the wall. Grayson watched
as she appreciated the painting by feeling it.

Hmmm. Tactile, Grayson thought. *I'll remember that.*

"Did you do this?" she asked, turning toward him,
a hand still sliding across the ridges of obsidian, in-
digo, and charcoal on the wall.

"As a matter of fact, I did. It was . . . several years
ago. I was going through a difficult time, and I took
my frustrations out on the vestibule."

Grayson sighed, trying to push away the memory
of what had driven him to seek a creative outlet for
his frustration.

"I had every intention of painting over it. But I was torn because I liked it and wished that I had painted on canvas instead of the wall so that I could frame it. And then I thought, why not frame it right here? So I did."

Sonji finished her intimate inspection of the Basquiat-like painting and continued from the foyer into the living room. Every time she thought she had Professor Gilmore figured out, he surprised her. And it was never a mild surprise. It was always jarring and commanding, like this burst of avant-garde expression, and on his wall, no less. She imagined the sunrays playing like ribbons on the wall where the brush strokes appeared to dance.

There was obviously more to him than his gruff and guarded exterior presented.

"Do you have other paintings?"

"I'm afraid not. This is the first and only thing I've ever painted."

"If this is the first thing you've done, I'd love to see what you could do with practice," she said, handing him the pan of peach cobbler that she had persuaded her grandmother to make.

"Thank you," Grayson said, smiling like a bashful young man and extending his free arm toward the living room area. "Please," he said.

Sonji tried to remember the number of times she'd seen him smile. They were few.

"You really should smile more often. It's very becoming."

Grayson stood still and crooked his head slightly. "Two compliments in a row. I'm not sure how much more of this I can stand."

How easy it would be for him to absorb the compliment of just having her standing by his side. He realized that since she had arrived, he had done little more than stare at her like a gawking teenager. His behavior embarrassed him.

"Make yourself comfortable. I'm going to check on dinner."

Sonji smiled and took a seat in a crimson wingback chair. She checked out her surroundings and felt spellbound. It was as if she had traveled back in time to the turn of the century. Nearly every piece in the room was antique, from the furnishings to the accents.

"Something smells wonderful."

"Thank you," Grayson said, emerging from the kitchen. "I hope you brought your appetite with you. I made plenty."

Grayson took a seat opposite her in a matching chair. Suddenly he became very self-conscious and wondered if he had made the right decision in inviting her to dinner. He looked at Sonji, who was fidgeting in her seat.

"So," he began, feeling the need to fill the silence. "Did you have any trouble finding the place?"

"No. Your directions were perfect. Besides, it's hard to miss. You've got the most beautiful house on the block."

"You should have seen it when I bought it. A realtor friend told me a long time ago to buy the worst house in the best neighborhood. Then fix it up. So I did."

Sonji smiled coyly. "What do you do with so much space?"

A flood of images and sounds materialized in Grayson's mind: a woman's warm smile, a child's laughter, Christmas decorations, cookies baking in the oven, toys. The stark memory felt like a cloud of pain hovering just above his head. It was heavy and rumbled with thunder and regret.

Sonji saw the expression on Grayson's face change

from pleasant to somber and wondered what could cause such a dramatic mood shift. Perhaps something about her question brought unpleasant thoughts. She would know not to probe that area again.

Grayson sat forward and stroked his chin. "At the time I bought this house, it was exactly what I needed."

He rose quickly and headed back toward the kitchen. "I'm going to check on the meal."

When he got in the kitchen, Grayson wiped his hand down his face. *What am I thinking bringing another woman into this house?* He worked to force the thoughts of hesitation down, telling himself that it was time he got on with his life.

He retrieved the tray of stuffed tomatoes from the refrigerator, sprinkled them with paprika, and walked into the dining room, refusing to be thwarted by shadows of the past.

"Are you ready for the first course?"

"Very ready," Sonji said, rising from her chair and joining Grayson in the dining room. She hadn't been able to eat all day in anticipation of dining with him.

From where Sonji had been sitting in the living room, she couldn't get a good look at the ornate dining area. But standing in it now, she found herself surprised again that Grayson would have such exquisite taste. "Your home is truly magnificent, Grayson."

"Thank you, again," he said, raising a just-opened bottle of wine from the table. "Would you like some Merlot?"

Sonji took a seat opposite of where Grayson was standing. "Yes, please."

Grayson filled the crystal glasses halfway and returned the wine to its holder. He sat down across from Sonji and placed his napkin across his lap. Sonji did the same.

"I'd like to say grace," he said, bowing his head. When Sonji bowed hers he began.

"Heavenly Father, we thank you for the blessings you have bestowed upon us this day. We thank you for our lives and the chance to be in each other's company this evening. We thank you for the meal we are about to eat, and I thank you for holding my hand as I prepared it. We know that it is through you that all blessings come and even though we may not always understand your will, we pray that we will always be guided by it. Amen."

"Amen," Sonji responded.

"I hope you don't have any dietary restrictions I should have known about."

"Are you kidding? People in my family call me the garbage disposal. I can eat anything."

They both dug into their first course with vigor.

"Mmm," Sonji said as the tastes of fresh salmon, pasta, and seasonings mingled in her mouth.

"I don't mean to be presumptuous," Grayson stated, "but do I sense another compliment coming?"

"Praise is more like it. This is delicious, Grayson!"

Grayson took a deep breath and released it. There were so many things he hoped she'd like when she came. He wanted her to feel comfortable in his home. He wanted his appearance to be pleasing. And since he'd offered to prepare the meal, he was hoping that she would enjoy his cooking. He had searched her face for any hint of disapproval since she had arrived. Looking at her expression of content now, so far so good, he thought.

"I was hoping I hadn't lost my skills."

Sonji burst into laugher at Grayson's statement.

Grayson raised a concerned eyebrow. "Is that funny?"

"Actually, yes," Sonji admitted. "Nowadays the word

skills is such a modern, hip-hop kind of phrase. It sounds unusual, humorous really, coming from you."

"Why?" Grayson asked, after finishing a forkful of tomatoes and pasta.

Sonji wasn't quite sure how to put it. She didn't want to hurt his feelings, but she didn't want to deceive him either.

"Because I'm such a hard ass?" he finished.

Sonji stopped chewing and looked up. Grayson was watching her with a wanton smile sitting on his face.

This time they both burst into laughter. And afterward, Sonji felt that it was the release she needed to relax and feel comfortable around this man that she was so incredibly attracted to. And she noticed a change in Grayson. He was less tense and smiled a lot more. She wasn't sure if it was their shared laughter, the wine, or a combination of both. But the gruff exterior of Professor Grayson Gilmore was slowly softening. As a result, Sonji felt herself being drawn closer and closer to him.

The rest of their meal progressed with buoyant conversation, laughter, more wine, and lots of food. Sonji talked about her major, her job, and her GrandmaZee. Grayson talked about his new literature class, life as a college professor, and the nieces he adored. By the time Grayson brought out the dessert, they were almost too stuffed to eat it.

"Let's have dessert in the den. It's much more relaxing," he said, handing a dish of warm peach cobbler to Sonji.

Sonji followed as Grayson led her down a long hallway and into another room. She should have known what to expect with him being an English teacher, but the sight of the den made her gasp upon entering. It was the size of his living room and was filled with shelf upon shelf of books. The mahogany bookcases were floor to ceiling and covered every wall except the one with an outsized, stone fireplace.

Sonji walked to where Grayson was sitting on the black leather sofa and sat down beside him, still staring at all the books.

"I, uh . . . like to read," he said, noticing her fascination.

"I see!"

They began eating the peach cobbler. The expression on Grayson's face told Sonji he was pleased with what he tasted.

"Now it's my turn. This is wonderful, Sonji. I can't remember the last time I had peach cobbler. And I certainly don't remember ever having one this good."

"I wish I could take the credit. Unlike you, my culinary skills are rather limited. So this wonderful cobbler is compliments of my GrandmaZee."

"Please extend my full appreciation to her for this wonderful desert."

"Will do," Sonji said, feeling the fullness in her stomach.

She settled back onto the soft leather sofa. She ate a bit of the cobbler and delighted in how content she felt.

"Everything was delicious, Grayson. The beef was fork-tender, the vegetables were fresh and flavorful, and the stuffed tomatoes were the best I've ever tasted. I have eaten tomatoes stuffed with crab before, but never salmon."

"Oh, my goodness, Phyllis and Alexandre!" Grayson rose and walked quickly to a ten-gallon terrarium in the far corner of the den. He reached above the tank to retrieve a small container from a bookshelf. He lifted the lid of the terrarium and sprinkled the contents of the container into a small bowl in the tank.

"I knew I had forgotten something," he said.

"What kind of fish do you have?" Sonji asked.

"I don't have any fish," Grayson answered, returning the container to its place on the bookshelf. "Phyllis and Alexandre are my crabs."

"Crabs!"

Grayson secured the lid, then turned around to face Sonji. "Yes, come on over. Let me introduce you."

"You don't really have crabs in that tank, do you, Grayson?" Sonji asked, approaching hesitantly.

The look that he gave her at that moment was both tender and serious. "I would never lie to you, Sonji Stephens."

Something about that remark made Sonji tingle all over. She walked up beside Grayson and peered down into the glass enclosure. And there, sitting on a bed of aquamarine gravel, were two golf ball-sized crabs. They were surrounded by several objects: a piece of wood, a lump of pink coral, a sponge, three shells, and bowls for water and food. Sonji could barely see them, as each appeared to be hiding inside its own exotic multicolored shell. They weren't at all what she'd expected.

"Sonji, meet Phyllis Wheatley and Alexandre Dumas."

Sonji bowed as if she were a geisha. Then she smiled up at Grayson.

"I thought they were going to be gross. Actually, they're kind of cute—in a creepy sort of way."

She returned her gaze to the two crabs moving slowly in their shells.

"Can I see what they look like?"

"You mean take them out of their shells?"

"Yes."

"No can do. If you remove them from their shells, they have the crustaceanal equivalent of a nervous breakdown. And then they die."

"Don't they ever come out?" Sonji asked looking up at Grayson.

His eyes said he understood that she was asking about more than just the crabs. "They come out whenever it's time for them to grow."

Sonji and Grayson walked back to the couch together in silence. They sat down and ate a few more forkfuls of peach cobbler.

Sonji reflected on Grayson's pets. Another surprise, she thought.

"What on earth made you get crabs?"

Grayson chuckled. "An argument with my brother," he responded, slightly embarrassed. "My brother has taken an annual fishing trip for the past fifteen years. I usually go with him. But for the last seven years, I haven't gone. Well, two years ago, Kyle was getting ready to go and asked if I was going to accompany him. When I said no, he called me a crab and accused me of turning into a hermit who refused to come out of his house.

"A couple of days after that argument, I was driving past a pet store that had a large sign in the window that said FREE CRABS. I don't know what it was, but something made me stop and go in.

"The store was having a special promotion. If you bought the starter kit, which included the terrarium, food, and, accessories, you got two free crabs. So I did it. And Phyllis and Alexandre have been part of my family ever since."

"What does your brother think of Phyllis and Alexandre?"

"Well . . . he's a psychologist. So he thinks they are a physical manifestation of my psychological disposition."

Sonji raised a curious brow. "And are they?"

Grayson thought about that question. Over the past

few years, he hadn't been the greatest person in the world. And he did keep to himself most of the time. He rarely saw his friends anymore. But even with all of this evidence, he still had fought, with himself mainly, to dismiss the notion that he was really what people said he was. Until now.

"Maybe. I . . . I don't know." He cleared his throat. "I'm worried about them." He transitioned back to the crabs. "They aren't as active as they used to be. Usually when I'm up late grading papers or doing research on the Net, I can hear them clambering across the gravel. But now, they're terribly quiet."

Sonji saw the concern in Grayson's eyes and became concerned herself. "Can you take them to a vet?"

"I have a good friend who's a vet. She told me to cut back on the snacks, make sure they stay moist, and just watch them. If they come out of their shells and don't molt, then they're preparing to die."

"Oh, that's awful!"

"I know. People are always taken aback when they find out I have crabs. But I don't care what kind of pet you have, if it's yours, you get attached to it."

Grayson didn't like the thought of losing his pets. He had lost too much already. "Let's change the subject, shall we?" he asked.

"Sure," Sonji said, noticing the fullness in her stomach. "I am *too* full."

"I think I'm about there myself. Shall I take this?" he asked, reaching for her bowl.

"One more bite," Sonji said, scooping a forkful of peaches and crust into her mouth. Then she handed the dish to Grayson.

"Be right back," he announced, and headed off into the hallway.

Sitting in the den alone, Sonji realized that she hadn't thought about what would happen after dinner. She had just imagined them eating and having a good time—which they had. But now that dinner was over, she was beginning to get nervous.

Grayson returned, brushing his hands together. "That's that," he said, seating himself next to her. She tried to focus on something in the room—the books, the fireplace, the speakers. His hot gaze prickled her skin.

"There's no stereo in here," she said, attempting casual conversation. "Where is the music coming from?"

"The stereo is in the living room. The speakers are wireless."

"I like the music," she said, without turning to him. Despite her attempt at casualness, she felt his body moving closer to hers. It caused her heart to turn over in response.

"It's courtesy of my brother. According to him, the world has changed since the last time I bought new music." Grayson turned toward her. "Sonji," he said, letting the passion he was starting to feel deepen his voice.

She turned and looked up at him. "Yes," she said in a barely audible whisper. Grayson's eyes peered intensely into hers and Sonji felt herself trembling softly.

Grayson wasn't sure what was happening, but he felt powerless to stop it. Whatever was drawing him to this woman was becoming harder and harder to stave off. And now, her very presence was stirring desires he hadn't felt in years. He moved closer until there was no room between them.

An electrifying shudder reverberated throughout Sonji's body. Grayson's nearness heightened her senses, and for the first time since she arrived, Sonji allowed herself to examine him fully.

She sat transfixed as he lowered his gorgeous face to hers.

His kiss was warm and rolled her like an ocean. She gave into his tongue, which glided gently over her lips until they parted, welcoming him. She felt swept up into a strong current of passion and longing. His arms closed around her, and the ensuing heat nearly levitated her from the couch. And then something, like a far-off memory, came to the surface and made her pull back from Grayson's embrace.

"I can't do this," Grayson said, pulling away as well.

Sonji felt flushed. "I'm sorry, Grayson."

"No, it's me," he said, increasing the distance between them.

"Maybe we're not ready. Maybe this is too big a step for us right now," Sonji offered.

"Agreed," Grayson said, running a hand down the front of his face.

Sonji put her hands across her forehead and pushed them up into her short, curly hair. "I think I should go," she said, rising.

Grayson rose beside her. "You don't have to go so soon, Sonji. I promise, I'll behave myself from here on."

"No, Grayson," she said, melting from the earnestness she saw in his eyes. "If I stay, I may not behave *my*self."

Grayson smiled and nodded his head. He walked her down the hall to the foyer. She paused at the front door. "Grayson, thanks for inviting me to dinner. You're a marvelous cook."

"It was your company that inspired me."

Sonji reached for the door and Grayson caught her hand in his. "Thank you, Miss Stephens. I haven't had an evening this enjoyable in a very long time." Grayson kissed the back of Sonji's hand softly, rever-

ently. Sonji felt small tingles igniting in her fingers
and wrist.

"Good night, Sonji."

"Good night, Grayson."

Grayson stood still in his entryway, chin in hand.
He couldn't figure out what had just happened. Sonji
Stephens, the woman he hadn't managed to get out
of his mind since he laid eyes on her, had been in
his arms. Then, before he knew it, an immense feeling of guilt had come down like a concrete wall between them.

He walked back to the den to confront the source
of his resigned feelings. He sat down at his roll-top desk
and turned on his computer. Even though he'd had a
flesh-and-blood woman in his house and in his arms,
his loyalty belonged to someone he'd met in cyberspace. Grayson logged on to Blackluv using his code
name of Osiris and hoped that there was a message
waiting for him from Nzinga.

Sonji was torn. The most handsome man she had
ever seen had just given her the most passionate
kiss she'd ever received. After fantasizing about him
for weeks, she finally got the chance to spend time
alone with him and what did she do? She pushed
him away.

I can't understand it, she thought as she drove along
the interstate. *I was with Grayson, and I was enjoying
myself.* But Sonji knew. Something in her thoughts reminded her of Osiris. "He's your soul mate," she
could hear Andi saying like a soft echo in her mind.

Well, he's definitely caught my feelings up in chaos, Sonji
mused. When she had kissed Grayson, a part of her
felt like she was betraying Osiris, and she couldn't
continue to be in Grayson's presence. As a matter of

fact, all she wanted to do right then was get on the Internet to see if Osiris had left her a message. So instead of continuing east on the interstate to go home, she got off on the Burt Street exit and headed toward campus.

Eight

Dearest Nzinga,

Tonight has been . . . shall I say . . . hectic? Something has happened. Something I'm not proud of but I feel as though I've come one giant step closer to you. Please don't ask me how. All I know is that I made a decision this evening. And whatever happens between us, know that I am committed to you—to us. All of this rambling must sound strange at best, but I know what I feel. And what I feel is beholden to you. And now that I've gone on and on about me, tell me, what keeps you busy these days? What makes you smile?

Osiris,

Believe me when I say that I understand. Our souls must be riding the same ascension for I, too, have had an . . . incident. Something that made me realize how important you are. I also made a decision. From this day forward, only your light will guide me. Only your song will move me; only your words will stir me. I share your commitment to us— whatever we become. As for what keeps me busy, imagining your face keeps me busy and you, Nubian man, bring my smiles.

Nzinga,

Hoping. Waiting. Believing. Looking—for you. It has been many days since I've heard from you. My mind is plagued with questions. Are you well? Has something happened? Has the Internet gone mad? Did you leave town? Or, Isis protect us, have I done/said/written something wrong? Have I lost you? Dearest Nzinga, tell me, please—I have to know. Since the lapse in our correspondence, I have entertained all manner of calamity. Please be well. Don't you know? We are fated now. And I am adrift without you.

Osiris,

Forgive me, O patient one. I am here, and I am well. I have been wrestling with a strange truth that has bound my fingers. And stricken my tongue. I wonder, as I write this, if you know how close we are. I didn't. In fact, I recently discovered that we are most likely within proximity. Closer than close. May I venture into uncharted territory and ask if your place of residence is Nebraska, dare I say Omaha? No . . . I haven't electronically traced your messages. A close friend informed me that our gracious Web hosts are Omaha natives. And since they have yet to offer their masterpiece to the public, members are most likely locals. I was unaware of our immediacy. This news scared me. Made this cyber experience more real than it has ever seemed.

My Dearest Nzinga,

No, I didn't know. But now that I do, my feelings are in turmoil. I must admit, when I read your last e-mail, I sat and lost track of how long I stared at the screen. And to be honest, for one, one-hundredth of a second, I considered ending our correspondence. Why, the thought of you here is maddening. We may have seen each other. Brushed against each other. Good heavens . . . we could have inhabited the same space. *"Call it off,"* my practicality insisted. *"Stop this now before it's too late."* But my dear Nzinga . . . I fear it is already too late. At least for me. And this most interesting news brings me to but one conclusion. We . . . must . . . meet.

Nzinga,
Now that I know we are—shall I say—proximate, I would like to send you something. I found it yesterday while browsing at a curio store. It reminded me of myself. And at the same time, it reminded me of you . . . of us . . . of what we've become. You don't have to send me your address. A post office box will do. But this gift is lonely without you.

Osiris,
I have asked myself one thousand times since receiving your letter what harm it would do to accept your gift. And one thousand times I have come up with no significant answer. So I accept. It will reach me at PO Box 35555, Omaha, NE 68111. I await your largesse with growing anticipation.

My Dearest Osiris,
It is exquisite and you are much too kind! I have never seen a piece of jewelry so intricate and radiant. I am wearing it now, and where it hangs, it warms my heart. Your thoughtfulness is touching. I will cherish your gift to me forever. Thank you.

My Dearest Nzinga,
You are most welcome.

Dear Osiris,
I pray you are of occasion to write back quickly. There

are many elements threatening my peace this evening. But I know a letter from you will banish all demons. I'm tired. And I need a lifeline, a glimmer in the darkness that promises a better dawn. My mind is clogged with the metaculture of hunter-gatherers and the physics of life. And to top that off, I need to talk to a linguist. Sometimes, experiencing the fullness of what life has to offer is overwhelming. Dear Osiris, send me some kind words.

Dear Nzinga,
I know very little about the metaculture of hunter-gatherers. As for the physics of life, not much more. But I can tell you about words. And I have taken the liberty of attaching a list of books, people and other resources of word origins. Use it as you see fit. And as for the kind words . . . your letters, this correspondence, our connection, has become such an important part of my being that looking for your letters is now as natural to me as breathing.

Nzinga,
My mind imagines you often. Are you well? Are you happy? Are you thinking of me? Why does the immediacy of the Internet take forever to bring me your words? Am I crazy? I feel I am baring my soul to a stranger yet not a stranger. Sometimes I regret logging on to BlackLuv that fateful night. For now, through our correspondence, I have begun a journey fraught with uncertainty and dread. But at the same time, I am empty until I read your thoughts. I am crazy. Nzinga . . . please . . . make me sane.

Osiris,
If insanity is a figment of a sane man's mind, then you, O Great One, have nothing to fear. I am here. I am well.

And you are the constant idea reigning in my soul. I am the crazy one. I was crazy enough to believe that there was no connection in this space. No possible linkage to joy, to contentment. You asked if I am happy. Yes. Each time we "touch" each other this way, I am overjoyed. But the opposite is also true. I am dismayed by keyboards, and screens, and Internet Transfer Protocols that might as well be miles and oceans and vast chasms. For they bar my way . . . to you.

Nine

If it weren't for the fact that she was finally going to meet Osiris, Sonji would be worried about her appointment with Professor Gilmore. The first A that she received in his class should have brought her great joy, but instead it brought her an uneasy and apprehensive feeling.

"I will not allow PG to spoil my evening," she said, looking at herself in the mirror. She had taken some much needed vacation time and was applying a light coat of foundation to her walnut-bronze skin.

She checked out her reflection in the bathroom mirror and was pleased with what she saw. Her natural curls were shining pristinely—a result of Andi's homemade olive oil, rosemary, and sage hair moisturizer. She also wore a small white lily just above her right ear, also courtesy of Andromeda Simmons.

Sonji turned to one side. She had chosen a herringbone coatdress. She liked the way its straight lines hugged her curves in all the right places. The wine color added just the touch of warmth needed on such a brisk day.

She sprayed herself lavishly with *Chez Noir,* a fragrance she saved for special occasions, and walked into her bedroom. She paused at her dresser. There, sparkling in its velvet case, was the scarab amulet sent to her by Osiris.

Sonji's curiosity had gotten the best of her when she had first received the elegant amulet. Her search led her to books on Egyptian magic. She learned that the ancient Egyptians wore amulets for protection. They believed that they were talismans with supernatural powers.

Then she discovered that the Amulet of the Scarab was an amulet of the heart. Egyptian priests placed the scarab, a desert beetle, in the heart-space of the body upon mummification to act as a source of life. It was a representation of new life and new beginnings.

Sonji felt as if she were on a journey of new beginnings. She placed the amulet around her neck, grabbed her purse and her favorite jacket, and headed out of her town house.

She pulled into the faculty-student parking garage determined not to let the impending appointment dampen her spirits. She figured that Professor Gilmore wanted to help her develop a plan to bring her grade up now that she had finally gotten an A. However, the seriousness in his voice and on his face made her wonder just what he had in mind.

She stepped out of the car, and her breath was whisked away by the night chill. As much as she wanted to be cute, she didn't want to be cold. She slipped on a jacket and trotted off toward the administration building.

Along the way, her hand rested lightly on the amulet around her neck. And a million questions buzzed through her head. Was he really coming? What would he think when he saw her? What would she think when she saw him? What if they didn't hit it off?

It's a good thing I'm wearing this necklace, she thought. That way, he'll know right away who I am. Sonji entered the building and climbed the stairs to Professor Gilmore's office. Because of the late hour, no one was around, and her footfalls echoed in the corridor.

When she got to his office and reached for the doorknob, she was halted by an errant thought. Why should Osiris have the upper hand? If she wore the amulet, he would know who she was, but she wouldn't have a clue about him. Without it, she could scope out Carrie's Café to try to figure out who he was first. Maybe then she would decide if she wanted to go through with the tryst.

Smiling, she took off the amulet, dropped it into her jacket pocket, and entered Professor Gilmore's office.

After straightening his tie several times, Grayson became disgruntled and removed it completely. All day he had been vacillating over what to wear, how to present himself, and just exactly what to say to the woman who had captured his heart. If it weren't for the fact that he had a late appointment with one of his students, he would surely have been suffering a hard case of nerves.

He would have liked to meet with Sonji Stephens earlier, but his hectic schedule did not permit it. And so he was forced to meet with her right before his date with Nzinga. Once during the day, he had thought about putting off his meeting with Sonji until a later time, but these things were better dealt with right away. Be that as it may, he would ensure that his discussion with her would not sour his mood, regardless of the outcome.

It was a simply incredible notion, yet here he was faced with the possibility that Sonji Stephens had cheated on her essay—plagiarized it or worse yet, paid someone to write it for her. How else could one go from a D+ to an A+? He hoped that Sonji could explain it.

Grayson placed the tie in his desk drawer and unbuttoned the top button of his field shirt. He stood up from his desk and walked to one of two four-drawer file cabinets.

He removed a mirror from the top drawer and gave himself the once over, for the umpteenth time that evening. He had covered his granite-colored shirt with a cream-colored, cashmere rope cable cardigan, and had completed his outfit with granite-colored tweed pants. He thought he looked okay. He just hoped that Nzinga thought so as well.

Before he replaced the mirror in the drawer, he smoothed his mustache and ran a hand over the thick waves of his black hair. He was pushing the drawer closed when he heard the door to his office open and close.

He turned around and was awestruck. Sonji Stephens was a vision of voluptuous womanhood standing before him.

He blinked and swallowed hard in an attempt to squelch the instant urge to ravish her body. And if he weren't mistaken, she was giving him an approving once-over as well. Perhaps his appearance was adequate after all. And if Nzinga was half as lovely as the beauty before him, Grayson would indeed be a happy man.

"Miss Stephens." Grayson pulled out his pocket watch. The face read 6:00. "You're on time. How refreshing."

Sonji stepped farther into the office. "Well, professor, I have an engagement that I need to attend shortly."

"As do I, so let's get started, shall we?" He motioned to a chair opposite his desk. "Please, have a seat."

Sonji sat down, and Grayson followed suit. These kinds of discussions were always difficult. He hadn't had many, and he regretted having to have this discussion with Sonji.

"Sonji, I asked you here because I wanted to discuss your latest essay."

"I thought so." Sonji said, sounding relieved.

"Yes, well, I'd like to know more about your paper."

Sonji crossed her legs. "Like what?"

Incredible. Her legs are simply incredible, he thought, forcing himself to focus on the discussion at hand. "Like how you came to write it."

"I don't understand."

"I think you do, Miss Stephens. I find it quite fascinating that you should make a sudden and most radical jump in letter grade."

Sonji leaned forward in her seat. "What are you saying?"

"Why, I'm not saying anything at this point. I'm merely asking." Grayson picked up a pen from his desk and rolled it back and forth between his fingers. "So, to what do you attribute the success of your last assignment?"

He saw her stiffen in the chair. "Hard work, professor. Research and lots of studying. Isn't that what students usually do to get good grades?"

Grayson wanted so much to believe her. But he had to be sure.

"Yes, but in this case the research and references were outstanding—scholarly actually. I'm surprised that a *student* would come upon such sui generis source material on her own."

He saw the expression on her face change from concern to outrage. She appeared to be genuinely offended by his accusation. He could all but see the hair bristling on her neck.

"I don't like what you're insinuating, professor."

"Sonji." Grayson sat forward in the leather chair. "Let's stop avoiding the issue, shall we?"

"And what *is* the issue?"

"Whether or not your essay is indeed *your* essay."

Sonji rose to her feet. "Of course it's my essay!"

"Now, Miss Stephens, there's no need to become agitated."

"No need!" Sonji shot back. "You sit there and accuse me of being dishonest. I know you don't expect me to remain calm!"

Grayson rose slowly. "And you sat in my class and handed me an essay with a list of works cited that would befuddle most research librarians. Don't expect me to believe you wrote your assignment without— shall we say—assistance."

"I'm telling you for the last time, professor. I wrote that essay myself."

Sonji faced her instructor-accuser and placed her hands on her hips. "Do you have any proof that I've been dishonest?"

He examined her bold stance and liked what he saw. "None," he said reservedly.

"So what—you thought by giving me the third degree that I would fess up?"

"I'm simply giving you an opportunity to be truthful." He walked around closer to where she was standing and sat on the edge of his desk. He wasn't sure what perfume she was wearing, but one thing was certain—it was dealing him a royal fit. He inhaled deeply and watched as her hazel eyes held him in their close scrutiny.

"For instance, Miss Stephens. Jolvin Covey's book on word etymology is quite rare and obscure. How exactly did you hear of it?"

For an instant, Sonji felt her resolve weaken. Of course she had obtained the reference from the information that Osiris sent her. But she wasn't about to admit that she had gotten the name of the book from an Internet beau.

She racked her brain for a believable explanation, yet could find none.

"Professor Gilmore, I did so much research for this essay, I'm not sure if it's something I just came across or something somebody told me about."

"I see," he said and perched himself on the corner of his desk. "It seems we've reached a stalemate."

Sonji was furious. "Stalemate! What stalemate? I expect an apology." Her hands aggressively punctuated her sentences.

"You can't be serious." He lifted an eyebrow coolly.

"I am most definitely serious. You have accused me of committing a vile and despicable act. And without proof! Purely on the basis of your . . . your . . . faulty suspicions!"

"And you, my dear, have conjured a document, much unlike your current performance level—which is a D-plus at best—using the kind of insider knowledge typically the domain of the learned, which frankly you are not, and expect me to accept on faith that you were led to the conclusions in your paper solely on the virtue of your what? Instinct and determination? I think not."

Sonji's mouth gaped open. Her eyes were as wide as saucers.

"Therefore, I believe—since as you point out, I have no unequivocal evidence—we have reached an impasse, a deadlock, a standoff, a draw, a dead end, a stalemate."

Now he's a walking thesaurus, Sonji thought. The only thing stopping her from ripping his head off was the fact that she didn't want her dress to be soiled when she met Osiris.

Her spinning mind latched on to that thought— Osiris. How much longer until they could be together? she wondered. She glanced up at the clock on the wall. It read 6:40.

"Oh, my God!" Sonji gasped, putting a hand to her mouth.

"What?" Grayson asked following the direction of Sonji's distressed stare to the wall.

"Good heavens!" he replied, bounding from his desk.

"I have to go!" they said in unison.

Grayson packed up the items on his desk as Sonji headed for the door.

"I'm sorry, Professor Gilmore. I really must leave."

"I understand completely," he said, shutting down his computer.

"This isn't over yet," Sonji said, turning toward him.

Grayson walked up behind her, a smug look riding his face. "Time will tell, Miss Stephens. Time will tell."

They walked out together, each caught up in a whirl of thoughts and emotions. Grayson held the door for Sonji to exit the Arts and Sciences building and held the door for her again when they both entered the student-faculty parking garage.

Once inside, they went their separate ways to their cars. Sonji's nerves leaped to life. In approximately twenty minutes she would come face-to-face with the man who made her heart pound like a jackhammer whenever she signed on to the Internet. Exhilarated, she started her car and headed for the exit.

One minute later, she was stopped several feet before the exit by a large barricade and a crew in work clothes. Grayson was arguing with one of the men.

"This is an outrage!"

"I dunno what to tell ya, mister. We're doin' all we can."

Sonji stepped out of her car and approached the two men.

"What's going on?"

Grayson looked pale and stricken. "The gate is mal-functioning."

"What?"

"That's right," the crewman said. "It's down, and it won't go up."

Sonji looked in the direction in which her professor was pointing. She could see the large metal gates in front of the entrance and exit. The gates stretched the full length and width of the openings like one mammoth chain-linked fence.

"I can go get the crew chief," the man said.

"You do that," Grayson growled.

Sonji's heart collapsed. She watched the men working on the internal controls and hoped that any second the gate would begin it's soul-saving ascent. After a few minutes, the crewman returned. Flanking him was a man of considerable size. He was tall and thick and reminded Sonji of a black Paul Bunyon.

"Gray!" he exclaimed, walking toward them.

"Bear!" was Grayson's response.

The two men clasped hands and then embraced.

"I guess you don't know nobody no more."

"Ah, man, you know how it is when you get busy."

Grayson's relaxed speech surprised Sonji, and she stared at him in disbelief.

"Bear, I really need to get outta here. If I don't get to my destination in the next fifteen minutes, I'm never gonna forgive myself. Now, what can you do for me?"

"I can call you a cab."

Grayson wrung his hands. Sonji put her head in hers.

"Out of the question," he said.

"Well then you and your lady-friend will have to wait until morning to get your cars out. We should have it fixed by then."

Sonji and Grayson looked at each other as if someone had poured lemon juice into their mouths.

"I can't wait until morning," Sonji replied. "And I am *not* his lady-friend."

"Suit yourselves," Bear said, rubbing his thick, bushy beard. "But y'all are the ones who are all dressed up and with no place to go."

"Call the cab," Grayson said.

The large man reached into the pocket of his green work suit and retrieved a cell phone. He quickly punched in the number.

"Yes, I need two more cabs at Barnett University—the Arts and Sciences building." Bear covered the receiver with his hand. "We've been callin' cabs for people for the last half hour."

"Yes," he said, looking at Sonji and Grayson. "Where to?"

"The Regency District," they both responded, then recoiled from each other in disgust.

Grayson's typically handsome face crumpled into a frown. "You are the proverbial bad penny."

Sonji's response was a swift talk-to-the-hand gesture.

Bear covered the receiver with his large hand again. "Since you're both going to the same place, they're only sendin' one car."

"Damn. Well tell them to hurry," Sonji retorted.

"Can this bucket go any faster?" Sonji asked.

The cab driver frowned into the rearview mirror. "Not if you want to arrive in one piece, lady."

Sonji's impatience was raging. It had taken the cab driver twenty minutes to get to the university, and now it seemed he was driving as slow as molasses even though she had asked him to hurry. To make matters worse, her instructor was sitting beside her as cool as a cucumber. He hadn't said one word since they had gotten into the cab.

At first, she was tempted to sit in the front seat with the driver. Being in the proximity of Professor Grayson Gilmore was the last thing she wanted right now. But when he gallantly opened the door for her and bowed like a prince, something in the regality of his movement made her climb into the backseat with him.

She glanced at him out of the corner of her eye. He sat, hand on his chin and eyes looking sternly ahead. For the first time this evening, she noticed that he was wearing a diamond earring in his ear. That was completely out of character. Just like his conversation with the maintenance captain earlier.

"You know, with the earring in your ear and the way you were talking to Bear a bit ago, you almost seemed like a real person." Sonji's words came out sounding as exasperated and as angry as she felt.

He turned to her, unblinking. "No matter how you insult me, I will not allow you to dampen my spirits this evening."

Sonji immediately felt bad. She was lashing out because she was severely late for her date with Osiris. She regretted what she had just said and wished she could take it back.

"I'm sorry, professor. I didn't mean to insult you." She took a deep breath and tried to relax. "It's just that with your accusation, and everything else that's happened this evening, I'm a little on edge."

"It's understandable," he said. "Yet I hope you can appreciate my position as your teacher. I wouldn't be performing my function adequately if I hadn't discussed the drastic change of grade with you."

Sonji hated to admit it, but she did appreciate his position. "I understand, professor."

* * *

As soon as Grayson stepped out of the taxi, he knew something was wrong. Carrie's Café, which had a loyal and regular clientele, looked strangely deserted. He saw Sonji reaching into her purse, and despite the fact that she had caused him significant distress this evening, he wasn't about to let her pay any part of the carfare.

"I'll take care of it," he said to her, taking a fifty from his wallet.

"I pay my own way," Sonji snapped, seemingly ready for another fight.

"Don't be absurd. What kind of gentleman would I be if—"

"Look," the cabby interrupted. "Somebody pay me so I can get the hell away from the both-a-yas."

Grayson handed the man the money and took his change. The cab driver sped off as if he were leaving the scene of a crime in the getaway car. Grayson stepped to Sonji's side as she stared aghast at the sign posted on the front door of the jazz bar.

CLOSED FOR REPAIRS. SEE YOU IN ABOUT THREE WEEKS. MANAGEMENT

"Oh, no."

"Oh, dear."

They both checked their watches in disgust.

It was now thirty minutes after the stated rendezvous time, and Grayson was furious. Because of this dishonest student, he had missed a date with the love of his life. Obviously she had been there, read the closed sign, and—since there was no one to meet her—left.

This Sonji Stephens had been trouble to him from the very start. Always disrupting class by coming in late. Always looking so alluring he often forgot the points he was making in his lectures. Then, there was the dinner where he had nearly betrayed Nzinga. And now this! This was the last straw. Now Nzinga was probably lost to him forever. Well, Sonji Stephens wouldn't get away with it. This time he would tell her exactly what he felt of her interference in his life.

"You bastard!"

"What?" he recoiled.

"Look what you've done! You've made me miss something, some*one* very important!"

"Me!"

"Yes, you!" Sonji paced back and forth in front of him.

"You have the audacity to blame this fiasco on me?"

Sonji's fists clenched and unclenched. She shuddered with rage and let out an anguished shrill. "If I've lost him, you're going to be sorry you ever met me!"

Sonji pivoted on her heel and turned away from him. She marched from the sidewalk and onto the grass, heading toward the street. Her forceful steps dislodged something in her pocket and Grayson watched as it caught the moonlight and fell into the grass.

He had a strange sense of déjà vu from that time in his office when the paper had fallen from her pocket, only this time there was something stirringly familiar about the fallen object. Grayson strode over to where it lay shining in the grass and felt a lump form in his throat. He bent down carefully and retrieved the scarab.

Grayson's moment of clarity was swift. Instantly, everything became unquestionably clear, and he was filled with a sense of understanding and euphoria.

His lips curved into a smile and delight sparkled in his eyes as he called out eagerly to his soul mate. "Nzinga!"

Sonji spun around abruptly in the middle of the street, her brow furrowed. "What did you say?"

Grayson's moves were agile as he closed the distance between them. He stared down into her winsome eyes and noticed, really noticed, how beautiful she was. And standing there at night, in the middle of the street, by God, she seemed to be wearing the moonlight!

He took the amulet, placed it carefully around her neck, and sighed.

"I am"—he swallowed apprehensively—"Osiris," he said, then stroked the side of her face.

"Wh-what?" she responded. But the light in her eyes told him she understood. He watched as a tiny tear escaped from her eye and rolled down her cheek.

"Now, now," he whispered. "Let's not have any of that."

Grayson wiped her tear away and then lowered his head to hers.

Their lips united into a swelling and raging passion. Their hands groped, raked, and rubbed each other's bodies recklessly. They felt all of the fervor and abandon that had been denied them online and devoured each other in a daze of exquisite need. Their long, lingering kiss was tumultuous, impetuous, and said what no words could say—that the space between them was finally closed. That the rapture of their bodies touching at last was almost more pleasure than their souls could bear.

When their soul-kiss ended, their eyes remained closed and their heads rested wearily together. Their breathing was fast and synchronous. Sonji felt the heat of Grayson's body approaching her again and prepared herself for another dizzying press of his lips. This time their exchange was slow and endearing. Grayson's tongue traced a perfect outline of Sonji's lips before sliding gently into her mouth. Soft moans emanating from someplace deep within her being came out in whimpers. Grayson echoed her sentiments with a deep moan of his own.

"Let's go," he said huskily.

Sonji said nothing, but nodded and held his hand when he offered it. They walked to a nearby coffee shop, called a cab, and rode in silence and love to Grayson's house.

"It feels as though I have waited an eternity for this moment." Grayson helped Sonji out of her coat and removed his own. He hung their coats in the closet and led her down the hallway. Hand in hand, they walked into Grayson's bedroom and embraced hungrily. Their desire for each other surprised even themselves, yet they were inextricably swept into a current of deep longing. Their clothes came off in flings and tosses. They fell down upon Grayson's king-sized bed like ancient lovers, apart for centuries and at last reunited.

Sonji's need was urgent. She relished the sweet, breezy taste of Grayson's mouth, neck, and arms. She pulled him closer and still closer, wanting them to become one—knowing she could wait no longer. And then she heard the words that made her soul collapse in anguish.

"No," he said. "This is wrong."

"W-what?" Sonji responded, unsure of what he meant.

Grayson sat up slowly, stroking Sonji's thigh in the process. His eyes roamed her nakedness in pure adulation. "Warrior woman, whose breath is truly softer than water, we cannot allow our lust to consume us."

"But Grayson—" she protested.

"Shh," he said, putting a finger to his lips and then licking them. "After all this time, we should relish our intimacy and make each second a delicious teasing into the next."

As he talked, his hands touched her ankles ever so

lightly. Sonji felt the delicate strokes moving to all of the sensitive areas on her legs as if his fingers were following a map of her pleasure zones. She wriggled sensuously. His mouth joined his hands as they worked their way inch by inch up her body. Eagerly she reached for him, and he took her hands in his and rested them carefully above her head.

All of his reservations, questions, and hesitancy were cast away by the ambrosial scent of Sonji's hair and skin. The passion in her eyes ignited a fire in him like no other. Just sensing her beneath him, wearing only the amulet, sent Grayson into heights of desire previously unknown. After wanting so badly to feel the caress of her body against his, he was possessed with an overwhelming need to touch, taste, and linger over every inch of her body. He reached for a foil packet in his dresser drawer, determined to do just that.

By the time their joining came, Sonji's nerve endings were ablaze. Their unhurried foreplay generated a slow burn on her skin that sent her senses spinning. Once Grayson was inside her, his movements were ocean-like—undulating in wave after wave of pleasure. Soon the waves turned into one mighty torrent, and Sonji knew it was not lust but love she was feeling. When the torrent broke loose inside her, she screamed his name and held on tight while Grayson filled her with a sense of completion like none she had never known.

Sonji awoke from an enchanted night's sleep to find Grayson lying snugly against her. His head was resting comfortably on her bosom as if he had been keeping watch over her heart all night.

She ran a hand gently through his thick hair and

purred like a tigress. He stirred beside her, and she
felt the subtle graze of his lips against her skin.

"Hey, you." His words vibrated on her chest and
caused a commotion in her lower torso.

"Hey, you," she said, smiling. And then a chord of
mischief struck her.

"So professor—do you still think I cheated on my
essay?"

"Oh, you!" Grayson responded and straddled himself above her. "Just for that, you're going to get it!"

Sonji batted her eyes flirtatiously. "I certainly hope so."

The new lovers kissed and nuzzled each other for
a time. Then Sonji looked up into his eyes.

"I can't believe it," she said. "It was you, all the time."

"Believe it," Grayson said, kissing her forehead,
nuzzling her neck, caressing her shoulders.

Suddenly Sonji became apprehensive. After all, she
had just slept with her English professor. There had
to be something not right about that. Grayson must
have felt her unease.

"We haven't broken any rules," he assured her.
"And you earned that A-plus. Even if you got the references from me, you still wrote the paper yourself."

"Grayson, I don't know."

"All right, my dear," he said, positioning himself beside her. "There are six weeks left in the semester. You
have three papers and a final due. If you earn an A on
each, you'll get a B in the class."

Grayson kissed Sonji in mid-sigh. "I promise not to
let our relationship influence your grade."

Sonji's heart did a quick-flutter. Did he say relationship? She tried to back track through Grayson's last
words, but found herself lost in a profusion of his
kisses. *Just this moment,* she thought. *I'll just focus on now,
and not think about tomorrow or the next day or that happily
ever after some people seem to achieve.* Sonji submerged her-

self into Grayson's passions and attempted to put her
past behind her.

"You are my *raison d'être.*"

"Ooh, I like it when you talk intellectually."

"Madam, if you are impressed by that, I have a body
language that will utterly enthrall you!" Grayson crept
toward Sonji like a panther on the prowl. "Come
here," he insisted, condom in hand.

"No, Grayson," Sonji responded playfully. For the
past two days the lovers had been inseparable. They
had filled the days with laughter, deep discussions,
gourmet food, and generous amounts of lovemaking.
They simply could not get enough of each other.

Now it was Sunday evening, and Sonji was contemplating her return to her town house. The prospect
seemed dreadful. She would much rather stay with
Grayson.

She watched him coming toward her in the den as
she backed away, smiling. He was truly magnificent.
His sleek and sinuous form looked delectable. She
had lost herself numerous times in the ripples of his
muscles, the sharp planes and angles of his chiseled
face, and the intoxicating power of his strength and
sexual prowess. And all he had seemed to want to do
all weekend was please her. She worried that her feelings were forming too fast and too soon. She
shouldn't let herself tumble into the abyss so quickly.
But the look in Grayson's eyes, so warm and golden,
turned her legs to jelly and made her want him again.

"Nuh-uh," she protested, laughing this time, and
continuing to back away.

Grayson was not swayed. "I don't think you understand the severity of the situation."

Sonji glanced down to see the full impression of

Grayson's manhood jutting out against his boxers. He continued his advance. Giggling, she bolted out of the den and into the living room.

"Oh, no you don't!" he said, running behind her. Swiftly, Grayson's quick reflexes and powerful biceps enveloped her.

"Grayson, we've enjoyed each other so much this weekend. Shouldn't we cool it off a little?"

"Never," he said, brushing his lips against hers. "You think I would let you get away that easily—when it took this long for me to find you?"

Sonji could barely contain her emotion. As sure as the beating of her heart, she knew she loved this man. She stuffed down the mighty feelings and swallowed hard. His embrace was almost more than she could bear.

Grayson pulled Sonji in closer and reveled in the tender sensation of her body contouring against his. They fit together perfectly. Now the words to one of his favorite songs made wonderful sense to him. He dropped his head and sang into Sonji's ear. "A thousand kisses from you is never too much."

"Oh, Grayson," Sonji said, reaching up and touching her palm to the side of his face. "You can't sing," she said, smiling.

"I know," he responded, nibbling along her neckline.

She moaned in response. "That's okay. Neither can I."

The way her fingers gently raked his back was heating his blood to a sensuously maddening temperature. He had to have Sonji. Now! He gently lowered her to the floor of his dining room and proceeded to make slow, passion-consumed love to her.

His unhurried attentions were deliberate, methodical, and careful. He surveyed her body like a cartographer mapping out his territory. As he moved, he committed every inch of her body to memory—the smooth slope of her stomach, the mole just above her right thigh, the brown flower that was her navel, the gentle rise of her breasts, and those dimples! He flicked his tongue back and forth across each one and then settled into her mouth as they became one.

Their eyes locked and neither could turn away as the need that filled them took over. He wanted to murmur, whisper, shout "I love you," but he was not certain of her feelings for him. He wanted to keep his feelings to himself, but alas, his body betrayed him. It was indeed speaking all of the affections he felt for her. And he was powerless to stop it. No matter what happened now, he belonged to this woman, this Sonji Stephens. Somehow he had to find a way to make her his own.

"Oh . . . oh, God . . . Grayson . . ."

"Yes," he breathed.

"Don't stop, Grayson."

"I won't stop, pretty Sonji," he moaned, kissing her on the left temple and then the right. "Not ever."

Ten

"Did you swallow a firefly?"

"No, silly! Why do you ask?" But Sonji knew the answer to her own question. The weekend she had spent with Grayson had been rapturous. Her skin still tingled from all of the places where he had ignited a passion so exquisite, their souls had become one. Her face was probably an unmaskable testament of joy.

"It's Osiris, isn't it?" Andromeda clapped her hands in front of her.

As the sociology students filed out of the room, Sonji quickly stuffed her books into her book bag. "Yes, it is. And I have to go." Sonji dashed away, smiling. "I'll tell you all about it later!" she called back, trotting off to class. Andi stood in the middle of the classroom smiling after her friend. She could tell something wonderful had happened.

Sonji halted her sprint at the door of Annex Seven. She stood still for a couple of seconds to catch her breath. She didn't want to appear too eager. A few students passed through the building entrance ahead of her, and she followed the last one in.

When she walked into the classroom, Grayson was standing directly opposite the doorway. It looked as though he had strategically positioned himself there to get the full effect of her entrance into his class. Instead of his usual tailored suit, he wore a micro-knit shirt. The butter-colored sweater was tucked into gray wool slacks. Their windowpane design and reverse pleats made Grayson's legs look long and powerfully strong. The sight of him standing there, welcoming her, made her euphoric. She took her usual seat in the front of the class and beamed with delight.

"Well, Miss Stephens," Grayson said, walking coolly toward her. "I do believe you are on time." He reached inside his pants pocket and pulled out a gold pocket watch. "With even a minute to spare." He walked past her desk to the other side of the room and the cologne that had intoxicated her all weekend played at the edge of her nose. *He did that on purpose,* she thought, smiling inwardly. Just then she realized how difficult the rest of the semester was going to be. How could she concentrate on learning the finer points of essay writing when all she wanted to do was disrobe her professor, call him Osiris—Nubian man of the bright sun—and make love to him on the classroom floor?

He turned his attention from her to the entire class. "I trust each of you had a . . . satisfying weekend." Amidst the low responses of "yes," "yep," and "uh-huh," Sonji's eyes widened like coasters at his insinuation.

"Good," he said energetically. "Then let's start with a quick review of Chapters Eight and Nine."

Sonji spent the remaining time in Grayson's class drifting in and out of attention. One minute her mind was completely focused on audience analysis, the next she was imagining Grayson's hands on her breasts. The fifty-minute class was arduous in coming to an end.

"Are you all right?" Byron asked, slinging his backpack over his right shoulder. "You seemed kinda fidgety today. Are you worried about the next assignment?"

Sonji appreciated the concern in her study partner's voice. "Yes, as a matter of fact, I am."

"Me too, Sonji." Byron shot a quick glance in Grayson's direction. "I haven't figured out what he wants yet."

Sonji realized that neither had she.

"If you like, we can meet in the library again this weekend. We seem to work well together."

Sonji watched the last of the students file out of the classroom. "That sounds great, Byron." Though she wondered if it would do anything to help her reconcile the dilemma of being Grayson's student and his lover.

"Sonji." Grayson's authoritative voice startled both her and Byron out of their conversation.

She turned and looked in his direction. "Yes, professor," she answered.

"There is a matter I need to discuss with you."

"Well," Byron said, heading toward the door, "I'll e-mail you so we can set up a time for this weekend."

"That will be great, Byron."

Before Byron was out of the doorway completely, Sonji found herself in Grayson's arms. His kiss was sudden and demanding. "Now, what's this about you and Mr. Moore this weekend?"

"Jealous?" she asked, donning her best innocent expression.

"Let's just say I don't want anything or anyone to take you away from me."

She reached up and gently touched the side of his face. *If he only knew what was in my heart,* she thought. *He wouldn't have to worry about me for the rest of our lives.*

"I think you're overreacting," she said instead of

the three words dangling precariously from the tip of her tongue.

"I'm sure I am, but I can't help myself. I was hoping you and I could spend some time together this weekend."

"Really?" she replied, wrapping her arms around his waist. She felt a thread of mischief move through her. "Doing what, professor?"

He lightly kissed her cheek. "Well, in addition to pleasuring each other beyond our wildest dreams, I thought we could go over to my brother's house for dinner."

"You're kidding!"

"I'm very serious."

And then a flush of crimson warmed the chestnut bronze of his face. "I would much rather invite you to my parents' house, but they live in another city. So instead of bringing you home to meet my folks, I hope you'll be satisfied with getting to know my brother and his family for right now."

"Grayson, are you sure?"

He kissed her gingerly on the forehead. "As sure as a Toni Morrison flashback."

"I'll have dinner with you at your brother's house this weekend under one condition."

"What's that?" Grayson asked, his eyes narrowing to playful slits.

"You have dinner with me at my grandmother's house next weekend."

"You've got me."

Sonji snuggled herself against Grayson's hard body. *I hope so,* she thought. *I really hope so.*

There was more food on the table than Grayson could remember ever seeing at one time. Jerika had outdone herself. When he and Sonji walked into Kyle's house, the mingling aromas of various southern dishes had greeted them at the door.

And not to their disappointment, everything was delicious. Serving bowls and platters were passed back and forth, and everyone had seconds. Grayson's jaws ached from smiling. He was happier than he had been in a long time. Sonji fit right in with his family as if she had been born his wife.

Suddenly everything in the room stopped on that thought. Sonji's head whipped around and took on a God-awful grin.

"Born your wife," she said and began to cackle.

"Born your wife," everyone in the room repeated, including baby Kya who was drooling a thick yellow goo.

Then piece by piece, Sonji's beautiful cocoa-tan skin flaked off her face and onto the floor. Grayson stared in disgust and tried to pull away. Sonji wrapped her arm around him and held him like a vice as her skin continued to fall in heaps to the linoleum. Where Grayson expected to see the skeletal outline of a skull came the face and features of Veranda Gilmore. The cackling increased.

"Here, Grayson," the Veranda-thing said, holding out the bloated body of a little boy. "Watch Gray Jr., darling. I *must* go comb my hair."

Grayson bolted upright in bed and shivered. He was ice cold. "Loosen me, demon memory!" he cried into the night. "Leave me be."

After splashing cold water on his face, he returned to bed. He reached over to the mahogany nightstand and pulled a flower to his nose. Its fragrance was still sweet, and its petals were damp from where they had been floating in water. The lily from Sonji's hair brought on sweet memories of their passion. Grayson returned the flower to its dish and turned over with thoughts of his beloved Nzinga settling him back into sleep.

Andi's dorm room was a wondrous sanctuary of flowering plants and sunlight. Even in the late autumn, the numerous windows on the south wall of the room transformed what could have been cold and dreary into a warm and relaxing atmosphere. Add to that the aromas of jasmine potpourri and herbal tea, and Sonji didn't know whether to meditate or simply take a nap.

"You are, like, pushing me totally to the edge."

Sonji stirred from her relaxed state. Her feet were propped on a flower-patterned ottoman and the sounds of Boney James surrounded her. "I could unwind here for hours, Andi. No wonder you have such a carefree attitude. Your home is the epitome of stress relief."

"Until now. Are you ever going to tell me what happened with you and Osiris?"

"Well," Sonji closed her eyes. "We met."

Andi, who was stretched out on the floor, sat up quickly. "Whoa! Why didn't you tell me you were going to do that?"

"I didn't want to get your hopes up. Or mine either. Just in case things didn't work out or we didn't hit it off."

"Well?"

"Well—Osiris and I have something in common."

"What!"

Sonji could not disguise her rascality. "Lust!"

The two women laughed, and Andi moved closer to her friend. "You mean you did it? Like on the first date?"

Sonji's eyes were open now. She vividly remembered Grayson's expertise with her erogenous zones. "Yes, yes, yes."

"Oh, my gosh." Andi blinked. "Sebastian and I waited before we did it."

"Really?" Sonji asked, suddenly self-conscious of her decision to sleep with Grayson.

"Oh, yeah. Since he had to go to work on the night we met, we had to wait until his day off."

Andi's dorm filled with the laughter of two blissful women.

"So what's he like? I mean, do I know him?"

How much should I reveal? Sonji asked herself. *What harm could it do to tell Andi who Osiris is? She could probably keep a secret.* Heck, Sonji wasn't sure if it needed to be kept secret. She wasn't sure of anything actually. "He's tall, dark, and handsome. And he makes me feel . . . like life is bursting inside me."

"Told you!" Andi proclaimed, and jumped to her feet. "Now, come over here." She pulled out the chair in front of her computer and beckoned Sonji to be seated.

"What for?"

"So you can sit down and declare your love."

"Who said anything about love?"

"You did, silly. Besides, Andi *knows*. Now come on over and tell Osiris how you feel."

What Andi was proposing was out of the question. Sonji couldn't consider opening herself so soon. Maybe what she was feeling wasn't love at all. Maybe it was an intense crush or a hard infatuation, or . . .

"Miss Sonji." Andi's insistence drew Sonji's attention to the computer screen where the home page to BlackLuv was already loading. "Haven't you heard that the thing you did to get him is the same thing you have to do to keep him?"

"Yes, but—"

"Then, like, sit down and at least tell him how much you enjoyed meeting him."

Well she could do that. After all, she had a spectacular time at his place. The weekend they shared was full of enchantment. She would remember it for a lifetime, even if nothing else ever became of their relationship.

She sat down at Andi's computer with her feelings for Grayson flowing sensuously inside her and began to type.

Treasured Osiris, paramour of my soul,
I thank you. Our days together burn in me like a new sun. Eager does not express my anticipation of our next shared moment. Nor does content explain my pleasure at our joining. But know this, I have no breath until I feel the warmth of your heartlight once more.

Andi gave Sonji a hug from behind and placed a small cluster of baby's breath in her hair. Sonji clicked Send and let out a sigh as her message disappeared and traveled through cyberspace. She had stepped out on a limb. As far back as she could remember, she had been stepping out on limbs. Sometimes it got her into trouble, like her relationship with Chad. But sometimes, like deciding to return to school, it was a risk worth taking. Unfortunately, she had never had a consistent streak. Her good and bad decisions always seemed to come one right after the other. She hoped with all her heart that *this time,* she would be lucky and seeing Grayson Gilmore would not only be a good decision but the best decision she'd made in a long time.

"Okay, move over," Andi insisted.

"What?" Sonji said, abandoning her thoughts.

"I might as well contact Prometheus."

"Who?"

"Sebastian. I haven't sent him a letter today, and I have some special news to tell him."

The two women switched places, and Sonji watched as Andi told Sebastian that Nzinga and Osiris had finally met. The story she wove in her e-mail sounded like a remarkable fairy tale—with two fated lovers finally coming together. *If only it were that effortless,* Sonji thought.

The longest week in Sonji's life finally came to an end. She stood at the window of her town home, looking out for the third time. Grayson was picking her up at four but she had started watching for him at 3:30. All week she had imagined what meeting Grayson's brother and sister-in-law would be like. She looked forward to meeting them with a mixed heart. She wanted very much to know Grayson's family, yet at the same time, she wondered if they were rushing things. In either case, she reasoned, she wanted to make a good impression on them.

Rushing to check herself once more in her full-length mirror, Sonji beheld a woman in love. Her dark curly hair was gleaming brightly in the light. She wore a light application of foundation along with a russet lipstick that made her mouth look moist. Her dress was a step down from the suits she normally wore, but definitely a step up from the jeans and T-shirts that were her usual attire on the weekends. It contoured around her modest frame with just enough give to allow her to walk freely, but not so much that it masked her shapely figure. She just hoped that its olive-and-gold brushstroke pattern didn't make her appear over-dressed.

When the knock at her door came, Sonji tingled

in anticipation. *Gee, I'm acting like a teenager,* she thought, walking to the door. *Compose yourself,* she ordered and opened the door. Grayson stood on the staircase looking completely dashing in an emperor sweater and black-and-cream tic-weave pants. His familiar cologne wafted into her nostrils and nearly made her swoon.

"Come in," she said, stepping aside. "I'll just get my purse and jacket."

"You can get your purse," Grayson remarked, coming inside, "but don't you dare cover up that dress. You look spectacular."

Sonji picked up her purse from the sofa. "Thank you, Grayson, but it is chilly out."

"My dear," he said, sweeping her into his arms. "I will see to it that you are as warm as you desire." Then he kissed her slowly, and gently varied the pressure to her lips in a rhythmic fashion that matched their lovemaking from the previous weekend.

Whatever resistance she might have had to fight his quick advance was vanquished. She gave in to a kiss that spun her in a million directions at once and yet kept her centered on the one truth that consumed her—she was in love with him.

"We had better go," he said finally. "Before we never make it to my brother's house." Sonji smiled, knowing he was right, and grabbed her jacket on the way out.

"Uncle Gray!" Klarice's familiar greeting lifted Grayson's heart like always. She opened the door and jumped into his arms.

"Hey, Crumbcake!"

Klarice's hair was plaited into numerous braids with multicolored ribbons and bows attached. Her red velvet dress was complete with delicate white lace on the collar and sleeves. She grinned broadly and swung her black patent leather–clad feet back and forth.

"Come on in, Bart." Jerika stood in the entryway and shook her head at her daughter.

Grayson stepped inside and guided Sonji in with his free hand. "Jerika, Klarice, this is Sonji."

Sonji stepped forward and shook Jerika's hand.

"Pleased to meet you, Sonji."

"Same here," Sonji said, wondering why she was so nervous.

Jerika frowned at her daughter. "Klarice, say hello."

Klarice buried her head into Grayson's shoulder.

"My little Crumbcake, shy? Nonsense!"

Klarice kept her head buried in her uncle's shoulder. "Hello," came her muffled reply.

"Let me take your coats," Jerika said, reaching toward Sonji and Grayson.

"I asked her not to wear that."

Sonji took off her jacket and rolled her eyes at him.

"I see why," Jerika said, giving Sonji the once-over. "He said you were cute, and he was right."

"Thanks," Sonji said, walking with them into the living room.

Kyle emerged from the kitchen with Kya on his hip. *"Somebody* had to have dinner early," he said. "And she got most of it on me," Kyle continued, pointing to various spots on his clothing.

The combination of the food stains on Kyle's clothing and the soppy grin on Kya's face struck Sonji as funny. She laughed heartily as Kyle extended his hand.

"I don't know what my brother has told you about me, but I assure you it's all true."

"Nice to meet you, Kyle," Sonji said as her laughter tapered off. The two shook hands and Kya held out her arms to Sonji. "I guess she's chosen a new victim. Do you mind?"

"Not at all," Sonji said, taking Kya into her arms. The almost toddler picked at the gold pattern on Sonji's dress. "It's easy to forget sometimes what it's like to be fascinated and absorbed by one small thing," Sonji added.

"Ain't that the truth," Jerika said.

"Can I get you two a drink?" Kyle asked, heading toward the bar.

"I'll have a Guinness," Grayson said.

"Make it two," Sonji responded.

Grayson looked at his lady-friend with surprise. "I didn't know you drank Guinness."

"I don't, but I've always wanted to try it."

"Maybe you'd better try Bart's first and then decide if you want one," Jerika suggested.

Kyle popped the top off a bottle of the dark lager. "It's definitely an acquired taste." He walked over and handed the bottle to Sonji. Everyone watched her with interest.

She took a small sip of the brown brew, and her face wrinkled into a grimace. She closed and opened her eyes, then gasped. "Aw, yuck!"

Baby Kya paused from her inspection of Sonji's dress to see what caused such a reaction. Sonji handed the bottle over to Grayson. "I'll just have a glass of wine."

"Sure," Kyle said, smiling. "White zin okay?"

"I'll take anything over that bitter concoction. How do you stand it?"

"Between you and me, I don't think they like it either," Jerika remarked, heading off into the kitchen.

"Man, will you put the checks and balances on your wife?"

"You must be kidding. I haven't been able to do that in years."

"Can I help with anything, Jerika?"

"Bart already told me you can't cook. But you can come in and keep me company."

Kyle's eyes widened at Jerika's remark. He looked at his two children in the middle of Sonji and Grayson and spoke with a concerned voice. "Do I need to remove my children from the battle zone?"

"No," Sonji said, standing. She walked over to where Klarice was sitting half-asleep in her uncle's arms and handed over Kya. "It's true. I don't have much success in the kitchen. And if you don't stop talking about me," she said, shaking a finger at Grayson, "you aren't going to have much success in the bedroom."

Grayson's jaw dropped, Kyle roared with laughter, and Jerika stuck her head out of the kitchen.

"I like her!"

Sonji whizzed around in Jerika's kitchen like a buzz saw. Her hands were constantly occupied, washing something, chopping something, handing Jerika something. Grayson's sister-in-law insisted that Sonji not cook, but she put her to use nonetheless. The two worked together like master chef and trusty assistant.

Before long, dishes were warming, pots were simmering, and bread was baking.

"I don't know how you do it, Jerika."

"Do what, honey?"

"All this," Sonji said, looking around the kitchen. She was speaking of preparing such a large meal, but she silently realized she also meant running a household, raising children, being pregnant.

Jerika wiped her hands on her apron. "Take a peek in the living room. You see that man with the ponytail?"

Sonji stood at the entrance to the kitchen and

looked out into the other room. Kyle was bouncing Kya on his knee. The child's face was a mass of giggles. Kyle's face shined like a high-beamed headlight. She also caught a glimpse of Grayson, who was, to her astonishment, playing on all fours with Klarice. Sonji felt her heart warm at the sight.

"I'm so in love with that man, sometimes it scares me," Jerika admitted. "But it also compels me to cook like food is going out of style. And do my part to make our house a home." Jerika's hand traveled quickly to her stomach. She smiled and shook her head.

"Is the baby kicking?" Sonji asked, childlike.

"He's always kicking. Sometimes he just gets a little carried away."

"May I?"

"Knock yourself out."

Sonji crossed the kitchen to where Jerika was now leaning against the sink. She extended her hand, and lightly pressed the spot where Jerika's hand had just been.

"Girl, you ain't gonna feel nothin' like that. Here." Jerika took Sonji's hand and flattened it against her enlarged abdomen. "Now hold still," she said.

Sonji did as she was instructed. She didn't feel anything. Even after a couple of minutes of being still and quiet. And then it happened. She felt a thump against her palm. And then another, and then a downright kick. Her eyes widened. She had never felt a baby kick before. She thought it was the most marvelous thing she had ever felt.

"It got quiet in here so I had to come see what's up." Sonji turned to see Grayson standing near the kitchen entrance with Klarice on his back.

"When women get quiet, that means trouble," he said, smiling.

"You can quit lyin' right now, Bart. You know the only reason you came in here is to catch a sniff."

"What?" Sonji said, frowning.

"Uncle Gray said he wants to smell the pots, Mommy."

"I knew it," Jerika responded, turning to Sonji. "Girl, I can't keep that man's nose out of my cookware."

Grayson sauntered over to the stove. "I gots ta get my whiff on."

Sonji watched in amazement while the Grayson she knew as reserved, diplomatic, and almost persnickety lost his cool over a simmering pot of greens.

"My sister-in-law can dip her toes in some greens," he proclaimed, grinning. Grayson walked past Sonji, but not before kissing her on the cheek. Then he returned to the living room, where Sonji could see that Kyle was setting them up with another round of Guinness.

Jerika eyed Sonji steadily. "You don't know anything about that aspect of him, do you?"

"Not a thing," Sonji admitted with her hand placed pensively on her chin.

"Don't worry, he's harmless. Just a little disconnected."

Sonji wondered what Jerika meant by her comment, but didn't feel it was her place to inquire.

"Jerika, this is delicious!" Sonji said.

"Told you she could burn," Grayson replied.

Jerika smiled at them both. "Thank you."

Grayson broke off a piece of biscuit and sopped up the gravy from his heaping portions of smothered liver and onions over rice. He popped the biscuit in his mouth and smacked loudly.

"Grayson!" Sonji exclaimed in shock.

"You haven't seen the half of it," Kyle remarked.

Just then Klarice got the giggles. "He licks his fingers, too."

Sonji shook her head. "I can't wait to see that." And then she felt like joining in the fun. "I'll bet he belches like thunder, too."

"Y-hes," Klarice said through her giggles.

"Forget y'all," Grayson responded to their laughter. He continued his aggressive assault of the food on his plate.

"He's like a bottomless pit," Sonji remarked, completely baffled. Throughout dinner she had to remind herself to keep eating, because she was so taken aback by Grayson's transformation. The moment he had gotten around his family, a new Grayson had taken over the one she knew. This new person was comical, relaxed, and homeboyish. It was fascinating to see the metamorphosis. Although Sonji was thoroughly enamored with the man she knew as Grayson Gilmore, she also found this latest incarnation equally attractive.

After dinner Grayson, Kyle, and Klarice cleaned up the kitchen while Sonji sat with Jerika in the living room holding baby Kya.

"You little gold-digger," Jerika admonished her child. "The girl is attracted to anything gold."

Sonji watched as Kya was once again fascinated by the gold pattern shimmering in her dress. Now and then she would glance back at her mother as if to make sure that it was okay for her to be poking around on a stranger's clothing.

"My child, my child," Jerika said pridefully. "You'll never get rid of her now."

"I don't mind. She's so precious." Sonji kept her

head turned toward the baby, but out of her periphery she could see Grayson standing a bit behind the doorway, watching her. He stood immobile for several seconds. At that moment he seemed lost, as if some gigantic hand had just snatched his soul from his body.

Sonji was beginning to get nervous. She decided against her better judgment to turn in his direction. Before she had the chance, Grayson moved from the doorway and retreated into the kitchen.

A few moments later, Klarice came skipping out into the living room. "All done, Mommy!" Her plaits bounced jauntily on her head.

Kyle emerged next with Grayson not far behind.

"Go get my coat, Crumbcake."

"Okay, Uncle Gray," she said trotting off toward the hallway. She returned seconds later with the coat in her arms.

"It's heavy, Uncle Gray."

Grayson knelt down so that he was almost the same height as his niece. "I know sweetheart. That's because it's got something very special in it."

Klarice clapped her hands together. "For me!"

He smiled at her happiness. "Of course for you. And Kya, too."

"Gray . . ." Kyle said, sounding slightly annoyed.

"Bart," Jerika said, crossing her arms in front of her.

"Don't trip, please. I like to do things for my family."

Grayson reached into his inside coat pocket and pulled out a large, multicolored lollipop. Klarice's eyes grew almost as large as the sucker. "Thanks, Uncle Gray!"

"Oh, my baby's teeth," Jerika moaned.

"Don't worry," Grayson said, standing up. "She'll get new ones."

Kya stared expectantly at the candy in her sister's hands. Right on cue, Grayson produced a smaller ver-

sion for her. He stepped to Sonji's side and knelt beside her. Kya's hands were already reaching for the
treat.

After handing over the lollipop to his niece, Grayson
stood and took a seat next to Sonji. Kyle and Jerika
glanced at each other with exasperated expressions.

"Well, I figured you wouldn't find candy as objec-
tionable as another toy."

Kyle huffed. "Gray, it's not what you buy. It's that
you buy all the time."

Sonji wanted somehow to lighten the mood. "I
guess they don't want their kids to be as spoiled rotten as you."

Although she didn't get a laugh, her comment
lightened the mood slightly. Now distracted from the
patterns in Sonji's dress, Kya straightened her legs
out, signaling that she wanted to get down. Sonji
obliged and off Kya crawled in a beeline to her father.

Despite the moment of tension concerning Grayson's gifts, Sonji had an enjoyable time. Jerika and Kyle
went upstairs to put the kids to bed after they finished
their snacks. That gave Sonji and Grayson a moment
alone.

"I have been dying to ask you something all evening."

He slid his arm behind Sonji's shoulders on the
loveseat. "What's that?"

"Why does Jerika call you Bart?"

Grayson chuckled. "I'm so used to it, I don't even
notice it anymore. Bart is short for Bartholomew.
That's my middle name."

"So she prefers to use your middle name?"

"She's never really said why she calls me that, but
I have an idea." The far away look returned to
Grayson's face. "I insulted her once, and even though
I know she's forgiven me, I think it's her way of re-

minding me how wrong I was." *There he goes—rubbing that place on his chin that he always rubs when he's thinking about something important,* Sonji thought. And then the moment was gone and he returned to her as quickly as he had left. *Maybe he'll share it with me one day,* Sonji hoped. She stroked the back of Grayson's hand as Kyle and Jerika returned to the living room.

Sonji couldn't believe what a wonderful time she had. When the evening began, she was a little nervous. Meeting Grayson's family was a big step and a step she was taking quite early in their relationship. But she soon felt so comfortable with them, she didn't recognize herself.

The reserved, subdued, almost shy Sonji Stephens had been transformed into a jovial, spontaneous, darn near boisterous new woman who felt like she had finally found her way home. All her life it had been just her grandmother and her. For years, she had longed for a family. Not that she didn't love her grandmother. She did with all her heart. But sometimes she wanted what others had, lots of people to love and be loved by.

"You're awfully quiet," Grayson said, momentarily taking his eyes off the road to glance at her.

"I'm just thinking about how much I enjoyed meeting your family this evening."

"I'm glad," Grayson responded. "I know they enjoyed meeting you." He rested a reassuring hand on her hers.

The highlight of the evening was learning about Grayson's other side. The side that loved greens, played on the floor with his nieces, and spoke more slang than most people half his age. Knowing that Grayson had an alter ego of sorts was intriguing and extremely arousing. And it was that other Grayson that Sonji wanted to make love to that night. Just considering it made her femininity moisten and throb. *Grayson is in for a treat,* she thought, checking him out behind the wheel. She licked her lips in anticipation of how she intended to seduce the other side of Grayson Gilmore.

"Have a seat," Sonji said, motioning to the sofa in her living room. "I have something to show you."

Grayson did as he was told as Sonji turned on the stereo. She selected a CD from the entertainment center, placing it carefully into the disc player. He recognized the music. The incomparable resonance of Anita Baker's sultry alto filled the room. With her back to him, Sonji turned down the lights and began the most sensual hip movements he had ever seen. Then she turned to face him, and mouthed the words to the prelude of "Rhythm of Love." Grayson felt the heated stirrings of lust and love mingling inside him.

As her lips moved to the spoken words, Sonji ran her fingers gradually through her hair and the look on her face matched the sultriness in Anita's voice. Grayson felt his manhood stiffen and grow harder with each movement of her mouth and each pass of her hand through her hair.

When Anita started to sing, Sonji started to sway and move her body in ways that suggested the passion of her lovemaking, of their lovemaking together. He wanted to comment on her soulful gyrations, but s-s-s-s was all he could muster. She looked so delicious that Grayson's mouth watered in anticipation of tasting her.

Sonji reached behind herself, unzipped the back of

her dress, and let it fall to her ankles. She continued her pelvic swirls and slid the dress behind her.

"Have mercy," Grayson moaned.

Sonji interpreted the words and glided before Grayson in a midnight blue camisole. The intricate lace hid just enough to make him ache to see what was underneath. His senses were heightened almost to the point of pain. He had to have her, had to touch her.

By the second verse, Sonji moved closer until she was only inches away. The scent of her floral perfume intoxicated him. He reached out but she stepped back swiftly and shook her head. She seemed determined to make him explode with longing. Grayson felt his resistance diminish and did as she bade by lowering his hand. She came back then, rotating her hips so gradually it hurt Grayson not to be inside her.

"Baby, *m-m-m-m,*" he moaned.

As if they were his own, Sonji's hands began to roam her body. Grayson's toes curled and uncurled as he watched her fingers slide smoothly down her neck and shoulders, over her chest, and across her breasts. She rolled her head back and around as her hands circled her sides and stomach. Then she let her head fall gently forward and stared deeply into his eyes as she parted her legs and rubbed the insides of her thighs.

Grayson could take no more. He reached out and pulled her to him. She straddled him and continued to rotate her hips in his lap. Her movements spun his senses dizzy. When her mouth descended upon his, he was so close to the brink of fulfillment that he cried out in ecstasy. He could feel himself pulsating against the warmth between her legs and almost toppled over the edge with desire. He kissed her again and again. At the same time, he deftly slid the fabric of her undergarment aside and inserted his fingers into her wet womanhood. Sonji's loud moan pushed him closer to the edge.

With his other hand, he unfastened his trousers and slipped them down his thighs. His hot organ was ready and waiting to receive her. Sonji helped him retrieve a condom from his pants pocket and hastily sheathed his large manhood. Then she lifted herself, pivoted her hips, and slid down onto him. Their joining was so rapturous that at first neither of them could move. Then together they created their own rhythm of love.

No longer slow and delicate like Sonji's erotic dance had been, their movements were swift and raging. Their urgent need catapulted them quickly to pleasure as they both announced their coming in loud almost animalistic moans. They had given into the raw passion they felt inside and satiated themselves in an exchange as carnal and perfect as sex and love combined. They were drenched in sweat and panting wildly. They held each other tightly for a long time, spellbound by the rhythm of their own new love.

"Tell me about him," she said.

"Who?" Grayson asked, cradling Sonji in his arms.

It was five A.M. and after another robust session of lovemaking, the spent lovers snuggled closely together.

"The Grayson I met tonight. Who is he? What's his story?"

Grayson sighed deeply. So much had happened in his life that he didn't know how to begin to explain it all to Sonji. And there were certain parts of his life that he dared not venture into, at least not now.

There was still too much pain and still some things yet undone.

"The Grayson you met tonight was a ghost. He died when I was young, but sometimes he comes back to haunt me. Forget him."

"But Grayson—"

"Sonji," he said, taking his arms from around her and sitting up in the bed, "that Grayson is a specter. A figment of an underactive imagination." He could feel himself bristling against the memory of his youth. He needed to relieve the pressure he felt building up because of it.

"I'm going running," he announced.

"I'll join you," Sonji said, sitting up.

"I'd rather go by myself," he said, rising from the bed. He couldn't expose Sonji to the frustrations of his past. She meant too much to him. He vowed right then and there to get his affairs in order once and for all. It was time that he started planning for his future—his future with Sonji.

Once again Sonji had broached the subject of Grayson's past and was met with resistance. She wondered what could have happened that troubled him so. As she prepared breakfast, she hoped that Grayson's run would help to dispel the wall she felt rising between them. She couldn't afford to have a bad ripple in their relationship so soon. If she was the cause of rehashing Grayson's pain, then she would do whatever she could to make the pain stop.

By the time he returned, she had breakfast prepared and was relaxing on the terrace. The air was brisk but not so much so that sitting outside was uncomfortable. She sat in a pair of sweats sipping on a mug of hot chocolate. Grayson approached her, his chest visibly rising and falling from his run.

"I'm sorry," they said in unison.

"I didn't mean to pry," Sonji offered, setting the cup down on a small table.

Grayson closed his eyes and then opened them. "It's not you. Please don't think that. I've got a lot of issues on my plate presently and instead of ignoring them, I need to tackle them head-on. When you asked me about my other personality, as it were, it was a stiff reminder that somewhere in my past is a guy I try not to think about. I mistakenly included you in the frustration I have with myself. Can you forgive me?"

Sonji walked into Grayson's arms. They hugged tightly and then Sonji stepped back.

"Are you hungry?"

"Ravenous."

"Come on, then."

Sonji led Grayson by the hand into the kitchen. Once there, she fixed him a heaping plate of bacon, eggs, and toast. She fixed a plate for herself as well and the two ate in silence. When they finished, Grayson took a shower and Sonji prepared for continuation of the amends she intended to make.

Grayson emerged with a towel wrapped around his waist. His skin was slightly damp and smelled of soap. Sonji watched transfixed as he walked closer to where she sat on the bed. His muscles were tight and firm from his run. Her eyes traveled from his calves up to his stomach tight with waves of muscle and finally rested on his hair, where a pearl of water dripped and slid down the side of his face.

"What's this?" he asked.

While in the shower, Sonji had gathered and heated her scented oils, turned off the lights, and lit several scented candles.

"Well, my running man, I wanted to treat your legs to a special toning service."

Oh, my God, he thought. *I love you, Sonji. Jesus. If I could just say it.*

She led him to the bed. He lay on his stomach and Sonji went to work. When she rubbed the heated oils in her palms and touched his skin, she heard him release an audible sigh.

She had finished the backs of his legs and was working on the fronts when Grayson became talkative.

"You know, I was thinking."

"Yes?"

"I was thinking that there is someplace I'd like to take you. Someplace . . . special."

"Where?"

"I want it to be a surprise. Do you trust me enough to go?"

Sonji thought she had never trusted anyone more in her life.

"Just say when, Grayson."

Grayson smiled, feeling the contentment only the attentions of a good woman could produce.

"My turn!" he proclaimed.

"What?" Sonji asked, finishing the massage on the fronts of his legs.

Grayson reached over to the scented oil. "Let me show you how special you've made me feel."

Sonji obliged, and they switched places. In short order, Grayson's capable hands were kneading her back and shoulders, sliding and gliding over her skin. Sonji was in heaven and prayed that she would never return to earth.

Eleven

Dr. Leigh Hoffman was having a long day. Unfortunately, it wasn't even noon yet. Already a therapy group session had been canceled because Mr. Smith had an episode, Lola Johnson was found roaming the halls naked, and Tommy Harris was caught trying to escape—for the fourteenth time.

She turned the lamp off on her desk and reclined in her large leather chair. Dare she prop her feet up? *Yes,* she told herself. *I deserve a rest.* The Mabel K. Staupers Hospital had been her place of employment for the past ten years. During that time, she had rarely used any sick days and always had vacation left over at the end of the year.

Leigh loved her job. She had seen such tremendous strides in medicine during her tenure as chief psychiatrist. And in the field of psychiatry especially, new treatments, therapies, and medicines helped people who would have otherwise been cast away by society return to full and productive lives. The downside, of course, was mornings like today. They were rare and nothing like what most people were familiar with in movies. But they did happen. And it was at times like those that Leigh felt the need to disconnect herself for a while.

It was quite easy to let the pressures of a psychiatrist's

line of work become overwhelming. Leigh had seen it happen. Instead of leaving work issues at the hospital, doctors sometimes brought psychosis, schizophrenia, depression, and suffering home with them. It ate away at them like water running on the surface of the earth. Pretty soon that ripple became a stream; the stream became a creek; the creek became a lake. Eventually an ocean of mental anguish wrapped around one's mind and before long the doctor became the patient. Leigh was determined to not let that happen to her. She would quit her job first.

As she relaxed in her moment of solace, she heard another commotion going on in the corridor. Leigh shut her eyes tightly and willed it to go away. After a few moments, she realized that whatever it was could not be wished into oblivion. She got up from her comfy chair and stepped out of her slightly dimmed room to see what the ruckus was.

"Dr. Hoffman," came the familiar voice of Veranda Gilmore. She was struggling with an orderly. "I have to go prepare for my dinner guests, and there's no one to watch Gray Jr. Can you help me?"

Leigh looked sympathetically at the woman. It was obvious that at one time Veranda had been beautiful. She was a tall and sturdy woman who sometimes gave the attendants a surprise with her strength. Her hair was cropped into a short Afro and there were brown rings under her eyes. But Leigh remembered seeing her for the first time.

She had come into the hospital with her husband. She was crying and couldn't stop. The death of her son had devastated her completely and a nervous breakdown was ensuing. Although she was quite distraught, she was clean and stylish and appeared well taken care of. From her long flowing hair to her manicured nails and two-hundred-dollar shoes, Veranda Gilmore exuded sophistication from the word *go*.

But the person before her now was quite different indeed. Seven years as a patient at the hospital had changed her into an alarmingly duplicitous woman. There was the Veranda who remembered that her son was dead and the one who did not. The one that remembered was actively involved in her own recovery. She had come a long way since being admitted and sometimes appeared ready for a visit home. And then there was the Veranda standing before Leigh now. The one that carried a doll with her at all times and insisted that others hold it, watch it, or take care of it, while she went off to prepare for an imaginary cocktail party.

"Are you sure you want me to take him, Veranda?"

The orderly appeared ready to force Veranda back to her room, but Leigh motioned with her hand for him to hold on.

"Yes, Dr. Hoffman. I trust you."

If I can just get you to trust yourself, Leigh thought. Leigh put an arm around her. "Veranda, I think Gray Jr. would be much better off with you."

"No!" Veranda yelled, yanking herself away. As she did, the doll slipped out of her hands and went tumbling to the floor.

Veranda emitted a blood-curdling shriek and collapsed on top of it. She continued to whimper and babble as the attendants took her away and led her back to her room.

Leigh closed her eyes for a moment and held her breath. Veranda had been doing so well. She let the breath out slowly and opened her eyes. She went back into her office and flipped her rolodex to a card with Grayson Gilmore's phone number on it. She would give him a call to provide him with an update of his wife's current condition. And then, she vowed, she would call her masseuse and tell him to meet her at her house by no later than six.

Forty-five minutes before Grayson Gilmore's Twentieth Century American Literature class was scheduled to start, several of the students from that class were gathering for a meeting in an empty classroom across the hall from Room 127, where they were scheduled for class.

As the students arrived slowly, Bill Hoft, a junior, stood at the front of the room. After waiting for a few stragglers, he finally addressed the assembled students.

"I'm glad everybody could make it." He looked around, a combination of nervousness and outrage egging him on.

"I don't have to tell anyone here how uncomfortable I am with what's being taught in our English Lit class. You all have heard me voice my opinion several times in class."

Several people nodded in agreement.

Bill continued. "What you don't know is that I even went to my adviser and an ombudsman about Mr. We Are the World, and you know what? They both said the same thing. 'Professor Grayson is an accomplished instructor, competent, and widely published.' They don't give a damn about *what* he's teaching—only that he's teaching."

"What's your point, Bill?"

"My point is that PG is a racist, and we are being subjected to reverse discrimination."

A young man in a bright red jogging suit spoke up. "Man, we talked about this before, and some of us don't care, just as long as we get good grades."

Bill sat down on the teacher's desk, eyes wide with

amazement. "You mean you don't care if that black man teaches us with substandard materials?"

"I don't get it," a girl in the back said while chomping on a wad of gum. "What's the big deal?"

"The big deal is that we white people are being excluded from the class."

The girl in the back chewed her gum with more vigor now. "Is that why there aren't any of the black students at this meeting? Did you ask me here because I'm white?"

Bill slid off the desk and over to the woman's side. He squatted down next to her so that they were eye-level. He placed a long arm around her shoulders. "I invited you here because you seem as concerned about our curriculum as I do."

One of the students stood and headed for the door. "Man, in any other literature class, we'd be studying dead white men and that's all. I'm not gonna sweat it." To Bill's fury the student walked out.

Adding insult to injury, many of the other students were getting up now too. Bill became incensed. He stood up to face them.

"It's inferior teaching, that's what it is. I mean, I've never even heard of most of these authors."

"I think that's the point, you dope." Another student walked out.

"No! The point is that if they were important writers, I would have heard of them, like Hemmingway, Faulkner, or . . . or Frost. I mean who the hell ever heard of Dorothy West?"

As the last of the students filed out of the classroom, one of them paused for a final comment. "It's the end of the semester, man. Just let it go."

And then Bill was left in the classroom alone. He grabbed his book bag from the floor and flung it against the wall. Papers, books, and pens scattered across the room.

He would not let it go. Not only had he been done a disservice in the classroom, but now some of his classmates thought him a fool. Well, PG would not get away with it. No way!

Sebastian Dupree lay contently in his bed, contemplating marriage. The woman in his arms was a constant source of wonder and satisfaction. She made him look at the world with new eyes and made him feel invincible. He wanted to make a present of the world and lay it at her feet.

Andi stirred and purred next to him. Her sleep was so peaceful, he could watch her for hours. No matter what had occurred during the day, she always slept with a slight smile on her face. And it was that smile that made him meet every day with a conquering attitude. She was the prayer of his days and the light of his nights. The idea of being without her was unthinkable.

At the same time, Sebastian considered his age of twenty-two and wondered if he was pushing the envelope—again. With his high IQ and exuberance for learning, Sebastian had graduated from high school at sixteen. Then he'd gone straight to college, where he had a triple major in American history, African-American history, and political science. And now he was back for a master's in political science. He was determined to learn everything there was to know about how America functioned so that he could make an impact on changing the circumstances of people of color in the country. Keeping him faithful to his dream was Andromeda. After a grueling five years pursuing his undergraduate degrees, he never would have gone back to college without Andi's confidence that he could be successful.

It hurt him to think that some people considered her slow. He even heard someone call her a black white person once. But no one knew the Andi that he knew. His Andi could blend her own herbs into wonderful teas, stretch her measly work-study check to make it last all month, and write programs in HTML and Java. She was a true delight to be around and a hellcat in bed. She was even a matchmaker. So far, Andi had created four couples, including them. Her latest success was their friend Sonji. One of the couples had already gotten married. Sebastian laid his arm gently around her and thought that perhaps they would be next.

"It comes and it goes, doesn't it?" Grayson peered into the glass cage at Phyllis. After several bouts of listlessness, Phyllis was active once again. She was by no means the raw ball of energy that Alexandre seemed to be—traversing the tank's length within a day's time or scuffing up sand against the glass—but she was mobile nonetheless. Grayson was hopeful.

And not just hopeful about his pet crabs, but also about this thing he had with Sonji. He wasn't sure exactly what to call it, except good. It was good for his mind—he had asserted himself past the doldrums of scholarly research for his latest paper. It was good for his body—not only was he running longer, but his stamina in the bedroom was heightened as well. It was also good for his soul—although he still had the occasional nightmare, he slept much better with Sonji beside him.

The reservations he had about Sonji and her feelings were fading like old jeans. And also, like old

jeans, he was feeling a comfortable fit with her—
something he hadn't experienced in its entirety even
when he was married. In the back of his mind, he
knew that he had been "settling" when he tied the
knot with Veranda. She was beautiful, smart, glamor-
ous, and assertive. The fact that she was willing to
marry him made it even better. So Grayson sacrificed
true love and married what some people would call
an arm decoration. Then he always worried whether
Veranda loved *him* or the lifestyle he could provide.

Being with Sonji had changed all that. Every day
that passed convinced him more and more that he
would not have to settle for companionship without
the magic of true love. The only thing that gave him
slight concern now was his English lit class. What had
started out as an assertive change of curriculum had
turned into an all-out crusade toward multiculturalism. Grayson hadn't planned it, but somehow he'd
gotten caught up in the desire to broaden the expe-
riences of his students no matter what the cost. The
more they seemed to resist it, the more determined
he was to insist on it. Although there had been no
overt rebellion so far, Grayson could sense one coming.

The trouble ticket was that he had no full explanation for his behavior. In his mind, he had approached
teaching the class with honorable intentions. To the
best of his soul searching, his intentions were still
honorable. But there was also something autocratic
and just a little too self-imposing about his approach.
And that's what tied his stomach in knots.

He knew what his brother would say—that he was
overcompensating, that his need to control his environment was shifting into hyper-drive because of what
happened to Gray Jr. He would say that perhaps some
unresolved issue was bubbling to the surface and had

been left unattended. He would also say that if ignored it would run amuck and eventually be his undoing.

Grayson emptied the last of the pet food into the dish for Phyllis and Alexandre. Animated Alexandre made his usual beeline for the bowl. He moved fast for a crab. Phyllis, on the other hand, moved slower and in a different direction. She seemed not to realize or care that what she needed to live and continue to get better was waiting for her at the other end of the tank.

When Nzinga Mae Stephens got a call from her granddaughter saying she was bringing someone for dinner on Sunday, she was happy as a lark. As long as she had been trying to get that child to bring somebody with her, she thought she wouldn't live to see the day, or would be too old to appreciate it when it came.

The last time Sonji brought somebody with her, it was some young man that worked her nerves. She couldn't see what Sonji saw in him. He wasn't that handsome, or that bright from what Nzinga could tell. He seemed more to her like a weasel with a false face. But this phone call—this phone call was different. Just by the sound of her baby's voice she knew someone special was coming.

"GrandmaZee?"

"What, baby?"

"I invited someone to come for Sunday dinner . . . is that okay?"

"Now baby, you know I've been tryin' to get you to do that for so long." Nzinga paused to clear her throat. "Now who is he?"

"I didn't say it was a he, Grandma."

"Didn't you? I coulda sworn—"

"Okay, okay. It's a he."

Nzinga felt her heart skip a glad beat. "Oh, baby. I'm so happy."

"Well, no celebrations yet. It's not like we're getting married. I just want him to meet you."

"Is it that Grayson fella you spoke of?"

"Yes, ma'am."

The yes in her granddaughter's voice sounded like a whole lot of happy. "Then you bring him on over. You want me to make somethin' special?"

There was a moment of silence, then Sonji's reply filled it. "I know he's fond of greens, and he really liked the peach cobbler you made before."

"Oh, that's easy stuff. I thought y'all wanted something fancy. Alright, baby. Grandma will be ready. You coming at the usual time?"

"Yep."

"Okay. Grandma loves her baby."

"I love you, too, GrandmaZee."

Nzinga didn't know what had happened with that Chad she was seeing, but she could tell by the pain in her granddaughter's eyes that he had done her pretty bad. Nzinga couldn't remember feeling more useless than when Sonji was hurting behind that fool. She would have given her soul to Old Scratch to take the pain away. But Sonji had gotten over him, it seemed. And the reason for that was coming to visit her this Sunday. Nzinga couldn't wait to meet him.

Another long week found Sonji tired and flustered. Grades from her sociology and world civilizations classes were holding steady at the A and B+ levels. Work was going well as they entered high season for the holidays. But her English class was still dealing her a fit. True to his word, Grayson did not cut her any slack in the grades department. For the last paper she turned in, she had worked harder than she had on any other paper. She received a B+.

She still struggled with seeing him three days out of the week in class. Although it wasn't as hard as it had been initially, Sonji occasionally discovered that images of her legs wrapped around his waist would overshadow his lectures. Yesterday, he had asked her a question in class, and she hadn't heard it. *There goes my class participation credit,* she thought.

Because of work and papers for class, she had not seen much of Grayson socially. One or the other of them was always busy whenever they tried to get together. That was why Sonji was looking forward to their dinner on Sunday. After several days apart, it would be good to spend some couple time with Grayson instead of student-teacher time.

"Slow down, son!" Nzinga counseled. "You don't want to choke."

"Yes, ma'am. I mean no, ma'am."

"You sure know how to enjoy greens."

"Yes, ma'am!"

"Sonji, I'm gonna have to let you do the Sunday cooking from here on out. You best to develop a good stirrin' arm for this one." Sonji's grandmother motioned toward Grayson as he devoured his food.

Grayson smacked his lips and licked his fingers, thoroughly enjoying himself, his surroundings, and most definitely his meal. Sonji had to focus on her own plate to keep from laughing. But her grandmother was bold. She laughed out loud.

"Ooh, he tickles me!"

Pretty soon they were all laughing and having a wonderful time.

"Zinga Mae, you must let me cook for you sometime."

She reared back in her chair, raised her eyebrows, and gave Grayson a quick once-over. "I'd like that. How about next Sunday?"

"Grandma!"

"You got it!" Grayson responded, before Sonji could get in a full protest.

"He offered. I accepted. Ain't no wrong in that."

Nzinga pushed herself up from the table. "Baby, you want anymore?"

"No, thanks, Grandma."

Then she looked over at Grayson with a crooked smile. "I know *you* want some more."

Grayson bowed his head in a bashful manner then looked up at her over the top of his glasses. "Yes, ma'am, I do."

Nzinga's shoulders bounced up and down. "He tickles me," she said again and was off into the kitchen with his plate and hers to get more food.

"She's wonderful," he said. His eyes were shining brightly at Sonji in a way she had never seen. She felt her soul go into meltdown.

"You're wonderful," she responded, touching the side of his beautiful face.

He brought his hand to hers, then brought her hand to his mouth. With a gentleness Sonji had never experienced, he bestowed delicate kisses on the back of her hand. Although the gesture could have easily been sexual, it wasn't. Instead it was reverent, like an homage to a princess. Sonji felt noble and validated.

"Ain't that sweet," Nzinga said, returning to the dining room. She returned the plates to the table and Grayson helped her into her chair. After eating a few more bites of food, she broke the silence.

"You give my baby that necklace?"

Sonji didn't realize she had been fingering it until then.

Grayson finished chewing a forkful of spaghetti. "Yes, ma'am."

"That's a mighty fine necklace, son. Mighty fine."

"She's a mighty fine woman," he remarked without hesitation. "As are you, Miss Zinga Mae."

"You somethin' else, mister," Sonji's grandmother said with a wiry smile. "Baby, bring the man some cobbler."

Sonji was elated that the two most important people in her life were getting along so well. "Yes, Grandma."

When their dinner of catfish, spaghetti, and greens was over, Nzinga insisted on washing the dishes. She assured them that keeping active kept her alive. And since she wasn't ready to go anytime soon, she told the couple they had better leave her to her activity. Grayson and Sonji gave up the fight and went outside, taking seats on an old porch swing.

Sonji suddenly felt melancholy. "I used to play on this swing when I was a kid. We were the first family that had one. But it wasn't long before several families had porch swings. Once, I broke it because I was mad."

"You? Mad?" Grayson teased. "I can't imagine such a sight. Why were you mad at the swing?"

"I wasn't. I was mad because I was too short to get up on it. I always had to have somebody help me or climb up on something to reach the seat. So one day I thought, I'm gonna get up here by myself. So I took a running start from the door and I jumped on the swing. Well, the whole thing collapsed. And my bottom was sore for days."

Grayson's infectious laughter chopped through the night air. "You know, if your derrière is still smarting, I may be able to alleviate the pain." Grayson claimed the lips he had come to crave with his own. The rhythm of the swing matched the beating of his heart.

"This is the first Thanksgiving I've spent away from my grandmother in years," Sonji said, thinking back. Even when she was with Chad, they had spent a great deal of time with her grandmother on this holiday.

"Come to think of it, I've made a tradition of spending Thanksgiving at Kyle's."

Grayson looked down at the woman lying beside him. She was wearing the top to his maroon silk pajamas and smiling like bright sunshine.

"We could go to your grandmother's house. We don't have to stay here." Grayson rolled the coils of Sonji's hair between his fingers.

"I'd like us to start making our own traditions, if you don't mind. Besides, GrandmaZee is spending today with her two best friends, Cora and Estelle. And when the three of them get together, look out!"

Sonji played with the hairs on Grayson's chest. "But what about you? Do you think Kyle and Jerika will miss you?"

"Kyle might. Jerika will probably be relieved to know that she might actually have some leftovers this year."

Sonji chuckled. Her man did have an appetite like no other. "So what are we preparing? I saw that the fridge was stocked. You've got enough food in there for three Thanksgivings."

"I don't know what possessed me to buy all of that, when what I really want is to feast on you." Grayson lowered his head to hers and his lips gently parted hers. His tongue descended judiciously into the warmness of her mouth, searching for its mate. Wantonly their tongues mingled until each of them moaned with need.

Grayson's kiss was hot and smoldering. It ignited Sonji's passion like an Olympic torch and made her craving for him seem infinite. She wrapped her arms around his neck. "I want to please you, Grayson." She brushed her lips against his. "Teach me," she said lustfully. "Teach me."

Grayson said nothing, but began the careful ritual of removing her top. He marveled at how beautifully formed she was. And he had made it a point to savor every curve, every twist and nuance of her flesh. His lips blazed a trail of kisses along her arms and neck. The scent of her skin drove him further into the depths of passion.

"If it's lessons you want, then you shall have them!" he said.

Sonji felt herself being lifted. Grayson's strong arms pulled her up until she was inches from his face. Then he traced an outline of her body with his fingertips. The slow movement touched off simmering sparks of heat in her nerve endings. She felt the center of her womanliness come alive.

Grayson continued his leisurely journey over her body. Seasoned with the occasional kiss and a surprise nip and suck, Sonji was breathlessly enraptured by his attentions. The way his mouth devoured her was overwhelming. And when his moist lips covered her nipples, she cried out in ecstasy.

"Grayson," she said in time with the throbbing between her legs. "I want to please *you.*"

"Lesson number one," he responded while keeping his lips against her breast. "Be quiet."

"But Gray—" the sensation of his fingertips entering her stopped her short. He lavishly, selfishly, rhythmically pressed against the orb of her desire until Sonji's whole world tilted on its axis. He guided her with the skill of a master craftsman into the realm of no return. Over and over she tumbled, feeling shock waves of sheer gratification. They rocked her like a mighty earthquake. It took several bliss-filled moments for Sonji to recover.

Grayson gently laid her back down on the bed. A smile brightened his lust-darkened eyes.

Sonji looked up feeling a tad bit guilty. "What about you?" she asked.

Then a look came over him like none she had ever seen. It was serious with a hint of apprehension lurking behind it. "Don't you know by now?" His gaze intensified, and he cocked his head slightly. "It's all about you. I get all my pleasure from pleasing you. All of it. Reaching the Big O is like extra credit. But Sonji, nothing satisfies me more than taking you over the edge."

She reached up and cupped his cheek in the palm of her hand. "That's the most beautiful thing anyone's ever said to me."

After a few minutes basking in the afterglow of their exchange, they got up, showered, and headed downstairs to prepare their Thanksgiving dinner.

"Are you sure you're up to this?" Grayson asked, playfully.

Sonji snickered. "Of course. I'm not all thumbs in the kitchen."

"Really? That's not what Jerika said."

Sonji slapped Grayson playfully on the behind. "You stop putting words in your sister-in-law's mouth."

"If you insist." Then a sober expression replaced his teasing one. "Only part of me was joking when I asked if you were ready. I take my cooking quite seriously. And if we are going to be in this kitchen together, then you had better learn the ropes."

"Yes, sir." Sonji gave Grayson a quick salute. First, he gave her a thorough tour of his kitchen. The cupboards were primarily birch wood with stainless-steel

handles and frosted-glass center panels. The walls
were adorned with utensils, pots, and oven mitts. The
reflection of the bright and airy room shone in the
freshly waxed maple flooring.

Then he demonstrated his preferred method of
preparation and how his kitchen was designed for the
logical progression from the refrigerator to the sink
to the counter to the oven.

"My favorite recipes I keep in my head. But if you
have a taste for something different, I can whip out the
ol' cookbooks." Grayson pointed to the shelf above the
microwave, which held at least ten cookbooks.

Sonji shook her head.

"So, what'll it be?" He rubbed his hands together
in anticipation.

Sonji surveyed the magnificence of Grayson's
kitchen. It was wonderful, filled with every modern
convenience. But for some reason, the thought of cooking in it didn't seem appealing right now. What she
wanted to do was spend some downtime with the man
she loved. And Grayson took cooking far too seriously
for them to relax and have fun while doing it.

"Why don't we eat out?"

"What!"

"Well, okay. Maybe we could go and get something.
You know, some restaurants offer complete dinners to
go."

Grayson rubbed his chin. "You mean, not cook on
Thanksgiving?"

"Precisely," Sonji responded.

"Why, that's uncivilized," Grayson said, smiling.
"But, all right, my lady. If you can find a decent place
that's open and has food not already spoken for, we'll
go get something."

Sonji was elated. This way she and Grayson would be
able to enjoy each other's company more thoroughly.

After giving Grayson a loud smack on the cheek, she dashed off into the living room to make some phone calls.

"I'll agree to this under one condition," he said, following closely behind her.

Sonji returned the phone receiver to its cradle. "What's your condition?"

"That I at least get to make dessert."

"It's a deal," Sonji replied.

Sonji eventually found a Family Market restaurant that was open. It was also nearby, so within an hour the hungry couple returned to Grayson's home with turkey and all the trimmings.

Together they set an elegant table and served up the meal. After Sonji blessed the food, they dug in. Grayson ate in a slightly more reserved fashion as they discussed some of their most memorable holidays. Grayson deliberately avoided any recollections that included his son. Now was not the time to drudge up painful memories. Their discussion of fond memories ultimately led them to the earliest days of their relationship.

"What was it like for you, at the beginning of our correspondence?"

It took only the briefest of thoughts for Sonji to be transported back to when she received her first e-mail from Osiris.

"At first, I felt exposed. And I tried not to take it seriously. After all, I figured that some people just e-mail everyone. But something drew me again and again to your profile and the first letter you sent."

Grayson nodded in understanding. "I felt as though I had taken a risk in contacting you. I questioned the sincerity of your letters at first. And I wondered what would become of such a linkage."

"I tried to read between the lines," Sonji continued. "When the computer is your communication vehicle, you miss out on subtle nuances like facial expressions and vocal intonations. So I had to make them up in my head."

Grayson jumped into her sentence. "I created a picture of you and your life in my mind. Otherwise, the essence of you would have been an enigma that I couldn't get past."

There was silence for a moment as the two finished the last of the food on their plates.

"Ready for dessert?" Grayson asked.

"Ready."

Grayson removed their plates and came back from the kitchen with two saucers of sweet potato pie. Sonji's mouth watered in anticipation of the treat.

"Was there anything else that went through your mind during the early days of our courtship, Grayson?"

Grayson took only a moment to think. "After we got past the getting to know you talk, things started to change."

Sonji took a forkful of the pie into her mouth. "Mmm, Grayson. This is exquisite."

Grayson remembered a time in their recent history when Sonji said those exact words in a moment of passion. He was sure the expression on his face revealed what he was thinking. Sure enough, Sonji spoke to it.

"I know what you're thinking, professor. Let's get back to the e-mail, shall we?"

"Well," he said, after swallowing some of the pie, "I expected you to discontinue our correspondence at any moment. Because everything in your letters was just too perfect. I couldn't have written better responses myself. That part was uncanny."

"Uncanny?"

"Yes, or more like—"

"Magic," she said. She sat back from the table and closed her eyes.

"It was like you were some sort of phantom, held together by mist and electricity, and by my wishes and dreams. I kept telling myself that I had fallen in love with a ghost in a machine."

Grayson closed his eyes as well. "Every letter you sent became a promise. I began to wonder if we would be able to transcend the technology. I wanted to know if the physical would match the spiritual."

The two lovers opened their eyes. They reached across the table and held hands in a silent testament that they had indeed transcended the technology. They gazed deeply into each other's eyes, knowing that the physical was one with the spiritual.

The MSO office was teeming with action. Students were making photocopies, talking on telephones, arranging packets, and typing away furiously on computers. Capiz, the Asian woman Sonji had met earlier in the semester, was issuing commands like a drill sergeant.

Sonji stopped Ricardo as he whizzed by her with a large stack of papers. "What's going on, Ricardo?"

He looked harried and elated simultaneously. "Angela Davis is going to speak at the Pantheon Gala tonight."

"Angela Davis? Here?" Sonji was shocked.

"Yes. She's a keynote speaker for the Pedagogy of the Oppressed conference in Lincoln." Ricardo hefted the fliers in his arms. "She's making a stop in Omaha to visit the Malcolm X birth site. One of the organizers for the event in Lincoln convinced her to speak at the Pantheon Gala and stay overnight in Omaha."

"Wow! That's terrific."

"But . . . we just found out about it this morning. So we're scrambling to get the word out."

"Where's Sebastian?"

"He's on his way to the Channel Seven television station. Jesus, who is an intern there, got him an interview on the midmorning news show. He's going to talk about the gala and how fortunate we are to have Angela Davis speaking."

Sonji felt the adrenaline in the room urging her to assist. "I want to help."

"You can help me put these fliers up."

"No problem," Sonji said, taking a handful of fliers. "Where do you want them?"

"Why don't you take the north end of campus, and I'll take the south end?"

"I'm on it!" Sonji said, exiting the office. She had originally gone there to find Andi. After much deliberation, she had decided to confide in Andi and tell her who Osiris was. *It will have to wait,* Sonji mused. *Maybe tonight at the gala,* she thought. *I'll tell her then.*

Sonji had heard about the Pantheon Gala. Andi had told her it was a yearly social sponsored by African-American fraternities and sororities. The all-Greek event began with a networking hour, followed by dinner and a step show. The gala concluded by closing remarks from someone in the community. At first, she wasn't going to attend. She and Byron had planned to meet at the library. But now that Angela Davis was coming to speak, she'd had a change of heart. She would contact Byron immediately and tell him.

She posted her last flier on a bulletin board in the computer lab. *While I'm here I might as well check my e-mail,* she thought. As she meandered between students seated at terminals, Sonji wondered if Grayson had answered her letter. She took a seat at an empty station, accessed the Web browser, and typed in the address for BlackLuv.

In a few moments the home page was displayed, and Sonji clicked on the hotspot to activate her e-mail. It had been a couple of days since she had checked her mail. She had one from Andi, one from Byron, one from someone named LoveMachine, and one that made her eyes sparkle. She took a deep, calming breath and opened the email from Osiris.

> *My Darling Nzinga,*
> *Can my heart beat any faster? Can my breath be taken more swiftly? Can my days be any more complete? I think not. Precious jewel, Nzinga, you have made my life magical! And I thank you for our time together, for the one we have become. You are the brightest star in the heavens. And I worship your loveshine.*
> *Yours,*
> *Osiris*

Sonji sat back in the chair and closed her eyes. She couldn't believe how happy she was. Grayson was intelligent, funny, handsome, and he adored her. Never in her life could she have imagined the bliss she was feeling. Sonji was bursting with her good fortune. She couldn't wait to tell Andi all about the love of her life.

Twelve

The gala started on a strong note with a welcome from Sebastian Dupree. Then dinner was served, and Sonji was treated to a mouthwatering plate of blackened catfish, asparagus spears, garden salad, and a roll. While Andi sat next to her and ate like a bird, Sonji was tempted to devour her food the way Grayson sometimes did—not because it tasted so good, but because of the freeing effect that he had on her. Once during the meal, she caught herself licking a smear of butter from her fingertip. She chuckled silently.

She wished that Grayson could have come with her, but he was at home grading a mountain of papers. It would have been their first time out as a couple. The last validation, she thought. Even though she believed in her heart that she and Grayson were a couple, the wonder of what they had almost didn't seem real. But to have him on her arm and have people see them as a pair would make it all real for her. Before she allowed her mind to wonder whether maybe Grayson was keeping their relationship a secret for a reason, she turned to Andi, ready to tell her the good news.

"Is this seat taken?"

Sonji looked up and saw Byron standing next to

her. "It is now," she said, happy to see him. She was so proud of him. He was doing so much better in English class. He didn't have to struggle nearly as much as she did to get good grades.

"Andi, Sebastian, this is Byron, my study partner from English class."

The three exchanged pleasantries, then Bryon turned to Sonji. "You look exquisite, Sonji."

Sonji took a quick inventory of herself—long black velvet dress, black suede pumps, and diamond studs. Sonji thought she looked attractive, but exquisite was a rather strong word.

"Thank you, Byron."

"You sure are welcome," he said, finally taking his seat.

As he sat, Sonji noted that Byron was crisply outfitted in a titanium gray suit. Its three-button jacket with peaked lapels made him look like a corporate executive. His black, silk tie made him look like a corporate executive with money to burn.

"You look like a man who owns the world," she remarked.

Byron ran his fingers across the smooth area of his upper lip. "If only that were true."

A server came over, offering him a dinner plate. He waved her away.

"The fish is wonderful, Byron."

"No, thanks. I'm not hungry."

When they finished dinner, the deejay charged the atmosphere with an electrifying old-school mix. Sonji rocked her head to "Let's Groove" by Earth Wind and Fire, "Joystick" by the Dazz Band, and "Word Up" by Cameo. When the words "Everybody get up!" rang out of the speakers, Byron asked her to dance to Teena Marie's bass-thumping "Square Biz."

The dance segment shifted into high gear as the

deejay spun tunes by The Whispers, Stevie Wonder, Chaka Khan, and Rick James. Sonji and Byron moved as if they were born to dance together. They fell into sync snapping their fingers, swaying rhythmically, and bobbing their heads in time.

"I haven't danced like this in a long time," Sonji shouted over the music.

"Really? I can't tell."

"Thanks," she responded, clapping her hands above her head."

Byron followed her lead with his hands pumping up in the air to the music.

In no time, some of the students had formed a Soul Train line. Byron and Sonji stood across from each other cheering on the young and not so young as, one by one, happy dancers took their stroll in the spotlight. Sonji just shook her head in disbelief at some of the ways in which people were able to move their bodies.

She and Byron reached the head of the line together and decided to go down as a couple. She decided wax retro and body-popped like The Lockers of the seventies. Byron chose a slightly more modern approach and breakdanced his way down the line. After all those in line had gone through, Sonji and Byron all but collapsed in each other's arms from the combination of exhaustion and exhilaration.

"This is DJ Diz, and I'm about to slow it up just a taste, 'cause after all that, y'all deserve a cool down."

Sonji's jaw dropped. She could not believe what she was hearing.

"Oh, that dude had to go through the Way Back Machine for this one," Byron remarked.

"Was he even born when this was out?"

They both smiled and watched as the sounds of Bootsy Collins's "What's a Telephone Bill" filled the speakers and drew people into snuggling couples.

Byron extended his arm. "Care to dance?"

"I don't mind if I do," Sonji responded, taking his hand.

He guided her to the middle of the dance floor and pulled her into his arms. They moved slowly and in perfect time with the song. After a few moments, Byron pulled back slightly.

"I'm having a great time, Sonji. Thanks for telling me about this."

She smiled in return. "Any time."

Byron's expression grew serious.

"Sonji . . . are you . . . seeing anyone?"

Startled, she blinked as if she hadn't heard him correctly. Sonji stiffened in his embrace, but looked him straight in the eye.

"Yes."

She felt his body deflate.

He closed his eyes and opened them. "And I suppose it's . . ."

"Serious," she finished. "Yes, it is."

"Of course it is," Byron said, holding her gaze. "Why is it that the good ones are always taken?"

"That's not true, Byron. You'll find her." Sonji remembered Andi's unwavering belief in soul mates. "I know you will."

"Do me a favor?" he asked.

"Yes?"

"Just for the rest of this song, let me pretend that I'm dancing with a woman who cares for me deeply."

Sonji was thoughtful, and then she moved closer to Byron and put her head on his shoulder. He sighed and swayed her gently until the song ended.

Sonji surveyed the crowd. MSO could be proud of their last-minute effort. There had to be close to three hundred guests at the gala. Everyone in attendance was dressed to impress. Even the younger students, who Sonji was accustomed to seeing in sagging jeans and oversized shirts, were dressed considerably more conservatively.

Suddenly, the crowd was drawn to attention by a male voice coming through the speaker system. "Ladies and gentlemen, do not attempt to adjust this audio broadcast. We have taken over the sight and sound system from here. We control the stop and the go, the hip and the hop, the funk and the funkier. You have now entered . . . the Pantheon!"

The audience applauded as a group of women dressed in red and white made their way to the stage.

The young women chanted, stomped, shouted, sang, rapped, danced and worked up the audience until people literally leaped out of their seats. The routine was fast, energetic, and so full of call and response that the founders would all be proud. Sonji was amazed and surprised at the clever songs and taunts each group presented. And she was impressed with the stamina with which the routines were delivered.

The room was electric with pride, creativity, and healthy competition. Her favorite parts of the show came when the Delta Sigma Theta sorority boasted their red and white colors while giving a high-spirited demolition of all the other sororities.

> This red,
> This red,
> This red,
> This red and white . . .
> Is mo' cheddar,
> Mo' better,
> Greek letter,
> Now sure you're right!
>
> Ain't no
> SGR

ZPB
AKA
Can step with me.
'Cause I'm a certified,
Bona fide
Lady DST
Ya see.

Somebody say Do Dat
(Do Dat)
Let the church say Do Dat Again
(Do Dat Again)
Somebody say Do Dat
(Do Dat)
We're DST till the end.

The other highlight of the show was the counterpart of Delta Sigma Theta Sorority, Omega Psi Phi. Their Sons of Thunder performance had the audience laughing, clapping, and shouting for more. Where the ladies had been elegant in red pantsuits with white gloves, the men took the stage shirtless with gold chains, open purple vests, and matching pants tucked into black spit-shined combat boots. Their high-stepping, super-charged performance was like nothing she had ever seen. Sonji thought she would remember their original chant for the rest of her days.

At the end of the show, the kings and queens of the Pantheon were crowned. Sebastian again took center stage as he announced the winners. Sonji's hunches were correct. Delta Sigma Theta and Omega Psi Phi were awarded the Royal Court trophies for 2001.

"Andi, why aren't you in a sorority?"

"They all seem so wonderful. I could never make up my mind which one I wanted to join."

"How about you, Byron?" Sonji turned to her left.

"You didn't display any loyalty to a particular brotherhood."

"I'm not much into the Greek stuff. It's just one more thing to do."

With Sonji's busy schedule, she could relate.

When Angela Davis walked to the lectern, she received booming applause, a standing ovation, and even a few whistles thrown in for good measure. Her impassioned reception was inspiring. Half of those in attendance weren't even born when she was kickin' butt and takin' numbers. Yet they greeted her as if they had all been there some thirty years ago, when the concept of black pride was as important to some as breathing.

Her wiry auburn hair adorned her like a fiery crown of confidence. She stood before the audience as a majestic lioness presiding over her pride. It was several minutes before she was able to coax the audience into quietly taking their seats. Sonji was enthralled as the woman with a dazzling gap in her teeth and simple gray suit proceeded to sweep the audience into the best speech she had ever heard.

She talked briefly of her days as a Black Panther and the time she was on the FBI's Ten Most Wanted List. She also mentioned her stint in jail, which led to the part of her presentation that Sonji was least familiar with, the harsh realities of the United States correctional system. She focused on the fact that in America you didn't have to do anything wrong to be arrested. The audience clapped when she said, "There is something about the U.S. justice system that is not *just*." By the time she finished, Sonji was convinced that she had to become more active in making the justice system more just for people of color.

As Ms. Davis took her seat, the robust applause returned, and Sonji was especially glad that she had made time to attend this event. Andi and Sebastian seemed pleased as well. And it didn't surprise Sonji one bit that they even clapped in unison. One glance at Byron, and she could tell that he, too, enjoyed the talk. But something behind his expansive smile looked dispirited. She wished she could change that fact, but she couldn't.

Sonji's mind drifted back to her dance with Byron. He was such a nice guy. He deserved someone as special as he. Sonji had no doubt that he would find that someone eventually.

Grayson could see his breath escaping in tufts and curls in front of him as he ran. The unseasonably warm weather they were experiencing had finally given way to an abrupt cold snap. *One more day of this and it's off to the gym for the rest of the season,* he thought. Grayson watched two young girls walking in front of his house before he took off toward the park. They were bundled up the way only Midwesterners could bundle their children, with lots of layers and plenty of bulk. Grayson glanced down at his light jacket and jogging suit and knew he wouldn't be running outdoors for long.

As he neared the end of the block, he detected the smell of burning wood. Looking up, he could see smoke coming from numerous chimneys on the street. Immediately, an image of himself and Sonji cuddled together in front of a fireplace warmed him. He smiled and continued on his run.

"Morning, professor!"

Grayson turned to wave at his neighbor ReTonya Laslow. ReTonya had made it a point to be up and outside every morning when he started his run. Coincidentally, she was also always outside whenever he returned from his run.

Grayson tried unsuccessfully to convince himself that the reason he hadn't been to the hospital to visit Veranda this semester was because he was too busy. The addition of the new literature class and his work with ESL classes were taking up a lot of his time. Add to that his evolving relationship with Sonji, and it seemed that it would have been difficult for him to squeeze in one more item on his agenda. But every time his mind created a visual image of that agenda, it dissolved into oblivion and was replaced by Sonji Stephens's ravishing face.

From the moment he saw her enter his class on the first day of the semester, his heart had been stolen forever.

The end of the semester was only two weeks away. Sonji felt even more confident that she had made the right decision in returning to school. She had two A's and a B+ for sure and with her final paper for Grayson's class, she was sure to get a B, perhaps even a B+.

Writing had never been her forte. She always said it used the wrong side of her brain. But math—give her anything to calculate and she could do the figures in her head.

The last paper she turned in was on learning styles. She had become so fascinated with the differences she saw in the way students learned, she insisted that she be allowed to do her final research paper on adult learning. Although Grayson had cautioned against tackling such a broad topic, Sonji assured him that she could do the subject justice and write in a way that would earn her an A. After he acquiesced, she threw herself into the final project with vigor.

Scanning the library now, it looked different from when the semester first started. Back then, there were so many students, the book checkout lines were seven to eight people deep, and the best research books were always checked out. Now, the students were still plentiful, but not nearly as much as before. Sonji surmised that some people had become frustrated, some may have had other pressing obligations, and then there were probably those who had simply flunked out.

Even in her classes, she had noticed at least a ten-percent reduction in students. In Grayson's class, the reduction had been more like one-third. And some of those that were still in his class often seemed as though they were barely hanging on. Not unlike herself. Because she had already been at the library for two hours, she decided to take a break. To revive her eyes, Sonji blinked repeatedly and stared off to the left at the shelves and shelves of books.

She stood, stretched, and then decided that she needed to get away from the books and notes if only for a moment. Without putting on her jacket, Sonji stepped outside into the cheerless winter air. Already she could tell that the day was a lot colder now than it had been when she first arrived at the library. She glanced at her watch. It would be noon soon, and her stomach emitted soft grumblings of emptiness.

"It's supposed to snow tonight," a familiar voice said. Sonji spun around to see Byron coming out of the library. His book-laden backpack rested heavily on his shoulder. Since their dance during the ball, Byron had been cordial and slightly evasive. She hoped that his admission of his interest in her hadn't caused a rift in their friendship. She was beginning to appreciate his company more and more.

"It's good to see you, Byron."

"You too, Sonji. You too." He looked away from her and out toward the dorms.

"How are you coming on your last paper?"

"I'm finished."

Sonji was undone. "Finished! I just started my research, and you're finished?"

"Yep. And I don't want to set foot in this library until next semester. As a matter of fact, I don't even want to see it from the street as I drive past the university."

Sonji giggled. He was vocalizing her sentiments. One reason she had come outside was that she just couldn't stand looking at those books any longer. The shelves and silence were starting to close in on her.

Byron smiled at her laughter and seemed more at ease. He shifted his weight from one side to the other.

Sonji felt compelled to broach the subject of Byron's confession. "Byron, about the other night—"

Byron interrupted. "I don't suppose you're going to tell me that you are suddenly unattached."

"No," Sonji said, smiling. "But I've felt slightly ill at ease since you shared your feelings."

"Me too," Byron said, holding her gaze for the first time since that night. "But I consider you a friend, Sonji. And as they say, this too shall pass."

"I was thinking the same thing," she admitted. "I'm sure that we can adjust and go on."

Byron wrapped his free arm around her. "Yeah. It just might take me a while to get over the way you dumped me."

"Oh!" Sonji protested with a scowl that did little to conceal the mischief in her eyes.

Byron released her and stuck out his hand. "Still friends?"

"Still friends," she replied, taking a firm grasp of his hand.

The two stood in silence for a few moments. Several students walked past them.

"Well, I'd better be going. I would like to spend some of this Saturday at home doing absolutely nothing!"

"That sounds like a great idea, Byron. I'll see you in class on Monday."

"Most definitely," he said, walking toward the parking lot. "That is, if we don't get snowed in!"

Sonji watched as Byron walked off and waved as he rounded the corner. He always managed to stay one step ahead of everything. After a rocky start, he was going to have no problems getting a decent grade in Grayson's class. She, on the other hand, had labored intensely just to get a shot at a B. Oh, well, she thought. At least it was only one class and not two or three that were beyond challenging.

And there was no study partner for this last assignment. Each student was on his or her own to do the research and present the most succinct documentation on their subjects that they could. It all came down to this paper. Everything that Grayson had taught up until this point—the brief grammar and sentence structure review, the examination of the essay and its parts, audience analysis and word choice, thesis statements and supporting references—would all become a part of her paper somehow. And she was determined to prove to Grayson that she had been an attentive student. She would use this research paper to demonstrate her command of the concepts and ideas presented in class. Relationship or no relationship, her paper would stand on its own, and she would get an A on it if she had to spend the night at the library to do it.

Before returning to her research, Sonji looked up at the sky. She saw clusters of steel-gray clouds forming in the distance. Byron could be right about the storm, she thought.

It started like a loud silence in the night. In slow motion delicate stars of white fell gently in straight lines. The flakes formed a coverlet—first large and then smaller pointed crystals—puffed up into mounds of powder. They shimmered in the moonlight looking thick and heavy and wet.

Grayson and Sonji watched the winter spectacle with warm mugs of cinnamon-spiced hot cocoa. They sat on the couch, covered by a large, thick Indian blanket, snuggling under its warmth. Grayson had stoked the fire into a comfortable and resilient blaze. The crackling of the wood lent itself nicely to the relaxed atmosphere of the evening.

They sat in silence for more than an hour, just enjoying the heat from each other's bodies, the falling snow, and the darkness of night. Each in their own thoughts, but both into each other, they nuzzled, cuddled, and snuggled as if they were a seasoned couple relishing an easy and familiar routine.

Now and again a sigh would traverse the silence between them and Grayson would kiss Sonji's temple or she would caress his waist. But all in all their silence was truly golden, and it shone in the contentment on their faces and in the way they nestled together in the flickering firelight.

Grayson hated to disrupt their quiet time, but he was starting to feel concerned about staying up so late on a school night. He spoke in a hush. "My darling, it's nearly three A.M., and we both have class tomorrow."

Sonji released a long, audible breath. The snow was coming down steadily now. "It's so beautiful," she said, staring out of the picture window.

"As are you, my warrior woman," he said as he bestowed deep lingering kisses across her shoulders and neck. "But I would be remiss as your instructor and your lover if I didn't at least mention the lateness of the hour."

The reference to him being her lover sent a ribbon of heat through Sonji's body sultry enough to melt every flake of snow outside. The sensation left her reluctant to move. "I'm not sleepy, but if you are . . ." she whispered. She was going to suggest that they retire, but the silken caress of Grayson's hands cupping her breasts stole her words. His fingers worked a mesmerizing spell on her nipples and set them like tender pebbles.

The silence that contented the two for so long gave way to Sonji's moans of surrender as Grayson leisurely tasted her back while rolling her now-hardened nipples smoothly between his expert fingertips.

"I thought we were going to have a quiet evening," she managed to say.

"I'm quiet," he said. Then he turned her toward him and pulled away the blanket. Slowly he unbuttoned her blouse and exposed the ample breasts he had awakened only seconds ago. "You are the one who insists on making noise," he added, and lowered his head to claim the ripe spherules that beckoned him like compass points.

Sonji's reaction was even more audible as Grayson slid his tongue over her breasts, stomach, and navel. He nibbled and sucked at her skin until her senses spun into a frenzy. She ran her finger through his hair as she felt him slide off the couch and onto his knees.

"You see," he whispered, unwrapping her skirt and sliding her undergarment down her legs. "I'm being very quiet. You, on the other hand," he said while parting her legs, "are quite literally disturbing the peace." Even the anticipation of his touch brought a soft moan to her lips.

And then his tongue descended to the center of her womanhood, and Sonji's soul took flight. Higher and higher he lifted her until she felt as if she had ascended above the stratosphere. Her moans became whimpers. Her whimpers became tears. And her tears became a scream until the need in her burst open like a million twinkling lights against the dark night sky.

When she returned to herself, she was sated and ready. "Now you know I can't let you get away with that."

Grayson's eyes widened in surprise as Sonji began the slow removal of his clothing. "Madam, just what do you have in mind?" he asked.

When he was fully disrobed, Sonji marveled at his dark muscles glowing a dusky brown in the firelight. She gently laid Grayson down on the carpet and placed a steady stream of lingering kisses on his chest and stomach. She paused momentarily. "I'm not the only noise maker here," she said softly and returned to her work. Before long a low murmur made its way out of Grayson's pursed lips. "Sonji," he said, stroking her skin.

"What's this I hear?" she asked, righting herself. "A sound?" And with that remark, she straddled him. As her hips descended to meet his, Grayson's deep moan of pleasure heightened her senses. And then she moved herself, slowly creating symmetry with him. Grayson was obviously fighting a battle with himself and losing. His sounds of pleasure accompanied her own in a duet of abandonment. Soon, she felt his manhood tightening inside her. She slowed down until her movements were nearly nonexistent.

Grayson's hands reached up and gently kneaded the round flesh of her breasts. "Don't stop, Sonji," he whispered. "Don't . . ." Before he could finish his sentence she was rolling him again. This time his moan was more sonorous. Raw passion consumed them as they guided each other to the edge of oblivion. One more sound broke the silence in the room when Grayson whispered, "I love you, Sonji," and they both tumbled over into rapture's divine abyss.

The snow continued to fall. After a few moments, Grayson got up to retrieve the Indian blanket. He covered Sonji and then added a few more logs to the fire. When he finished, he joined her under the covering and cradled her in his arms. It was morning before either of them moved again.

Sonji awoke first, having slept more peacefully than she could ever remember. The fire in the fireplace had long since gone out, but the fire in her heart was another matter. It burned as brightly as any star in the heavens.

Did I dream it? she wondered nervously. Then she looked longingly at the man in whose arms she had slept. She listened to the sounds of his breathing and realized that no, she hadn't dreamed it. She heard him say the words that filled her with overwhelming jubilance. "I love you, too," she said.

Sonji inhaled deeply as remnants of smoke from the fireplace still permeated the air. She sat up slowly so as not to disturb the man sleeping beside her. The room temperature was significantly cooler than beneath the blanket and her skin prickled with the chill in the air. She blinked against the brightness, and then gasped.

"What is it?"

A groggy Grayson raised up beside her. "What's with all the lights?" he asked still coming out of his sleep.

"There aren't any lights, professor. Look."

Grayson sat all the way up and followed Sonji's gaze

toward the picture window. There must have been three feet of snow outside. Possibly four.

Sonji raised her hand.

"Yes, Miss Stephens?"

"May I be excused from class?"

"Certainly," Grayson responded. "Now lie back down."

Sonji looked dejected. "But Gray—"

"Ah!" he interrupted. "I feel like I've been ridden hard and put away wet." Then he raised a knowing eyebrow. "Oh, that's right. I have."

Sonji reached under the covers and lightly pinched him on the behind.

"Ow!" he protested. "Don't get mad at me Miss three A.M. and she's gotta have it."

Reluctantly, she returned to Grayson's side beneath the blanket. "You started it."

"I was merely trying to enjoy the silence last night. It was you who insisted on making those libido-inspiring lamentations."

Sonji wrapped her arms around Grayson and pulled herself to him snugly. "You mean like this?" She uttered a sultry moan that increased the temperature under the blanket by ten degrees.

"You're not playing fair," Grayson said, snarling mischievously.

Remembering Grayson's comment to her in the heat of their passion, Sonji held him even more tightly. "Who says I'm playing?"

Grayson shifted his body so that they were facing each other. "I meant what I said last night, pretty Sonji." He ran a finger down her nose and across to one of her dimples.

Sonji swallowed hard. "Grayson, I . . ."

"Don't say anything now—especially if you can't return my feelings. I don't think I could bear it." He closed his eyes and pulled her even closer. "Just wait awhile before you respond. That way you'll be sure of your feelings when you do."

Sonji felt her heart melting with each second they were together. She was sure about her feelings. Wasn't she? At least she was grateful that he wasn't pressuring her and decided she would take the time to sort out her emotions.

"Thank you, Grayson."

"No, thank you. For being here, for being with me, for . . ." He let his voice trail off and his lips finished his sentence. Their kiss was a sweet-tender exchange of understanding. They were standing at the threshold of change. And Sonji held the key to the next step in their relationship. Grayson was asking for a serious commitment. Sonji knew that as surely as she knew her own name. And he was willing to let her take the time she needed to decide if a serious commitment was what she really and truly wanted.

When their lips parted, Sonji could feel the confirmation of Grayson's emotions throbbing against her lower body. She gave him a delicious smile.

"Here we go again." He sighed slyly and began the slow, pleasurable journey of dispatching her to the stars.

"Baby girl, I'm fine. Why do you think I spend so much time cannin'? I got enough supplies to survive more than this little bit of snow, and I got plenty of quilts."

"Okay. GrandmaZee. You're sure?"

"Sure I'm sure! You don't worry 'bout me. Now *you* on the other hand—how are you gonna make it? I know all you've got in that house to eat probably comes out of a box. Do you have enough boxes, baby?"

Sonji shifted in the living room chair and looked at Grayson, who was seated across from her watching her intently. She wasn't sure how much to reveal. But since the city had declared a state of emergency, she decided honesty was the best policy.

"Actually Grandma, I'm at Grayson's house."

"How'd you get over there in all this mess?"

"Well . . ." Sonji twirled the phone cord around her finger.

"Ooh, never mind. You young folks do thangs differ'nt than when I was coming up." Nzinga chuckled. "Well, you just be careful."

Sonji smiled, letting the love for her grandmother mold a wide grin on her face. "I will. We will."

"Okay, baby. Bye."

"Bye, GrandmaZee."

"Is she all right? Does she need anything?"

"No, she's fine."

Grayson's curiosity got the best of him. "What did she say when you told her you were here?"

"She told me to be careful."

"And are you?" he asked, stepping forward. He hadn't meant to blurt out his feelings for her the way he had. But it was too late to take the words back now. All he could do now was give her space and hope that she would eventually come to love him as he did her. But how could he wait? He was risking her leaving him right now by not demanding a response. Maybe the only reason she had stayed around this long was because of the blizzard. What if his declaration had scared her?

"Am I what?"

"Being careful?"

Sonji smiled. "I stopped being careful the moment I stepped into your classroom, professor."

Grayson wasn't sure whether to laugh or scoop her

into his arms, carry her off to bed, and make love to her for the fifth time that day.

"I have something I want to show you," he said.

Sonji detected a serious undertone in his voice and decided against making a suggestive comment.

"What is it?"

"It's something you have to see to understand. I can't really describe it."

"Oh?" Sonji responded, her curiosity fully piqued.

"Yes," he said. "But you'll have to get dressed."

After their loving interlude that morning, Sonji had only bothered to don one of Grayson's shirts to lounge in. "Why? Are we leaving?"

"Yes."

"In this weather!"

"Where is your sense of adventure?"

Sonji pointed to a drift of snow just outside the door. "Under that snow bank."

"Nonsense. I'm going to shovel the driveway while you shower and change."

"Grayson, you need a snowblower for all of that snow."

"Since I didn't have my morning run, the exercise will do me good."

"You're serious."

"Quite."

"Okay, Apollo."

Sonji did as Grayson insisted. Her shower was quick and invigorating. It didn't at all surprise her that Grayson had a large soap-on-a-rope hanging from his showerhead. It created a rich lather on her skin that smelled of musk, earthy patchouli, and sage. It was Grayson's smell, and she wanted it all over her.

After her shower, she changed into the clothes she brought in her overnight bag. He hadn't been gone that long and already she missed his company. The thought occurred to her to join him outside, but something told her that, much like his early morning runs, shoveling away the mounds of accumulated snow was something he needed to do alone.

She watched him from the living room window hefting and hoisting the snow with little difficulty. He looked reasonably warm in a black ski jacket. His facial expression was stern. And then she saw it, the look that meant Grayson had just gone someplace far away. He looked distant and sad; angry and remorseful.

It usually occurred when he was doing something physically strenuous—that his entire demeanor would change. And Grayson could very well have been on the other side of the world, because during those times nothing Sonji could say or do would reach him.

She had asked him about it once over dinner. Despite her minimal cooking skills, Sonji was quite proud of the meal she had prepared. She had happily treated Grayson to heaping portions of spinach salad, fettuccini carbonara, and garlic bread. Again he surprised her with his healthy appetite and how energetically he could apply himself to eating.

When the dinner dishes were loaded, they discussed many things: music, cooking, favorite movies, Grayson's favorite recipes, Alexandre and Phyllis, and Sonji's dream of becoming a college professor like Grayson. Sonji also talked about some of the incidental things on her wish list like painting her kitchen and rearranging her furniture.

The next thing she knew, she was standing in the far corner of her living room while Grayson moved her couch, love seat and sofa table until it was exactly where she wanted it.

At first, the mood was lively and a little playful as Sonji asked Grayson to try the furniture in one place and then another. He did as she asked and gave Sonji the opportunity to explore all the possibilities of various arrangements. But once, when hauling the sofa from the south side of the room to the east, an expression took over Grayson' face that disturbed Sonji greatly.

It lasted only a few moments, but in that time Sonji saw a sadness so deep and painful that it hurt her.

"Grayson," she said pensively, "what's wrong?"

He shook his head slowly. "Nothing," he said, and the expression was gone.

They went back to moving furniture, but something was off. Like a half-step in a tango, their playful dance was out of sync and missing rhythm. Although she never pressured him about it, Sonji wished that he would share whatever it was that caused him such profound remorse. She would have done anything to be able to prevent him from ever being that sad again.

It was like a cold wall dropping between them. It had happened more than a few times, and Sonji remembered each time vividly. She turned away from the window, unable to watch the expression take Grayson to a place she couldn't go.

She decided to check on Alexandre and Phyllis while she waited for Grayson to finish shoveling. She had become accustomed to watching them move slowly across the gravel in their tank, or curl into their shells until she could barely see them. She walked into the den and over to the terrarium. They were resting on opposite ends of the glass encasement. Sonji watched quietly as periodically a brown leg would move about in the shell. "I still don't know what he sees in you," she said, reaching up for their food. She filled their dish with pellets and gave them fresh water. This made them cast about a little more, but not much.

Finished with her pet chores, Sonji was drawn to

the exquisitely preserved rolltop desk in the room. She sat down in front of the computer and ran her fingers softly across the keys. She fantasized that this was where Grayson signed on to the BlackLuv Web site and sent her the most romantic love notes she had ever read. Sonji's melancholy turned into curiosity when she noticed the photo sitting next to the keyboard. She picked up the ornate frame and stared into the eyes of the boy in the picture. They were Grayson's eyes. But the picture was too recent to be a photo of him. She brought the picture closer. This child was a smaller version of Grayson, there was no doubt. A son, she wondered?

"Maybe I'll need a snowblower after all."

Sonji didn't even hear him come in.

"What are you doing?" Grayson's voice sounded heavy and harsh.

"Grayson, who *is* this?" she asked, apprehensively.

Sonji held up the picture in her hand and saw a look of surprise and anger cross his face.

"Put that down!" he said strongly.

"Grayson, who is it?"

Grayson strode over to where Sonji sat at the desk. His arms made an angry *swish, swish* sound inside his ski jacket. He snatched the picture from her hands.

Sonji leaned backward, suddenly wary of his actions. "Grayson!"

"It doesn't concern you," he snapped.

A muscle trembled in his cheek, and she felt her stomach muscles tighten. "Grayson . . . I thought we were—"

"Were *what*?" he questioned, sternly.

His remark made her unsure of herself and their relationship. Had she been wrong all this time? "Well, I guess I don't know."

"Ask next time before you go snooping around in

my things." Grayson turned to walk out of the den. "I'm going to finish the driveway."

"Good!" Sonji remarked standing. "When you finish you can take me home."

Her words made him pause at the doorway for a second, but only for a second. And then he was gone.

Thirteen

Grayson couldn't believe what he was seeing. The snow had barely melted from the storm a few days earlier, and the ESL students were at the community center. Almost every person on the list had shown up. In his literature class that same morning, half the students were absent.

It was just as well, Grayson thought. The ones who were absent were the ones who had the most objections to the class anyway.

Members from MSO were again present to set up materials and check people in. However, this time, Sonji was not among them. She had probably found out that he was teaching tonight's session and decided against volunteering. Not that he blamed her. There was no excuse for his behavior the other day. He had been a cad. And Sonji had not spoken to him since. So Grayson's greatest fear, that Sonji would be taken away from him, had been realized. But it wasn't by some baneful outside force. It had been his own panic and overreaction that had driven her away.

He watched as the Sudanese students came in and helped themselves to refreshments. Despite his enthusiasm for conducting the session this evening, something in the pit of his stomach turned over every time he thought of his mistake and prevented him from circulating among the student arrivals. He sat in the back of the room analyzing the memory over and over until he was nearly groggy with sadness.

Why had he reacted so vehemently? Reviewing it in his mind now, his behavior seemed outrageous. But at the time, seeing the picture of his son in Sonji's hands struck him as a violation of a sacred bond. To see the essence of his progeny in the hands of someone else was a painful shock. For years, Grayson hadn't shared the memory of his son with anyone except Kyle. And the realization that he might have to share that memory with Sonji hit him as the invasion of a life that he had kept closed all this time. So he had lashed out. And Sonji had suffered the repercussions of his long, silent agony.

He yawned for the umpteenth time that evening. Sleep had been elusive since the incident. And last night was worst of all. His recurring dreams left him exhausted and drained. He remembered them vividly. Black-and-white images of him alone and searching. Around every corner, there was nothing. In every room, there was nothing. Behind smoke and curtains of mist, still nothing. And after endless walking and running, the object of his pursuit was nowhere to be found. Just as he was about to abandon the hunt, he would wake up barely able to move.

This happened so many times throughout the night that at four A.M. he was reluctant to return to sleep. Rather than put himself through additional torment, he had gotten up and gone to the gym where he ran on the treadmill until his heart thundered in his chest for him to stop.

Snap out of it, he told himself. *I can't maintain this kind of despondency and lead a good session.* He got up from his seat, forced a smile, and mixed with the assemblage. In a few minutes, his faux smile was replaced by a genuine one as Zaina and Sahar entered the room. Their sincere dedication to this project from the start was always a refreshing comfort. He walked over to where they were standing and extended his hand.

"Professor, always a pleasure to see you." Zaina's African accent rolled over her words as if she were singing.

Instead of shaking her hand, Grayson instinctively kissed the back of it. "My sentiment as well, madam. And Sahar." He extended his hand once more to the woman forever walking in Zaina's shadow. He also kissed the back of her hand. "Your presence honors me." Sahar smiled in response and her dark cheeks warmed at his greeting.

"I understand you are presenting this session."

"I am."

"Then it is we who are honored." Zaina's response was pleasant, but perfunctory nonetheless. Grayson sometimes got the feeling that behind Zaina's many pleasantries was an ulterior motive—one that Grayson had no desire to uncover. He admired her commitment to the ESL project, her accomplishments as a previous student, and now her presence as an associate. Anything beyond that was out of the question. As always, Grayson would make sure that their interactions were professional.

He retrieved his pocket watch: 7:00 P.M. "Ladies," he said, offering them a princely bow. "Please excuse me. It's time to begin."

"Certainly," they responded.

Grayson reached the front of the room and took his place behind the lectern. "Ladies and gentlemen, if you will take your seats, we will begin." The murmur from the crowd died down as the students took their seats and waited patiently for Grayson to continue.

"Welcome to the Midlands Literacy Council's Project Sudan. My name is Grayson Gilmore, and I am honored to be your facilitator this evening." Grayson looked around at the many faces in the room. He thought the the Sudanese were such a regal-looking people. Many of them were tall and slender and carried themselves with a quiet dignity that was awe-inspiring. He could tell from the looks on their faces that their expectations were high. He would do everything in his power to exceed their expectations and set them on the path to greater learning.

Grayson's thoughts were disrupted by the fleeting memory of Sonji, who hadn't answered or returned any of his calls. Determined not to ruin the students' experience with his own woes, he pushed the memory from his mind by focusing on the lesson plan before him. First he would start with his traditional quote and question for the evening. Then he would get the students warmed up by having them tell stories about their names. He had planned to follow that activity by providing them with a unique human-interest article from *USA Today*. He hoped that out of that article, they would identify and discuss words that were new to their vocabulary. Afterward, he would finish the evening with a game of Taboo. With all of that to occupy his mind, Grayson hoped to keep away musings of Sonji, at least until he could make the time to deal with the unpleasant rift between them.

On the other side of the city, Sonji Stephens was mad as hell. Her car battery was dead and not even responsive to a jump-start. Her grandmother was right about her boxed, microwave meals, and she had run out of them. All that Sonji had to eat was a can of salmon and a bag of animal crackers that had been in her cupboard since who knew when. And the pièce de résistance—the heavy ice and snow had snapped her phone line. She couldn't call for help if she wanted to. And boy did she want to. "This is all your fault, Grayson Gilmore," she shouted to no one. "If you hadn't been such a butthead about a stinking picture . . ." Her thoughts trailed off as she popped a bite-sized elephant into her mouth. The graham taste she expected had been replaced by the flavor of dust and old cinnamon. "I don't believe this!"

Sonji tossed the ancient cookies into the trash. She had been cooped up in her town house ever since Grayson had dropped her off two days ago. What little food she had was gone now, and Sonji had no way of getting to the store. Frustrated with the whole situation, she decided to take a nap. Perhaps an hour of sleep would clear her head and help her plan what to do.

Sonji didn't think she had been asleep that long, but the clock on the wall read 10:00 P.M. Was that a knock? she wondered, righting herself on her couch. She listened for a few moments and sure enough, the knock came again.

"Just a minute," she called, rising and clearing her head. *It must be someone wanting to shovel the snow,* she thought. *Well whoever it is can have at it.*

"Miss Sonji," the two voices sang in unison. She opened the door to find Andi and Sebastian at her doorstep. Sebastian was holding a medium-sized box and Andi had a covered flowering plant in her hand.

"May we come in?" Sebastian asked.

"Of course," Sonji replied, stepping aside.

The two stamped their feet on Sonji's interior rug.

"What brings you two out in this weather?" The way they were bundled made them look like African snow bunnies.

Andi smiled her bright Andi-smile. "We heard how some people were without power and phone service. So we made survival kits for all of our friends that we couldn't reach by phone."

"It was her idea," Sebastian said. Then a smile revealed all his teeth. "Do you see why I love this woman?"

"Yes, I do," Sonji replied, honestly.

Sebastian set the box on the floor. "You've got a first-aid kit, flashlight, batteries, candles, matches, a blanket, a can opener and enough canned food to last a week."

Sonji could have jumped for joy. "You don't know how much I needed this. As you can see my electricity is still on, but the food—"

"Well, I know how you hate to cook."

"An-di!" Sebastian reprimanded.

Andi covered her grin. "Sorry," she said.

"So is your phone out?"

"My phone, my car, my patience. It's all out."

"How about if we stop by tomorrow evening to see if you need anything?"

"Yeah, and you can ride to school tomorrow with me if you want."

"You two are lifesavers. And I'm ill-mannered. Let me take your coats."

Sebastian shook his head. "That's okay, Sonji. We've got a few more deliveries to make tonight."

"This is for you," Andi said, grinning.

Sonji took the plant from Andi. She looked at it through the plastic. Its white flowers looked as though they had been folded inside out and backward.

"It's beautiful," she said, admiring the unusual petals.

"It's a cyclamen. The leaves grow out and then they reverse."

"I've never seen anything like it. I'm not sure I'm going to be able to take care of it. I'm not as good with plants as you are."

"This one takes work, but it's not difficult work." Andi helped Sonji unwrap the plant. "Keep it in a cool place with indirect sunlight until it's finished blooming. When it completes it's bloom cycle, the leaves will die back and the plant will go to sleep."

"Wow, then what do I do?" Sonji asked not taking her eyes off the plant.

"Then, water it from the bottom once per month. When the weather gets warmer, it will bloom again."

The sight of the plant's leaves turned backward reminded Sonji of the state of affairs between she and Grayson. Since the picture incident, she felt as if their relationship had been turned inside out and backwards. Maybe what they needed was a cooling off, like the plant.

"Thank you, Andi. I—" The doorbell interrupted her. "Well, I'll be. It's Grand Central around here tonight. Excuse me."

Sonji opened the door, and Grayson stood on her front steps, picnic basket in hand.

Sonji frowned. "What do you want?"

Grayson took a deep breath. "To talk and"—he raised the picnic basket slowly—"to eat."

No better time to talk about the cooling off than now, she thought, and stepped aside so he could enter.

Andi watched in surprise as the professor entered. "PG?"

"Baby." Sebastian again reprimanded.

"That's all right," Grayson responded. "I've heard all the names. Pathetically Grim. Pretty Gross."

"Positively God-awful," Andi added.

"Baby!" Sebastian shook his head, yet smiled just the same.

Andi put her hands on her hips. "Well it's true, and it's about time somebody tells him about it."

Grayson looked only at Sonji, who had been staring at him with disapproval the entire time. "Believe me, I know what an idiot I've been."

Andi looked from Sonji to Grayson, then from Grayson back to Sonji. She grabbed Sebastian's arm. "We've got to go now."

"Why?" Sebastian asked, frowning.

"Because, Prometheus, he's Osiris." Andi smiled with knowing.

Sebastian gave Professor Gilmore a once-over. "I don't believe it."

"Believe it," Grayson snapped, still looking at Sonji.

Andi and Sebastian left without another word, and Sonji was left alone with the object of her displeasure.

"We need to talk, Sonji."

Sonji thought about how Grayson had shut her out for the second time. Once when she had asked about his change in demeanor at his brother's house and then again when she asked about the picture. She was tired of trying to talk to this man.

Sonji crossed her arms. "I'd sooner talk to Alexandre and Phyllis."

Grayson dropped his head. *This is it,* he thought. He put the basket on the floor and took off his coat. The look in Sonji's eyes was ice cold. She was about to protest, but he interrupted.

"He had . . . an airplane spoon," he said, staring directly into Sonji's eyes. "When he was eight months old, the only way to get him to eat was by using that spoon."

The features on Sonji's face softened a little, but only a little. "It was blue and white and all I had to do was make a propeller sound and his toothless grin would spring open."

Grayson took in a strong breath and released it slowly. "Grayson Bartholomew Gilmore, Junior. That's who is in the photograph, Sonji."

Sonji's features relaxed even more. "Why didn't you tell me you had a son?"

"Because I miss him."

"Is he with his mother? Does he live in another state?" Then Sonji saw that faraway look over take him again.

"He's dead, Sonji."

Sonji felt as if the room was spinning. The angry lump in her throat dissolved into a nauseous knot in the lowest part of her stomach. She could see tears suspended in Grayson's eyes.

She went to him. "I'm sorry."

Their embrace was swift and urgent. "It was seven years ago. He was only two."

"How did it happen?" she asked, clinging to him tightly.

"It was an accident. He was playing in the backyard and fell into a large storm drain."

"Oh, my God."

"He died of complications from head trauma."

"Oh, Grayson." Suddenly the faraway looks made sense to her.

Grayson pulled out of their embrace. "I was wrong the other day." Now the expression on her face was softer than he had ever seen it. "I snapped, and I'm sorry. It's just that—"

"No, don't be sorry. I can't imagine the pain you feel. It must be overwhelming."

"Sometimes, I know I'd give anything to bring him back."

Sonji stared into Grayson's eyes, and the emotions she had felt for weeks tumbled out of her mouth. "I love you, Grayson."

He stared back at her, aghast.

"I know this is probably the most inappropriate time to tell you."

"No," Grayson said. He pulled her into his chest and enveloped her in his arms. "It's not. It's not."

They held each other silently for a long time. Sonji finally broke the silence.

"Grayson, what about the food? It's getting cold."

He looked down at the basket as if he didn't remember placing it on the floor. "I'll serve."

He knelt and began unpacking the food. Sonji knelt beside him. "And while we eat, will you tell me about your son?"

"I'd like that."

"Mr. Gilmore, the doctor will see you now."

Like an echo from his dream, Grayson rose from the leather seat and followed the nurse into the patient-care facility.

Hospitals always made him feel ill-at-ease, as if the sickness contained inside them was a monster to be shunned or destroyed. He took a deep breath and prayed for the resolve he needed.

"Professor Gilmore."

The mild voice of Dr. Hoffman filled the room. She extended her hand, and he grasped it firmly.

"Thank you for coming."

"Please," Grayson said, following her to her office. "Don't thank me. I should have been here months ago."

Dr. Hoffman's office was always the same. White, textured ceiling, sparsely covered walls, and bookcases galore. The subdued lighting made the leather furniture look older and darker than it was.

Grayson took a seat opposite the doctor. "Your message sounded important. Has there been a change in her condition?"

"I'm afraid so."

He could tell by her tone of voice that it wasn't a good change. He sat back in the studded leather chair.

"You know how well Veranda's been doing."

Grayson nodded.

"I was beginning to have serious hope for a home visit soon."

"Yes, doctor. I remember discussing that the last time I was here."

"Three days ago, she had an episode."

Grayson's disappointment was audible. He rubbed the tips of his fingers across his furrowed brow.

"She hasn't had once since, so perhaps this is a temporary episode. But it bears watching."

"Can I see her?"

Dr. Hoffman leaned forward in her chair. "Of course. But we'll have to have someone in the room with you as a precautionary measure."

Grayson said he understood, but he really didn't. How could someone he had once loved so deeply, the mother of his child, be so far away from him? Sometimes on his visits, he would sit right next to her, and he could tell she didn't have any idea who he was. And other times, they talked as if there was no tragedy between them. In all the times he had come to see her, he had never mentioned the divorce. He wasn't sure if she would understand it. And if she did understand it, could she withstand it?

Since he had bared his soul to Sonji, he had felt lighter than he had since his son's death. With each sentence, he was freed of the dark regret that had pressed him for seven long years. He owed it to himself and especially Veranda to finish the purging of his soul that he began at Sonji's house.

"I'd like to see her," he said.

The dayroom was small and designed to be relaxing, with warm yellow walls, paintings with tempered patterns, and soft Muzac piped in through small stereo speakers. Most of the space in the room was taken up by two overstuffed chairs and a matching loveseat. The plush carpet muffled the sounds of his shoes and the doctor's when they entered.

Grayson sat on the loveseat, anxiously awaiting Veranda's arrival. The sun had been covered over by clouds, and the room made eerie shifts from light to dim, like a strobe on a slow blink. When was the last time he had seen Veranda? Five months ago? Six? He knew no one in her family visited her. To their bourgeois conscience, she was too much of an embarrassment. He had been her sole support for years, but now . . .

The sounds of people entering the room broke him from his thoughts. An attendant, whom Grayson recognized as Stanley, stood in the doorway. At his side was the woman who had been his wife for fifteen years. Her dark, flowing mane of raven hair was gone. Stress, the doctor had said. In its place was a complex tangle of tight curls. Their bedeviled tendrils twisted around each other like a skein of wool yarn.

The hospital held the philosophy that when residents look like patients they tend to act like patients. Despite the floral-print dress she wore, her vacant stare made her indeed patientlike. Instead of appearing vibrant, the dress with pink, yellow, and purple butterflies merely hung from hollow, hunched shoulders like a heavy shroud. Grayson sighed at the frail-framed woman and rose to greet her.

Dr. Hoffman entered the room then and gave a

nod to the orderly to step back. She stepped gently to Veranda's side and smiled.

"Veranda, Grayson is here to see you. Would you like to visit with him for a little while?"

Veranda looked slowly from the doctor to Grayson. Her vacant stare wavered but never really came into focus.

"I'm going to leave you two alone, unless you want me to stay," Dr. Hoffman said, glancing at them.

Veranda's mouth remained closed. Grayson shut his eyes, pained by her silence.

"Here," Dr. Hoffman suggested. "Let's take a seat over here. Okay?"

Grayson moved to his ex-wife's side. "Please, let me," he said first looking at the doctor and back to Veranda.

He guided Veranda to the loveseat. She sat without protest. He took a seat beside her and willed himself to smile. The doctor nodded and took one more look at Veranda before leaving them in the room with Stanley watching nearby.

Grayson ran his fingers through his hair. He looked on as Veranda's attentions were caught by a nearby window and the hospital grounds that lay beyond. He remembered each visit to the hospital as if they were stacked before him like dominoes. And the patterns of each visit were written in his memory. Sometimes Veranda was almost the Veranda he had fallen in love with. Lively, vibrant, with a smile that would melt the coldest of men. And then there were other times when he couldn't tell if she even knew he was there.

It was at those times that he talked the most. He tried harder to make a connection with her and to help bring her out of the prison she had created.

"What did you think of that snowstorm? Quite annoying, I'd say. Thank heavens it's melting already."

Veranda continued her gaze through the window. Grayson was undaunted.

"I saw ReTonya the other day. You know she still gets up at the crack of dawn. Maybe you were right about her having a crush on me."

Still no response.

"Veranda," he said, and placed his hand on top of hers. She still had some of the softest hands he had ever felt, but now they were always cold. "Did I tell you the latest escapade with Alexandre and Phyllis? Well it seems that perhaps they should be monkeys, for whatever Phyllis does, Alexandre does. When Phyllis gets sick, Alexandre follows suit. When Phyllis's health improves, Alexandre's recovery is not far behind." Grayson forced himself to chuckle. "Well if *that* isn't monkey see, monkey do, I don't know what is!"

Grayson caught Stanley smiling in the corner. But he was wearing the smile of a man trying not to let on how pathetic he thought the situation he was watching really was.

When Grayson turned his attention back to Veranda she was looking at him. But the expression on her face was volatile and cloudy, as if at any moment she might burst into tears or erupt into thunderous anger.

"Veranda," he said, touching the side of her face. She closed her eyes in response, and he knew he had broken through at least one barrier.

"I haven't been here to visit with you in a long time. I apologize. And I have no excuse."

He looked deeply into those almost-bright eyes and hoped he was doing the right thing.

"Now that I'm here, there's something that I need to talk to you about." Grayson tightened his hold on her hand slightly to brace them both for the announcement to come.

"My dear, I will always love you. I hope you know

that. Some of my most cherished memories are times I've spent with you. But my life is different now. With you working on your recovery these seven years, it caused me to make some important decisions."

Now the "poor man" look was gone from Stanley's eyes, replaced by understanding and concern.

"Veranda, what I'm trying to say is . . . we are no longer married. I filed for a divorce two years ago and six months after I filed, it was granted."

The muscles in Grayson's stomach tightened into a guilt-ridden knot the size of a fist.

"Now, please don't think that I'm abandoning you. That's not the case. And know this, I understand the meaning of for better or worse. But I also know that the current situation is debilitating both of us, and has been for years. I sincerely believe that my decision was the first step in healing for both of us."

Grayson searched Veranda's face for any sign that he may have broken through another barrier. There was none. Only an expression that made him want to grab her shoulders and shake her into consciousness. But instead of relenting to his urge, he covered her hands with both of his.

For the remainder of the afternoon, Grayson spun stories for Veranda of his nieces' latest exploits and some of the students in his ESL class.

"Professor Gilmore." Dr. Hoffman's voice interrupted his discussion. He looked up toward the door. "I'm going to have to ask you to bring your visit to a close."

"Thank you, doctor."

Grayson took in the sight of Veranda once more. She had now become fascinated with the fabric on the furniture and had turned her attentions there.

"Well, I guess this means we'll have to continue our discussion some other time." Grayson rose slowly and then stretched. "Next time I won't allow so much time between visits." His smile was not returned.

As he walked toward the door, he gave Stanley a firm pat on the shoulder. This time Stanley's face showed only respect.

Before he left the dayroom, Grayson watched as Veranda turned her head back to the window, as if she was waiting for him to pass by it.

"May I see you for a moment, doctor?"

"Would you like to go into my office?"

"I'd appreciate that."

While Grayson followed the doctor through the narrow hallways of the patient-care facility, he had an unsettling wave of déjà vu. Once in the doctor's office, his unease subsided significantly.

"I want to discuss the arrangements regarding Veranda's account."

"Yes," the doctor said.

Grayson took a manila envelope from his coat pocket. "I will no longer be making the payments for her treatment here."

"Oh?" the doctor said, sitting up. "Would you like to look into state subsidies for her care?"

"No," Grayson responded. He handed the thick envelope over to her. "I believe this will take care of it."

The streets were slushy and wet with melting snow. Traces of the recent storm were quickly fading due to rising temperatures and lots of sunshine. So much snow had melted that muddy puddles were everywhere, and where the snow hadn't melted completely random patches of ice made it slick going for drivers and walkers alike.

Sonji watched the road intently as Andi's car splashed standing water in a jet stream from her tires.

Now and then she would slow down so as not to douse pedestrians with the wild tire-spray.

"Please thank Sebastian for sending the tow truck this morning."

"No problem," Andi said. "I just wish the guy could have gotten your car started, ya know?"

Me, too, thought Sonji. "It's just as well. This way I get to spend some time with you and tell you all about Grayson."

Andi beamed with delight. "I was hoping you would, like, go there. Sebastian made me promise that I wouldn't bring it up if you didn't. But it was getting hard not to say something."

Andi spared a quick glance at Sonji, then turned back to the road. "So . . . tell me everything. Especially the juicy stuff."

Sonji laughed. "We'll be at Sears before I get to the juicy stuff." Sonji looked down at the battery sitting by her feet. It was a generic brand that had come with the car. Considering the Nebraska winters, Sonji wanted a battery that would withstand the extreme elements.

"Then we're going to the Sears in Colonial Heights."

Colonial Heights used to be a suburb of Omaha until it was annexed ten years ago. It would take them twenty minutes to get there.

"Okay," Sonji conceded. She could not conceal her happiness. Even after her short rift with Grayson. And now that he had disclosed some very personal information about his son, Sonji felt closer to him than ever. The one thing that still troubled her was the mother. Of course Grayson Jr., had to have a mother. But Grayson hadn't talked about her. And Sonji wanted him to talk about her of his own volition. She refused to force or push anything. But after their serious talk, they seemed closer than ever.

"Hel-lo!"

"Sorry, Andi. I was just thinking about how close I feel to Grayson." She smiled at the woman responsible for bringing them together. "And I really want to thank you for setting things in motion for us. If it hadn't been for you—"

"Nuh-uh. You two would have found each other. I can feel it."

Traffic was light for a Saturday morning. Many of the cars were so splattered with muck, they looked like they had been part of a mud derby.

"Sooo, when did you figure out it was PG?"

"I didn't. It wasn't until the necklace he gave me fell out of my coat that we realized who we were." Sonji took a deep breath. The memory of their revelation still made her sizzle with excitement.

"What happened after that?"

"It was like the last piece to the puzzle. We fit together as if we were created together. Sometimes I'm overwhelmed at just how wonderful he is."

"Wonderful enough to, like, give you a break on your grades?"

Sonji smiled. "Wonderful enough *not* to."

"Wow," was Andi's awe-induced response. "So he must be way different off campus."

Sonji's mind filled with images of Grayson stuffing his face with her grandmother's cooking, smacking his lips, licking his fingers, and sending her virtual flowers. She chuckled at the image. "Like Dennis Rodman and Denzel Washington."

Andi shot her another glance. This one was gleaming and slightly crooked. "So, you like him, huh?"

"Are you kidding?" Sonji responded. "Yesterday I said the *L*-word."

"Oh, whoa!"

Sonji thought Andi's response was to her comment

and then she saw the flashing lights. Andi slammed
down on the brakes and her Geo Metro came to an
abrupt halt. An ambulance sped quickly and silently
through the intersection directly in front of them.

"Oh, God," Andi said, visibly shaken.

"What?" Sonji asked, seeing the coloring fade from
Andi's chaste face.

"Don't you know?" she responded.

Sonji shook her head.

"A silent ambulance is a bad omen. It means
death."

Sonji felt a sliver of chills walk up her spine. "I've
never heard that before."

"It's true," Andi assured her. "Once when I was a
kid, I was walking home from school with some
friends, and we saw a silent ambulance. When we got
home, an ambulance was at my friend's house. Her
father had just, like, dropped dead. Out of the clear
blue. Just *blam*. He was gone."

Sonji's stomach muscles tightened slightly. "Yeah,
but Andi, that was probably a coincidence. A fluke."

Andi shook her head. "All I know is bad things
happen whenever I've come across a silent ambulance. And someone's death is usually involved."

Sonji looked down at her feet. "Maybe it means
this battery!"

The two laughed, just enough to cover the unease
left in the car by Andi's pronouncement.

After they got moving again, it wasn't long before
they reached East Park shopping mall where Sears was
housed.

"Now I know why the streets seem so deserted."

"Why?" Sonji asked.

Andi frowned at the inordinate number of cars in
the parking lot. "Because everyone is here."

After several minutes of searching for the closest

spot, they gave up and parked in a space that looked nearly five blocks away from the entrance.

After trekking for what felt like the length of a football field, the two arrived at the Sears automotive department. A new battery that had a reputation for starting in the coldest weather imaginable replaced Sonji's old, sparkless battery. By turning in her old one, she happily received a ten-percent discount.

Because of finals week, neither of them had time to shop like they would have wished. "And besides," Sonji said, "Grayson's supposed to stop by soon." So, after she paid for the battery, they left the store and headed for home.

"Well, the storm may have delayed our plans, but they are not scrapped."

The three people who showed up for Bill's clandestine meeting nodded their heads in agreement. Mary Carl, Pat Wilkens, and Ted Maten. They were all seated in a neat half-circle around him.

They had arrived at his apartment only a few minutes earlier. So far, they had been treated to caramel-crème cappuccinos, a meat and cheese tray, and instrumental background music. Bill sat in a bar chair in the middle of the semicircle.

"Do you all agree that something must be done about this impostor posing as an instructor?"

"Yes," they said.

"Then we've got to come at him as outrageously as he has come at us all semester." Bill pushed the morsels of food around on his plate absentmindedly. "Giving him a poor evaluation isn't enough. Lodging an informal complaint isn't enough." He smoothed a square of cheese back and forth between his thumb and index finger. "The English department must be made aware of his ineptitude as a teacher." A squish with his fingers and the cheese cube was squeezed flat. "He might even be barred from teaching that class again."

"Well he needs to be. I've never been so insulted," Mary replied.

"Let me ask you all a question. have any of you earned anything higher than a B?"

No one spoke.

"That's what I thought. It's reverse discrimination. That's what it is."

Ted perked up. "Yeah. First there was multiculturalism, then there was affirmative action, and now they've just taken us out all together."

"But is there still time to do anything?" Pat asked.

"Yeah, it is the end of the semester," Mary agreed.

"I know. That's why I asked you to come over tonight. Besides, there's always time to do what's right."

Pat frowned. "So what do you have in mind, man?"

"A formal protest."

"What?" The three gave each other curious glances.

"I say we go straight to the top." Bill could tell he had their full attention. "I say we air our frustrations to the dean of the Arts and Sciences college."

"Oh, that's too perfect," came Mary's reply.

"I'll type up a complaint. I think I know how you all feel. And then I'll set up a meeting with Dean Waters to present our grievance.

Bill's heart responded to the smiles he saw slowly emerging on his cohorts' faces. "So, are you in or what?"

"In."

"In!"

"In."

"I was hoping you'd say that." Bill walked to the other side of the room. From the top of a desk he retrieved several papers. "I took the liberty of typing up some things for you to say and the order in which you should say them." He passed out the folded papers.

"This looks like a script."

"I guess you've thought of everything."

"I guess so," Bill said, smiling. "I guess so."

Veranda's pulse was racing. As she sifted though the items in her closet, she forced her mind to focus. It was difficult because it had been so long since she had tried—really tried—to herd all her loose thoughts into coherence. Several times she had to stop just to remember why she was in the closet. At first, the reason was slow in coming. But now it drove her to places, physical and emotional, she hadn't been in weeks, months, years.

"Where is it?"

She was getting anxious now, tearing at scarves and socks, pouring through sweaters and panties.

"Oh, God. What if I only imagined that I put it here?"

Towels, pajamas, a hat. Last pile, she thought. Shorts, T-shirts, more socks, how many socks? And then—before the panic could set in and take her to the dusky place her mind sometimes went—a wallet.

Veranda clutched it to her breast, heaving air in gulps. *Calm down,* she told herself. *Clam down. Everything is all right now.*

Grayson was swelling with joy. As he checked his reflection in the mirror, he actually liked what he saw. The handsome man he'd been years ago had returned, and returned with a vengeance. He was looking good for his woman today, if he did say so himself. Navy European cut Nehru suit. Black woven Lazio shoes. He was ready for a day with his warrior woman.

Grayson's happiness bubbled up into a laugh as he remembered the shocked faces of the students in his English class as he had come in last week, smiled, and asked in a quite buoyant voice, "So, what shall we do today?" He couldn't remember the last time he had devoted an entire session of one of his classes to open discussion. He used to do it. But at some point, he had lost enthusiasm for teaching that way and no longer deemed open discussions necessary for the students to learn. But the old Professor Gilmore had taken over his classes recently. And that Grayson Gilmore had a light inside, a light that he wanted desperately to create within his students. God, how he had missed that.

But there was also another source of fulfillment. He glanced hopefully at the two articles on his roll-top desk. The first was a palm-sized box enclosed in gold-and-black wrapping paper. A gold bow was tied prominently on top. The second item was smaller than the first. The object in this little black velvet box made Grayson's heart do a loop-the-loop.

"First things first," he said, scooping the larger of the boxes into his hand and heading outside.

"Stop right here," she said, a half smile taking over her lips. As the cab slowed, Veranda pulled a twenty-dollar bill from her wallet with shaky hands. She had made it, and without incident. She remembered the entire trip from the hospital and now she was home. It was almost as if she had never left. Remnants from the recent storm made the front lawn look fit for building snowmen or falling backward into the remaining drifts and making snow angels.

"That'll be fifteen dollars even," the cab driver said.

Veranda's anxiety grew until her face was dotted with pearls of sweat. Her hands trembled so badly, she struggled to put her change into her wallet.

"Are you all right, ma'am?" the cab driver asked.

"Yess, y-es," her voice came out as shaky as her hands.

Her home. She was seeing her home. It was difficult to contain the sensation of fear and eagerness that made her hot and dizzy. *But why am I here? Oh, no, not now. Hold on,* she ordered herself. *It can't go now.*

"I'm here to stop the end," she said, smiling. Her mind had not gone blank. She had remembered. And the view of her home came even more clearly. It resembled a snow bungalow she and Grayson had once stayed in. That was one of the reasons they had liked the house so well. So many memories.

Veranda watched as a man emerged from the house.

"Grayson," she said, clutching the car door handle.

He walked jauntily down the stairs, despite the slick remnants of the storm, and stepped into a black BMW. Before Veranda could get her jumbled thoughts together, he had backed out of the driveway and was headed down the street.

"Where's he going?" she asked, stunned. "He can't be gone."

The cabby turned around. "You want me to follow that car?"

"Y-yes."

"I've been waiting for years to get a call like that."

The cab driver put the car in gear and took off behind Grayson. Veranda put her hand to her throat, unsure of how to proceed now that her homecoming plan had been altered. Through her fuzziness, she was certain of one thing, Grayson knew where Gray Jr. was, and she had to find their son. Then they could be a family again and forever.

The cab ride took Veranda to a part of the city she was only vaguely familiar with. Grayson drove up into the driveway of a cozy-looking town house. *Is this where Gray Jr. is?* she wondered.

The cab driver parked across the street. Veranda watched closely as Grayson climbed the stairs to the front door and knocked vigorously. She kept her eye trained on the package in his hands. Something from the wrapping reflected gold in the light. She opened her wallet once more. "How much?"

"Are you kidding, lady? This one's on me." The cabby laughed to himself. "If you had said 'Step on it!' I would have given *you* some dead presidents."

Something about that word *dead* made Veranda's stomach twist inside out.

Grayson had given up knocking and placed the package he was carrying into the mailbox on the side of the stairs.

"Wait!" Veranda insisted, still inside the cab. But it was too late. Grayson had gotten back into his car and was backing out of the driveway.

The cabby looked back. "You want me to follow him again?"

Now the thoughts in Veranda's head seemed slightly misted over. She had to get out of the car before she blanked out again.

"No," she said, opening the door. "Thank you. Th-th-thank you." She stepped out of the cab and closed the door behind her. The cabby tipped his hat to her and sped off, leaving her alone and apprehensive.

For a few moments, she just stood on the sidewalk

with her arms wrapped around herself, uncertain of what to do. She worked diligently to clear her mind and to focus. *What's the last thing you remember?* she asked herself. Grayson. Grayson was at that house. And he put something in the mailbox. Maybe it was something that would tell her where Gray Jr. was.

Veranda walked quickly across the street and up to the town house. She pulled open the mailbox and retrieved the package wrapped in black and gold. She sucked in her breath, marveling at the delicate look and feel of the box. "Gray?" she muttered tearing the box open. Inside, she found a pair of gold earrings. They were molded into the shape of what looked like a beetle. There was a note inside the box.

> *My Love, please accept these earrings as a testament of my unending devotion to you. I know we've hit a rough spot recently, but believe me when I say that our love can and will bear out this tempest in my soul. I cannot, will not, see you unhappy. Wear these and remember that truth.*
> *Forever,*
> *Grayson*

Veranda thought that perhaps she should cry. But her tears had dried up long ago. It was enough to know that Grayson still cared about her and her journey had not been in vain. And now, if she could just find Gray Jr., everything would be back to normal. He must be here in this house, she thought. Grayson led me here for a reason.

"Thanks, Andi!"

Sonji waved as Andromeda backed out of her driveway. She walked up the stairs to her town house, picking up several torn pieces of foil wrapping paper. "Kids," she said, letting herself in.

All she wanted to do was flop down on the couch and rest from her ordeal. She would have much to tell Grayson. She regretted missing their rendezvous, but it couldn't be helped. On the way home from the shopping mall, she and Andi had witnessed a terrible accident. An older gentleman had lost control of his car and his El Dorado went careening into a Volkswagen Beetle. The driver and the passenger of the Beetle were pinned inside for what had seemed like an eternity.

The paramedics had to use the Jaws of Life to free the passenger from the wreckage. Sonji and Andi stayed at the scene to give statements to the police and to see if the accident victims were all right.

Miraculously, the driver and the passenger only suffered cuts and lacerations. The paramedics said that they would probably be released from the hospital the next day if not that evening. For a moment, Andi almost had Sonji convinced that the events they witnessed were a result of the bad omen from earlier coming to pass. When they found out that the people would be fine, including the driver that caused the accident, they both breathed a deep sigh of relief.

After hanging up her coat, Sonji decided to call Grayson and let him know why she wasn't home for their date. Before she could reach the phone, there was a knock at the door. *He must have come back,* she thought.

Sonji opened the door wide, and an unfamiliar woman was standing on the stairs. The woman looked harried and distraught.

"Is he here?" she asked and bounded into Sonji's town house.

"What the . . . ?" Sonji's shock and anger boiled into one. "Look, lady, I don't know who you are, but you'd better get out of my house, and I mean now."

The woman stepped nervously from side to side. "I'm Veranda Gilmore. Now is Grayson here or not?"

Sonji blinked and frowned as if she hadn't heard the woman correctly. "You're who?" she asked, feeling a queasiness building in her abdomen.

"Veranda Gilmore. My husband is Grayson Gilmore. Now where is—"

"Your husband!" Sonji swallowed hard. Déjà vu couldn't begin to describe the sick sense of repetition she felt occurring. As her queasiness intensified, she felt like everything that held her body together as a cohesive unit was falling away.

The woman before her looked as though she had spent the last few years of her life in constant tears. And she was sunken, frail-looking actually. Her close-cropped hair looked as though it could use a stiff combing. The only air of normalcy about her was the earrings she wore. They seemed out of place on her ears and . . . Oh, God! Sonji thought as the room spun beneath her. *They're scarabs.* The same kind of scarab as her necklace.

"Where is he?" Veranda insisted. "I must find him!"

Before the room could swallow up all of her air, Sonji answered the woman solemnly. "He's not here. I don't know where he is."

Veranda's hand flew to her mouth. "I must find him," she repeated and charged out Sonji's front door just as she had come in.

Sonji closed her eyes and gasped. A tidal wave of dizziness threatened to overpower her. She had full-blown nausea now. With tears flowing, she cradled her stomach and ran into the bathroom.

Fourteen

It was two hours before Sonji felt well enough to do anything besides lie down. After several bouts of nausea and vomiting, she believed her stomach was finally settling. It was flu season. And so far, Sonji hadn't had as much as the sniffles. *All good things must come to an end,* she thought, wincing. When she got up, she made herself some Alka-Seltzer and followed that with a cup of Andi's green tea.

Sonji released a deep and remorseful sigh. Love had made a fool of her once again. She couldn't fathom why she above all people had been singled out for such enormous pain. She knew if the doorbell rang again today, she would rip the chimes right off the wall. She wanted no more intruders in her life.

The tears came again, and she was powerless to stop them. They shook her body and made her gasp for air. She curled up into a ball on her couch and wondered how anyone could be so cruel.

The call of a train's lonely whistle reverberated in the distance. It was the last sound Sonji heard before drifting off to sleep. It seemed to her so hollow and ghostly, like the faint echo of a dream traveling to nowhere.

When Sonji awoke, it was evening. She sat up feeling much better. Andi's tea had done the trick.

Memories of the events of the day came rushing into her mind. But instead of tears, Sonji felt anger tightening her throat. "You need to be told where to go and what to take with you," she said, rising from the couch.

A quick change and Sonji was headed to Grayson's house. The car battery worked fine and installing it was just the occupation her hands needed. *Now I'll be less likely to choke you when I see you. Though you do deserve it.* Sonji had finally reached her boiling point. His betrayal was the last straw, and he wouldn't get away with it.

When Grayson opened the door, it took everything in Sonji's power not to slap his face.

"Exquisite timing," he said, smiling as if everything was okay between them. "I just arrived."

"I'm not staying long," she said through gritted teeth. "I just came to return this." Sonji snatched the scarab necklace from around her neck and threw it at him. "Give your wife back her jewelry!"

Grayson stared at her in shock. "My what?"

Sonji placed her hands on her hips. "I know all about Veranda, Grayson. And you know what? Men like you are sick, vile, and disgusting creatures. You don't deserve me or her or *any* woman for that matter. I hope you one day experience the same kind of hurt that you've made me feel. I . . . ." Sonji could feel the anguish churning inside her. It spilled out of her eyes and down her cheeks. She pointed an accusing finger at Grayson. "Don't you come near me ever again, you . . . you . . ."

"Sonji!" Grayson shouted grabbing her shoulders. "What in God's name are you talking about?"

"Grayson?" a weak voice came from inside the house. "Who's at the door, dear?"

Grayson spun around, releasing Sonji. "Veranda?" he said, mouth gaping. "How did you get here?"

"No!" Sonji said, wrenching herself from Grayson's grip. "The question is, how did *I* get here?" Sonji turned and ran to her car.

"Sonji!" Grayson yelled out, but to no avail. She started her car and sped away.

Veranda walked up to Grayson's side. She was holding a small, brown boy doll in her arms. "Darling, who was that?"

"Uh-oh," Nzinga said. She needed only one look at her granddaughter to know that something was mighty, mighty wrong.

When Sonji stepped into the house she enveloped her in her arms, swaying gently back and forth. She felt her granddaughter hug tighter and tighter. Nzinga gently stroked her curly head. When the sobs came, she shushed her like she had when Sonji was a little girl.

"Grandma's here, baby. Whatever it is, I won't let it hurt you no more. You just cry it all out. And when you're done, then be done with it, child."

Sonji's hold grew even tighter. "That's right. Now you just get all that sadness out. You hear? Get it all out."

After a few moments, they locked arms and walked into the kitchen.

"You don't have to tell ol' GrandmaZee about it, but sometimes talkin' is the best thing." They sat down and Nzinga crossed her arms over her hefty bosom. "Now is it that man of yours? 'Cause if it is, you know every couple gets dealt their share of rough times."

Sonji looked up with watery eyes. "He's married, Grandma."

"Humph. I'd say that's way too rough. Oh, I'm sorry, baby."

"Me too, Grandma. Me too."

"You want me to round up Cora and Estelle? We can go over there right now and give him a good talkin' to!"

The thought of her grandmother and company going over to Grayson's house to give them a piece of their wise, old minds struck Sonji as funny. It wasn't enough to make her laugh, but it did make her smile a little.

"You know in some African villages, the women would get together and handle a situation like this."

"They would?" Sonji asked, although she had heard the story numerous times. But her grandmother liked telling it. And she liked hearing it.

"Of course. There would be no relations with the men until the dirty scoundrel had been punished! Hee, hee, hee, hee." ZingaMae's shoulders rose and fell gently with her laughter. And Sonji's smile broadened just a bit.

"Now that's Momma's baby peekin' through that sadness. Let me whip up some banana pudding, and you can tell me all about the troubles you havin'."

While her grandmother cooked, Sonji told her the awful tale of her ordeal with Grayson's wife and her subsequent confrontation at his house. When she got to the part where she had been physically ill, her grandmother paused momentarily, gave her a swift appraisal, and returned to her cooking. Sonji ended her tale by talking about finals week and how she had worked so hard to get a decent grade in Grayson's class and how it had been all for nothing. She didn't see any way that she could possibly finish her final paper. Unfortunately it was worth thirty percent of her grade. She would have to repeat the class next semester.

"You mean you'd get left back?"

"No, GrandmaZee. Not exactly. I would just have to take the class again." Sonji was determined to register early so that she wouldn't have to take the class with Grayson.

"Sounds like bein' left back to me." Her grandmother stopped stirring the contents of the large bowl. "Sonji baby, you ain't never been left back before. Why can't you just go on and do your assignment?"

Sonji took a peek at her grandmother's concoction. As she looked over the bowl at the creamy banana mixture, the smell of vanilla and fresh fruit wafted in her direction. "I don't want to do anything that will remind me of him."

"Humph," Nzinga snorted. She resumed her stirring. "Sounds to me like you givin' up."

"Grandma . . ."

"Don't Grandma me. I have a good mind to keep this banana pudding all for myself."

Sonji leaned back in surprise.

"That's right. Things is comin' too easy for you, little girl." She stirred the contents of the bowl more vigorously. "Them other classes you told me about, you had no problems with them, did you?"

Sonji shook her head.

"But this man's class, you been complainin' about from the get-go. See, Sonji baby, when it's something you have to struggle with, that's when your heart will tell you what kind of person you are."

Sonji realized that the well of her tears was bottomless, and they were threatening to overtake her again.

"The question you need to ask yourself is, who are you doing this for? When you started school, you were doing it to get back at that no-goodnik, Chad. When you stayed in school, you did it for Mr. Appetite Gilmore. Somewhere in all this, you gotta find *you*. When you do that, then nothing will keep you from wanting to do your best. Because you'll be doing it for yourself."

Nzinga poured the pudding into a baking dish lined with vanilla wafers. "You see, sweetie?"

Sonji held her tears at bay. "I see, GrandmaZee."

"Good. Now get outta that chair and help me with this pudding."

Kyle sat on the sofa in anguish. It pained him terribly to see Grayson so tormented. He had been at his brother's house all afternoon, watching the man he had looked up to all his life pace and shout. Occasionally he threw a book or whatever happened to be within reach. Luckily nothing was physically broken. But Grayson's sensibilities were in desperate need of repair.

"I know what it is. The world has just gone completely mad! That's what it is."

"Why do you think that, Gray?"

Grayson pointed an angry finger at Kyle. "Don't you even try that psychologist crap with me! I don't deserve that."

"I'm just trying to help, here."

"The only person who can help me won't even speak to me."

Kyle scratched his head. "Then why did you call me?"

"I called you because you're a good listener. And right now I need to be listened to."

Grayson's brother crossed one leg over the other.

Grayson relaxed his shoulders just slightly. "I called

because you're my brother. Can you be a brother now? Not Dr. Gilmore. Just Kyle Ellington."

"Yeah," Kyle said, relenting easily. "I can do that."

"Thank you."

"Okay, man. Start from the beginning. I need to listen with a different ear this time."

Grayson recoiled. How often would he have to re-live this nightmare? He sat down in a chair across from his brother and began again.

When Sonji came over, he had just come back from running at the gym. Since they had missed their engagement, he had taken that opportunity to get in some track time. He was feeling invigorated and re-freshed. When he saw Sonji standing at the door, he hoped she had found the earrings he had left in the mailbox.

And then came the accusations.

"Kyle, I couldn't figure out for the life of me what she was talking about." Grayson rubbed the sides of his temples with the palms of his hands. "That's when I discovered that Veranda was in the house."

"Gray, if that had been me, I would have jumped out of my skin seeing her there."

"That was nearly the case. And don't ask how, but she found a doll. It must have been somewhere in the house."

"Oh, damn."

"Tell me about it. She must have hidden it before she went to the hospital. But seeing her with that doll . . . it was like she had never gone to the hospital at all. I expected to look around the living room and see it full of all those dolls she bought before the breakdown."

"Did you go after Sonji?"

"Go after Sonji? Man, by that time, I was trying to go after my mind. Because I was surely losing it."

"How did Veranda get in the house?"

"She's had the keys to the house in her purse since she went into the hospital. I just never thought to take them back. I mean . . . I couldn't." Grayson shook his head. "Who knew that something like this could happen?"

"And the hospital just let her go? She just walked out?"

"She just walked out. She's been a voluntary patient—up until now. So she was never in a locked facility."

Grayson got up and resumed his pacing. "Somehow she must have followed me to Sonji's house and accosted her. I don't even know what she said. But I know one thing. I'm going to make Sonji know the truth if I have to camp out on her steps for weeks."

"Now wait a minute, big brother," Kyle said, frowning. "Haven't you been seeing the girl for a while?"

Grayson didn't like the way Kyle used the word *girl,* but he answered his question. "Most of the semester. Why?"

"Well it seems to me that if she really cared about you, she would have given you the benefit of the doubt."

Grayson stopped in his tracks. "What are you saying?"

Kyle sat back against the sofa. "I'm saying that she can't be all that if she was so quick to judge you without hearing your side. Maybe you should be glad she's gone."

"Now look here, little brother." Grayson snatched the collar of his brother's shirt, jerking him upwards. "You will not ever again in life disrespect Sonji Stephens. Do you hear me?"

Kyle's eyes widened.

"I love that woman, and she loves me. And if she'll

have me, I'm going to make her my wife. Which," he said, releasing his grip on Kyle's shirt, "will make her your sister-in-law. You got that?"

Kyle smoothed the front of his clothing. "Got it," he said, smiling.

"What's that grin for?"

"For the psychology you told me not to use. I just wanted to see if you were serious about her or if you were still grieving over the idea of suffering another loss."

"What!"

"Besides," Kyle said, standing. "I owed you one for Jerika."

"You're never going to let me get past that, are you?"

Kyle slapped his brother across the back. "Not on your life. Now, let's figure out a plan to get my future sister-in-law to talk to you. You say she won't answer the phone or come to the door."

"That's right. The last time I knocked on her door, I thought she was going to call the police on me."

"Then we need a different approach."

Grayson saw a familiar look in his brother's eyes. It was the same look he had as a child when Kyle was about to stir up some mischief. Usually, he got blamed for whatever his little brother did, but today, the promise in that look gave him hope of winning back the woman he loved.

For the first time in two days, Grayson felt hopeful. He and Kyle had talked at length about all the things he might do to get Sonji back. Although he wasn't quite sure what approach he would take, he was certain that he would not give her up without at least trying to salvage what they had.

Grayson pushed his chair away from his desk and looked at his appointment schedule. For finals week, it was unusually light. Only a few students seemed to require his attention. This was a welcome change from the usual hustle and bustle of the semester end. Typically, there was a monolith of papers to grade and back-to-back appointments with students who wanted to know what they could do in the final hour to bring their grades up. This semester it appeared he would be able to grade all his papers during office hours instead of having to take them home to finish.

When the phone rang, it startled Grayson as he realized that even lurking in between his thoughts of students and grading papers, his relationship with Sonji occupied his mind, demanding to be put center stage.

"Gilmore speaking."

"Grayson."

He recognized the voice of the Clarence Waters, the Dean of Arts and Sciences.

"Clarence. What can I do for you?"

"I'd like you to come to my office. We have a situation here."

"A situation?" Grayson asked, sitting bone-straight in his chair. "What kind of situation?"

"The kind you need to come to my office for. See you in ten."

Grayson heard the click of the phone line as it disconnected. *See me in ten,* he thought. *You'll see me right now.* He got up from his chair and headed out into the hallway.

Less than a minute later, he was in the dean's office. Valencia Tyree, Clarence's secretary, was where she had always been for the last fifteen years. She smiled brightly at Grayson.

"Professor Gilmore."

"Good morning, Valencia. Clarence is expecting me."

"Go right in then, professor."

Grayson walked in without stopping. The dean of the college was seated behind a massive mahogany desk. His high-backed leather chair swallowed the diminutive man with its fullness. The chair's bright red color was a startling contrast to the browns and blacks of the other furniture in the room.

"You said there was a situation," Grayson said, raising an eyebrow.

"Yes. Please, have a seat."

"If you don't mind, I'd rather stand."

"Suit yourself. Here," the man said, handing Grayson a folded piece of paper.

Grayson drew the paper up to examine it. "What's this?"

The dean remained silent as Grayson read though the ten-page document. It only took a few moments, but when he finished, he took a seat in the dean's office after all.

Grayson was fuming. His first reaction was to rip the accusatory note to shreds. He ran a hand though the waves in his hair.

"What do you propose we do about this . . . situation?" Grayson asked, anger lowering his voice.

"That's why I called you. I want to hear your side of it."

"My side of it is that these kids have too much time on their hands. They should be studying instead of writing nonsensical garbage like this. Or perhaps they should have taken a creative writing class, because this is the worst piece of fiction I've seen in a long time."

"You deny their allegations?"

"Emphatically!"

"So if I were to ask you if you were passing off`

insignificant writers as writers of merit, you would say . . ."

"Absolutely not."

"And if I were to inquire about the significance and application of your required readings, you would respond . . ."

"My students are provided with a rich resource of readings and activities that contribute to a well-balanced appreciation of twentieth century literature."

"And if I were to challenge that balance by pointing out that you have no writers of European decent featured in your class . . ."

"Look, Clarence. I won't lie and say that I'm teaching an ordinary lit course. Most literature classes present dead white men as the canon literati. I presented the best of the best in this class. They just happen to be people of color. But great literature is great literature, no matter where it comes from."

"You have a point, professor. I will take your position under advisement before I make my decision."

"Decision? Decision to what?"

"My decision on whether to formerly reprimand you for your teaching strategy in the class."

Grayson was flabbergasted. First Sonji, now this.

"Clarence, you can't be serious."

"I'm afraid I am, Grayson. These are some serious charges here."

"Then at least let me face my accusers. If they were bold enough to sign that letter, they should be bold enough to take it up with me."

"I don't know. That's highly irregular."

"Is there anything in that letter that states that they would rather not confront me?"

"I think the mere fact that they wrote a letter in the first place says it all."

"Well, then ask them! Hell, demand that they say these things to my face!"

"Calm down, Gilmore. You know I can't force them to do anything, especially if they specifically ask that they not have to address you." Clarence rubbed the top of his small head. "But I can ask them if they would agree to a meeting. How's that?"

"Better than nothing I suppose."

"Fine. I'll have Valencia contact you if it gets set up. Otherwise, you and I will be meeting again, privately."

"I understand."

When Byron burst into the MSO office, the students inside were busily preparing organizational reports for the end of the semester. As president, Sebastian was reading and signing. As secretary, Andi was typing and printing. As a new member, Sonji was copying and filing.

Ricardo was assembling the signed reports into documents to be filed with the student government. He saw the expression on Byron's face and became concerned. "Can we help you, man?"

"I think something terrible is about to happen, and I'm going to try to stop it." Byron let his backpack slide from his shoulder and slam to the ground.

Sebastian perked up from his seat behind the desk. Several other students who had been studying in the back turned in Byron's direction.

Sonji had never seen Byron in such a state, not even when he thought he might flunk out of English class. "Byron, what is it?"

"It's Professor Gilmore."

Andi and Sebastian glanced in Sonji's direction. Sonji closed her eyes.

Sebastian rose from his seat. "What about Professor Gilmore?"

"A guy from his literature class told me that some of the students have lodged a complaint against him. They've accused him of being a racist."

"A racist?" Andi said, surprised.

"That's ridiculous!" came Capiz's outraged response.

Byron raised his hand. "Hold on. Here's the head-splitter. There's some sort of a hearing today. And Professor Gilmore is going up against a bunch of students in the dean's office."

This time Henry piped up. "That's not fair."

"Yeah. I mean, it sounds like he's being freight-trained."

The students in the office shot curious looks at Andi. Sebastian just smiled. "That's railroaded, baby."

"That's what I thought too." Byron said. "So I'm going up there. Professor Gilmore needs somebody to represent his side of things."

"Now hold on . . . Byron, is it? You can't go charging into the dean's office like that."

"I know. I was hoping to take some folks with me. Professor Gilmore may be hard-boiled, but he's no racist."

"I'll go," Jesus said from the back.

"Me too," replied LaShay.

"I'm there," Andi said.

Sebastian held up his arms in a gesture to quell the incited students. "Before we all go storming off to demand justice, we need some kind of plan. And we need an all-student effort. Not just the students of color."

"Byron, did this person tell you what time the meeting was?"

"Two o'clock."

"Good. That gives us just about an hour to round up some other students and to strategize."

"What is there to strategize?"

"We can't just show up and then when they call him a racist say 'No, he's not' and leave it at that. We need to think through our response, so that it has conviction and merit."

Henry walked briskly toward the door. "How about if Andi, Jesus, and I round up all the students we can find who will support PG? The rest of you can stay here and work on a plan."

Sebastian made a deferring nod toward Byron.

"That sounds good," Byron said.

During the entire interaction, Sonji remained transfixed in her seat. Grayson was a one-hundred-percent Neandrathal, but a racist? Never. Her loathing for his behavior in their relationship grappled with her respect for him as a teacher. How could a man be so good at some things, and so poor at others?

Three MSO members left the office quickly and the remaining students huddled together. All except Sonji.

"Miss Sonji, we're going to need your help," Sebastian said, looking in her direction. If you don't mind me saying so, you probably know him better than all of us combined."

Sonji's stomach did a somersault. Who was the bad penny now? she wondered.

"Sebastian, I'm afraid I can't help you. You all will have to plan Grayson's rescue on your own." She gathered her books and papers and walked out of the office.

Not one more thing, Grayson thought pacing in his office. Not one more thing can go wrong. "I won't let it!" he said to the empty air.

When it rained in his world, there always seemed to be a hurricane not far behind. So far, Veranda had found her way out of the hospital, Sonji had cast him aside like an old sock, his students had accused him of the unthinkable, and to nail the lid on the coffin, one of his crabs had died.

Well, Grayson had had enough. And if the dean and those accusatory students wanted a fight, he was in the mood to give them one, a good one. It was a hard lesson, but Grayson had learned it. Like in the book *Beloved*, when you cling to a dead past, it's bound to come back to haunt you. He knew now what he had to do, and as soon as this business with the dean was finished, he would take care of things once and for all.

When Grayson walked into the dean's office, the offending students were already there. He glanced at the clock: 1:50. If he was early, what did that make these students? Misled, he thought and stood near the dean's desk.

"Sit down, professor," Dean Waters ordered.

"I'll stand, thank you."

The students sat across from where he was standing. They looked agitated and slightly fidgety. All except for Bill. He looked as sedate as a medicated patient at Staupers Hospital. *So that's who's behind this,* Grayson mused.

"You know the students?"

"Yes, Dean."

"Bill Hoft, Mary Carl, Pat Wilkens, and Ted Maten have filed a formal grievance against you, professor. Do you understand the nature of their complaint?"

Grayson crossed his arms in front of him. "I know what they wrote in the letter."

"Good. Good. Then the purpose of this meeting is to allow both parties to present their side of the issue in question. After hearing from you, I will make a decision whether to pursue further action or simply to add the memo to the professor's personnel record. Do you all understand?"

"Yes!" Bill said, seemingly speaking for all of the students.

"I understand, Dean Waters."

"Very well. Let's begin with you, Mr. Hoft. Will you please review the contents of this document?"

Bill passed a condescending glance over Grayson and then began. "Well, it's like we said in the memo, Dean Waters. All semester, the man has been teaching us with inferior materials. He's been requiring us to read obscure authors. I mean his whole teaching methods have been, well . . . not conducive to a proper learning environment."

Grayson didn't want to hurt the boy. He really didn't. But he could visualize his fingers tightening around his neck, real easy. The kid was obviously distraught about something, perhaps his own ignorance. And although all of the authors in the literature class were people of color, Grayson knew his teaching methods were sound. He would bet his life on that.

"Do any of the rest of you have anything to add?"

The students with Bill Hoft shrugged their shoulders. Then one of them spoke. "We agree with Bill. The guy's topics were lame."

"Yeah," another student said. "He's just an inferior teacher, and I haven't learned anything worth applying. How can studying someone named Zora Neale Hastings possibly help me in the real world?"

"That's Hurston," Byron said, entering the Dean's office. "And if you knew anything about social anthropology, you'd understand that chronicling a people's folklore is the doorway into preserving and studying culture."

Fifteen other students followed behind him. They filled the Dean's office like a world rainbow.

The dean rose from his chair. "You weren't invited to this meeting. You students will have to leave."

Sebastian spoke up then. "We leave when they leave."

Fifteen

Grayson stood with his mouth gaping open. He couldn't believe what he was seeing. The multicultural coalition that he had been trying to build in his classroom was standing at his side.

Byron spoke again. "We believe that Professor Gilmore is underrepresented at this meeting, so we decided to level the playing field."

A miracle. He was witnessing a miracle. Grayson shook his head and blinked. No, he was not dreaming it. The very students that had labeled him everything except Grayson the Good were standing up for him. Maybe things weren't has bleak as he had earlier imagined. Despite this wonderful turn of events, he couldn't help wondering about Sonji. She had obviously not accompanied the others in his defense. He wondered what she was doing.

"Are you crazy!" Bill shouted at the dean. "They can't just come in here like that!" He was on his feet huffing and puffing like a spoiled child. His fists were balled at his sides, and he was turning as red as Louisiana hot sauce.

"Yes, they can," Grayson said. "This is a public disclosure. Any student on campus is welcome."

"Dean Waters, all fifteen of us are here to tell you that Professor Gilmore is not a racist. If he were a racist, he would have been turned in a long time ago, by any one of us." Byron gave the students from the literature class the once-over. "Now don't misunderstand me. The man is no walk in the park. If you don't give each assignment your all, he'll let you know. I've never worked so hard for a B in my life!" Byron smiled at Grayson, and Grayson smiled back. "But everything he does, he does because he cares—about all of us surviving that thing they call the real world. He's just helping us make our own life jackets."

Bill appeared livid, now. The students with him were more agitated than ever. "Jesus holy Christ!"

After Byron's inspired speech, Grayson felt compelled to speak on his own behalf. "I make no apologies for the passion I have for literature and writing. The day I stop feeling passionate about the subjects I teach is the day I stop teaching." He gave an acknowledging glance to the students at his side. "My goal is not unlike the goal of my colleagues, not unlike your goal, Dean Waters, to make a difference in the lives of others. To inspire them, to stimulate them, to fuel their curiosity. Sometimes, my zest for doing so may cause me to seem a bit overbearing."

"That is so true!"

Grayson smiled in Andi's direction. "Thank you, Miss Simmons."

"Are you going to let this *incompetent* continue?"

"Easy, Mr. Hoft. You've had your say. Let him have his."

"I may have been overzealous when creating the curriculum for the Twentieth Century Literature course, but my objective was a simple one—to provide my students with a rich experience like none they have encountered, an experience that would open their eyes to new possibilities. And to help them be more coming out of the class than they were coming in."

The dean took a deep breath and released it. "I see." He looked at the students who had come to Grayson's aid. "What I need is a document that attests to the professional nature of Professor Grayson's teaching. Are you prepared to deliver that?"

"It's already done," came a voice from the back of the room. Grayson's heart beat double time at the sound.

The MSO students and their friends stepped aside as Sonji Stephens approached the dean with a memo in her hand.

"And you are?" The dean asked, curiosity furrowing his brow. "I'm one of Professor Gilmore's students. And this," she said, handing the dean the memo, "is a letter stating the ways in which he enlightened his students and dedicated himself to raising their level of performance. Even if his methodology seemed rather strict. Everyone here," she said, motioning toward the students near Grayson, "will sign it."

"They can't do that!" Bill insisted.

"The thing is, Mr. Hoft, if I let your little group submit a document and not let this group submit a document, *that* might be called racism."

Dean Waters stepped back and addressed the entire group. "I thank you all for taking the time to address this issue today. I will review these two documents and contact the primary parties involved when I've made a decision."

"This is outrageous! I came here to see him squirm the way he makes me squirm every time he holds up those stupid writers like the rest of us are supposed to bow down or something."

"Contain yourself, Mr. Hoft!"

"No," Grayson said, moving closer to the student.

"Let him continue, so we'll all know who the *real* racist is."

"Why you black mother—!"

"That's it!" Byron said, lunging for Bill.

Grayson grabbed him and held him in check. "I've spent my life trying to turn people to the truth." He realized with dreadful finality that some people could not be saved.

The other students with Bill Hoft restrained him, while Dean Waters called campus security. In a matter of minutes, Bill was being escorted off campus.

"That young man is so expelled, it's not even funny. I apologize for all of this, Grayson," the dean said.

"No apology necessary. You did what you had to do."

Hoft's other cronies had exited when he did. And that left Grayson with the MSO Students and company. He quickly expressed his gratitude and shook the hands of all the students there. All except Sonji. She refused his hand when he offered it. As the others began a congratulatory banter while leaving the office, Grayson jogged to catch up with Sonji, who was well ahead of the crowd. "Sonji, wait!"

"Leave me alone, Grayson. I didn't show up here for you."

"No?" he said, catching up with her. "I want to thank you anyway."

"Don't bother. I came because of me, so get over yourself."

"But there's so much to tell you. So much to explain."

"Save it for your wife!" Sonji spat out, increasing her pace.

"Ex-wife," Grayson responded.

Sonji refused to look at him. "That doesn't explain why she was at your house."

"She has . . . had a key."

"A key!" Sonji took a corner fast and nearly collided with a custodian. Now she was running.

Grayson stopped. He couldn't keep up. All of his recent life events had exhausted him. "Sonji, Veranda's ill!"

"You're the one who's ill, Grayson!"

A couple of seconds later, Byron had caught up with him. He saw the look in Professor Gilmore's face and recognized it as the look he must have worn when Sonji turned him down on the dance floor of the Pantheon gala. He wrapped a brotherly arm around his instructor's shoulder.

"You look like you could use a stiff drink."

"Man, you said it."

"I know the location of a great juice bar. They make this concoction called Face Up. I have no idea what's in it, but it's supposed to improve your mood."

Grayson almost smiled. "Lead the way."

"I should have done this a long time ago."

Dr. Hoffman sat at her desk across from a dejected Grayson Gilmore. "Grayson, it's not good to second-guess your decisions."

"I know."

"I'm not going to step lightly here. Your wife has suffered a serious reversion."

Grayson nodded.

"We've moved her to the guarded wing of the facility, and we've increased the dosage of her medication."

Grayson ran a hand down the front of his face. "She seemed so lucid when I brought her in. She looked at me and the clouds were almost gone from her eyes." He looked up at the ceiling, noticing with perfect clarity that the paint that was curling in some spots and completely absent from others. "She said, 'I keep remembering it, even when I don't want to.' And then she just broke down. I had to carry her in."

"Veranda's a fighter. She hasn't given up on her recovery. We see it often—the old Veranda peeking through the tormented surface. That's what gives us hope that one day she will recover completely." Dr. Hoffman leaned forward in her chair.

"But I won't paint any false pictures for you. Veranda is suffering from acute post-traumatic stress disorder. Right now, she feels extreme guilt, and she's on a mission to roll back time. Our job is to continue to help her release the guilt and keep her energies focused on the present."

"That sounds a lot like the first discussion you and I had."

"I wish I could say it wasn't. We may be starting from scratch. At this point, we don't know."

Grayson was still for a few comfortless moments. Then he reached beside him and retrieved his briefcase. When he opened it, he took out a small stack of papers and handed it to Dr. Hoffman.

"This is the annuity contract I mentioned. It belonged to Veranda's father. He died shortly after she was hospitalized. Before he passed away, he asked me to use this money to take care of any expenses. It matured just a few months ago, and since then I've been struggling with turning it over to you."

Dr. Hoffman nodded slowly. "It must be saddening for you. You've taken care of her for so long."

"I know," Grayson said. "But like Veranda, it's time for me to focus my energies on the present."

"A wise decision, professor."

Grayson stood and extended his hand. "I would still like to visit from time to time."

The doctor smiled. "As soon as she's up to seeing you, we will contact you."

"Thank you, doctor." Grayson turned to go.

She offered him a knowing smile. "Good luck, Grayson."

It was the seventh book she had started reading in three hours. This one was on the Maroons—slaves who had escaped and established thriving communities. Sonji's eyes scanned the words, but comprehension was a distant wish. Why had she waited so long to do her research paper?

It was no use. She couldn't focus. Images of her in Grayson's arms, then him in his wife's arms, invaded her thoughts. "Snake!" she yelled, hurling the book across the table and onto the floor. Several students glanced in her direction.

"Sorry," she said and picked up another book in her pile. This one was entitled *When You're the Village: A Single Parent's Guide to Raising Healthy Children.*

"I thought I might find you here."

Byron's familiar voice lifted Sonji's spirits somewhat.

"What are you doing here, Byron?"

He handed her the book she had tossed away. She took it and placed it on top of the one she'd just been reading. "I've been appointed deputy in charge of book protection."

Sonji felt the first stirrings of a smile.

"Madam, you've been accused of the inappropriate throwing of a book in a public place. How do you plead?"

"Guilty." It was there now, a full-fledged smile. In a moment it would be a silly grin.

"Very well. I sentence you to one year's reshelving duty at the Barnett University library." Byron sat down at the table with her. "I e-mailed you several times, but you never responded."

Sonji lowered her head. "I know. I've been . . . pre-occupied lately."

"I'm sure this is going to sound selfish as hell, but I really wanted you to review my research paper before I turned it in. I've gotten used to your feedback on our assignments."

"I can read it now," she said, grateful for the distraction.

"Thanks, but I already turned it in. I've always been fascinated by weather. So, I did my report on global warming."

Sonji nodded.

"What did you do yours on?"

The smile drained from her face. She tapped her pencil on the table. The rubber eraser made a dull thud against the wood. "I haven't decided yet. I keep changing my mind."

The warm brown coloring drained from Byron's face. "You're kidding."

"I wasn't even going to do a research paper until today."

"Sonji, tomorrow is the last day to—"

"I know. I know. As soon as I narrow down a subject, I'll get started. And write all night if I have to."

Byron glanced at the pile of books on the table. "What can I do to help?"

"How about if you bring me some more books on this subject?" Sonji reached over and picked a book out of the pile of many.

Byron read the title. *"As Punishment.* What's it about?"

"It's an exposé on crimes that take place in jails and penitentiaries."

"Hmm. Angela Davis must have had an impact on you."

"You can say that again."

Byron wrote the call number down and handed the book back to Sonji. "I'll go see what I can find."

For the first time that afternoon. Sonji dared to feel hopeful about her assignment. "Thanks, Byron."

While Sonji skimmed the chapters of the book, Byron went off in search of others. Several times she came across an important idea or concept. When she did, she would place a Post-it note on that page and write a few notes in her note book. By the time Byron returned, she had the beginnings of an outline.

"That section of books is huge," he said, smiling. "But I found five books that I thought really addressed some of the issues Angela brought up in her speech." He set them on the table and took a seat opposite her.

She looked up, encouraged. "This book focuses on the definition and role of punishment in a capitalist society. The author draws some interesting conclusions about when punishment becomes something else."

"Like what?"

Sonji glanced down at her notes, feeling a bit flushed. "Like castigation or vengeance."

"Kinda like what you're doing to Professor Gilmore."

The pencil in Sonji's hand snapped. "What are you really doing here, Byron?"

Byron let out a long breath. "I came to see if I could talk some sense into you."

"You'd be better off minding your own business. I thought we were friends."

"That's exactly why I came. Because we are friends. And I don't want to see you discard your future happiness."

"Listen—"

"No, you listen. I've seen the way you look at Professor Gilmore. Heck, everyone's seen it. And more important right now, I've seen the way he looks at you."

"Have you seen the way he lies to me? Now that's a sight to witness!"

Byron got up, walked to the other side of the table, and sat down beside her. "Sonji, PG never lied to you. And regardless of what you may think, he is not married."

Sonji felt her face getting warmer. She tried to brace herself against the headache she felt coming.

"The woman you saw—Veranda—she is Grayson's ex-wife and she is also a patient at Staupers Hospital. She's very disturbed, Sonji."

"Having made Grayson Gilmore's intimate acquaintance, I can see why! Now if you please, Mr. Moore, I have work to do."

Byron stood and gave Sonji a concerned look. "Good luck with your paper."

As he walked off, Sonji rose quickly and headed for the rest room. By the time she got there, her head was spinning and her stomach was determined to show her who was the boss.

Sonji sat in front of her new computer. A couple of weeks ago she had decided to take out a loan from the credit union at her company and purchase a computer to replace her old one, which, as it turned out, wasn't worth repairing. She figured if she was going to spend the money, she might as well go all out. So she had her new computer loaded with the latest in word processing, research, and Internet applications. It came complete with a printer, scanner, and digital camera.

If it hadn't been for her impulsive decision to buy,

she knew she wouldn't be able to finish her research paper. A quick glance at the wall clock told her that it was 3:30 A.M. She had been working for more than twelve hours straight. After she had regained her composure in the library, she had checked out the books Byron found for her and came home.

She defined, described, and cited the ramification of the prison industrial complex. Her thesis statement was that corporations benefit substantially from the prison system. In proving her thesis, she then identified ways that punishment had become profitable. Overall, she was satisfied with what she had come up with. And although she knew she would be mule-tired tomorrow, she was determined to finish her paper. And not only finish it, but get a good grade on it.

A deep yawn overtook her. She stood and stretched. Just a little while longer, she told herself. Sonji walked to the fridge. She was dying for a diet soda, but she reached for the orange juice instead. She filled her glass and returned to work on her paper.

Sonji reviewed her notes. So far, she had followed her outline and presented strong arguments in identifying the legal definition of punishment and explaining the difference between a criminal going to jail *as* punishment and, what so often happened, going to jail *for* punishment. Now all she had to do was describe her idea for correcting both the perception and administration of punishment. She had planned to end her report with a call to action.

When she finally finished and read over the nine pages she had written, she felt better about this paper than any she had written previously. She had found a way to channel her anger and hurt into something positive. She felt an A coming for certain.

* * *

He could barely see in front of him. It was too cloudy, too foggy, too misty. All he could make out was shadows, curling around him, making him spin and lose his sense of direction.

Where? he asked in his mind. Turning. Walking. Searching. He was traveling through layers of confusion and doubt. The road was bumpy and uneven under his feet. But something beyond his own comprehension drove him on. Where? he called.

It was as if the night was disguised, wearing some obscure veil, concealing everything around him. No stars. The clouds were the brightest objects in the sky. Still he knew he had to press on. "Where are you!" he shouted. His voice echoed in front of him. As if watching himself on a screen, he could make out black-and-white images of himself, alone and searching. Around every corner, there was nothing. In every room, there was nothing. Behind smoke and curtains of mist, still nothing. And after endless walking and running, the object of his pursuit was nowhere to be found.

Oh, God, please, he said rushing forward. *Please, I can't lose her. I can't.* He drove faster into the darkness and his search increased. He could almost feel her presence. He could sense that her heart was lurking someplace in the dark night. If only, through his haggard rummaging, he could see her, touch her, taste her once again. His soul-quest would be over, and he would wander no more.

"Sonji!" he yelled, wrenching himself out of a deep sleep. He sat up slowly and swiped the sweat from around his neck. Grayson Gilmore looked at the cold, empty space beside him in the bed. "Sonji," he said softly.

"Hello?"
"Miss Sonji!"

Sonji smiled at the sound of Andi's familiar innocence-rich voice. She had long given up the idea that Andi, or for that matter Sebastian, would call her anything other than Miss Sonji. She wasn't sure if it suited her, but she was certain that it suited them.

"What's up, Andi?"

"I called to ask you that. Are you coming? Because we need to give LaShay a count. She's cooking, you know."

Sonji removed her propped feet from the ottoman and sat up. "Coming to what?"

"Our Kwanzaa celebration. Sebastian and I have one every year. Didn't you get our e-mail?"

Sonji hadn't looked at her e-mail in more than a week. She hadn't felt much like being on the Internet. "I haven't read my e-mail in days. I'm sorry. When is your celebration?"

"It's at Sebastian's, next Friday. It starts at six."

Sonji hadn't felt much like celebrating anything recently. Since her breakup with Grayson, down in the dumps didn't begin to describe her mood. *At some point, I'm going to have to rejoin the land of the living,* she thought. *Just not now.* "Thanks for the invite, but maybe some other time."

"But there isn't any other time. Unless you mean next year."

"Well, for this celebration, I guess it's going to have to be next year."

"Gee. It sounds like someone bought a ticket on the bitter bus!"

"I have a right to be bitter, Andi."

"Well, suit yourself. But holding grudges only causes ulcers."

Sonji wasn't sure how to respond to that. After a moment of silence, Andromeda spoke again.

"Well, in case you change your mind, I'll send you

a reminder about the celebration. So check your e-mail, okay?"

"Okay."

Sonji hung up the phone and stretched. She had been neglectful of a lot of things recently. She hadn't gone out except to school, work, and the store. She had only called her grandmother twice that week, and the leaves of her plants drooped like sad lips. She picked up the nearby watering can and filled it. She added a few drops of fertilizer and gave her fern and rubber plant what their dry roots needed.

Finishing her task, she headed to her bedroom and sat at her computer. Turning it on, she decided then and there that her moping must end. She had indulged herself in the mourning of her relationship long enough. Any more grieving would drown her forever. Andi was probably right about the ulcers. Although her upset stomach lately was due to something else entirely.

Sonji activated her ISP and selected *BlackLuv.net* from her bookmarks. When the familiar screen loaded, she recoiled and vowed to get another free e-mail account that day. She would notify all of her Internet friends and give them her address change as soon as she had a new one.

A couple more clicks, and Sonji was into her account, scrolling through the letters waiting to be read. Some of them were SPAM. Ever since the guys who created the site listed it on major search engines, suddenly the junk mail came soon after. There was a note from Byron. Sonji opened it.

One more thing and then I'll leave it alone. I know a good thing when I see it. Do you?

Sonji huffed and clicked Delete. A couple more SPAM letters: *Lose 20 lbs. in one week. 30 Hours free and then 2 cents per minute.* And one that just had a series of x's in the subject line. Then there was a letter from Andromeda marked INVITATION. She was about to open it when the sound of a knock came through her speakers. Surprised, Sonji sat back and stared at the screen. Then a box appeared. The top read DIGITAL DISPATCH. A message scrolled across the inside.

Greetings, Nzinga! This message is from Handley, one of the site designers. How are you today?

After Sonji's initial shock, she realized that this must be the moderator that Andi had told her about. Thinking back to the botched relationship she had with Grayson, she didn't think any form of intervention could have helped them. She hoped she could make this quick. In the response box, she typed,

Fine. What can I do for you, Handley?

His reply came seconds later.

Part of your agreement as a BlackLuv member states that you will make yourself available to periodic surveys and questionnaires by me, the MatchMaker.

Too little, too late, Sonji thought. *"Thanks anyway, but I no longer require your matchmaking services. And as of today, I will be utilizing another service for my e-mail."*

Oh, that's too bad. Came the response. *Then our correspondence now is more important than ever. We pride ourselves on customer care and our ability to provide the most professional personals service on the Web. Would you mind taking a few moments to give us your opinion of your experience as a network member?*

Sonji thought for a moment and decided to go on with the questionnaire.

All right.

Wonderful. Let me just start by asking about the layout and navigation of the site. How would you rate it? Exceptional, Satisfactory, or Poor?

Sonji glanced at the color scheme and the arrangement of objects, text, and buttons. She had seen better, but it was obvious that the designers had put a lot of thought into it.

Satisfactory, she typed.

How about your ability to send and receive e-mail? Exceptional, Satisfactory, or Poor?

Exceptional. She was very pleased with the service.

And our personals service. How would you rate the number of potential correspondents?

Exceptional. There were a lot.

Did your profile provide you with someone to correspond with?

Sonji's jaw tightened. *Yes.*

And for archival purposes, did you find him attractive?

She thought that a rather odd question to ask. *Yes.*

And did you by any chance meet your correspondent in person?

Yes.

And your initial meeting, was it Exceptional, Satisfactory, or Poor?

Thoughts of their passion-consumed kiss in the middle of the street gave her goose bumps. Memories of the sensuous assault of his touch on her body made her tingle in places she hadn't thought of in days.

Nzinga?

Exceptional, she typed, honestly.

And because so many of our matches become couples as a result of our service, I must ask you this. Do you love him?

Her fingers quickly typed *no,* but stopped before pressing the Enter key. As hard as she had tried to cleanse her soul of Grayson's hold upon it, she had been ineffective. After images of their lovemaking lingered with her like infinite echoes of the past. One of the reasons she stayed so close to home was that so many things reminded her of him.

Nzinga . . .

The kids playing reminded her of the child he had lost. The people holding hands in the park revived her starving erogenous zones and made them throb for his touch.

The heavy traffic made her reflect on the time she and Grayson were stuck in traffic and decided to take the opportunity to kiss like teenagers.

Nzinga?

She could only imagine what would have happened in his car if the traffic hadn't started flowing again.

Sonji!

I can't agonize over this anymore, she thought. "Snap out of it," she said, refocusing on the screen. When she saw the moderator's response, she blinked. *Oh, my God . . . how does he know my name?* Quickly she clicked her mouse and left the Web site. Startled and shaken, she signed off of the Internet and shut down her computer.

Something's wrong. She could feel it. Her skin prickled as if the air had just been iced. When her doorbell rang, she jumped straight up out of her chair. Cautiously, she approached her front door. She looked through the peep hole, and a hurricane of emotions nearly levitated her off the ground. Anger. Relief. Resentment. Gratitude. She was almost dizzy. Slowly she opened the door.

"How did you do it?"

For a split second, Grayson considered not telling her, and then banished the thought. From his inside pocket he pulled out a handheld computer the size of a thin paperback book. He flipped up the antenna.

"It's wireless," he said.

"So is this something else about you that I don't know? Now you're a personals moderator?"

"No, Sonji. It was the only way I could think of to contact you. To get you to see that we've made a mistake."

"We!"

"Sonji, at least let me come in. It's cold out here."

Sonji supposed that the only way for her to get him out of her system for good was to have some sort of closure. Otherwise, she'd never be able to leave the house without thoughts of him cloying at her subconscious. "It's even colder in here," she said, letting him in.

How long had it been? Two weeks since they'd been this close? It seemed to Grayson like two lifetimes. And now more than ever he had to be rational and reasonable and talk this thing through when all he really wanted to do was reach out, pull her into his arms, and hold her forever—or at least until she came to her senses.

"Do you have something to say, or are we wasting our time here?" Sonji's hands were on her hips, her beautiful hips.

"I owe you an explanation, and—"

"I don't want an explanation, professor. But what I do want is for you to understand that what we had is . . ."

"What? Over? I will not allow you to turn this into a requiem for our relationship. What we've had is a grave misunderstanding."

"No, what we've had was an invention, a dream, make-believe. What we've been doing for the past few months is playacting. And you," she said with a dismissive gesture, "are a specter, a figment. As far as I'm concerned, you're not real, I only imagined that you were."

"Nonsense! I *am* real. And by heavens, Sonji, you *know* me."

"Really? Then why is my mind brimming with questions like, who are you? Are you Grayson? Are you Bart? Are you married with children? You're just too hard to figure out!"

"That's it, isn't it? It's too hard. I hate to break it to you, but most things in life are difficult, fraught with rapids and pitfalls. Half the time it's like pushing water. But you can't cave in at the first sign of hardship." .

"Do I look caved in to you?"

"You said you were a college student years ago. Why did you drop out?"

"I had obligations!"

"Oh, I don't doubt that. But I would also be willing to wager that being a college student was much more difficult than you had ever imagined. And that's the primary reason why you quit."

"You've got a lot of nerve."

"Yes, I have. For the first time in seven years, I've got plenty of nerve." He stepped closer. "Ever burn something, Sonji?"

"What?"

"While you were cooking . . . ever botch dinner? You probably decided at some point in your adult life that cooking was just too big of a hassle, and so rather than apply yourself in the culinary arena, you just decided to forgo it. Makes things quite a bit smoother, wouldn't you say?"

"Grayson, this is about you. Don't try to turn the tables here."

"I beg to differ. This is about *us*. And I'm not leaving until you realize that. So tell me. How soon after your first day in my class did you consider dropping it?"

She reached out to slap his face, but he grabbed her hand and held it in midair. "How soon?" he said more intently. Sonji struggled for a while and gave in. "I wanted to drop it that first day." She wasn't sure which had weakened her, the urgency in his eyes or the thought that she was carrying his child. But something had shaken her loose from the anger she held for him.

"It's taken me a long time to let go of my past. For the most part, I had severed my emotional ties. But I've had no real sense of closure until now. I've made sure that Veranda's welfare is no longer my responsibility."

Sonji's brow furrowed in confusion.

"Don't misunderstand. She will continue to be taken care of. It simply will not be by me."

"Grayson, is she really ill?"

"I'm afraid she's very ill. And for seven years I've felt responsible for her well-being. But her father was a good provider. The interest from his annuity alone is enough to take care of her for the rest of her life, if necessary.

"But I'm telling you this because I know I was wrong. I shouldn't have kept that aspect of my life hidden. But I couldn't take the chance that I would lose you. Please don't tell me I've lost you anyway."

She turned away. "Maybe if you had told me in the beginning. Maybe then I would have been prepared."

"Prepared! How does anyone prepare for the kind of love we have?" He walked around to face her again. "I don't know about you, but sometimes, when you touch me, I feel as though I've been hit by a Mack truck. Nothing on this earth could have prepared me for that."

He held her and pulled her close. "My Nzinga. My Great Elephant. My warrior woman."

She closed her eyes as if wincing in pain.

He pulled her closer. "Woman, don't you know I look for you in my *sleep?*"

She opened her eyes and stared into his. Everything she could have ever wanted was there. Hope. Tenderness. Fervor. Love. Adoration. And yes, honesty. And she knew she felt the same. She had since the beginning. But now she had more to consider. There was a child. And they had been so careful. But somehow, it was true. Now, she was determined to do what was best for the life developing inside her.

"It devastated me to think that you had hidden such important things from me. So now, I have to be honest with you."

The tears were coming. She could feel them approaching from the corners of her eyes and even somewhere below her stomach. How would he react? Having been through one tragedy, she was certain he would want to do everything in his power to prevent another, which probably meant he didn't want to bring another child into the world. But it was too late. And she was going to have this baby.

"What?" he said, concern wrinkling his face.

She couldn't speak. The tears were overflowing now. Slowly she looked down and placed her hand where the fruits of their love was growing. Then she looked up.

His eyes followed to where her hand rested. At first, he seemed even more confused. And then the realization widened his eyes and made him gasp. "A baby?" he asked, the words barely escaping his lips. Sonji nodded.

Grayson closed his eyes and dropped to one knee. He hugged Sonji to him and buried his head in her abdomen. She hugged him back and was surprised when she felt small tremors coming from his body. When he looked up, his face was as wet as hers.

She reached down slowly and cupped the side of his face in her hand. Then she used her thumbs to wipe away his tears. And in doing so, she wiped away all of the turmoil that had come between them recently in her heart. She wanted to give their love a clean start.

Grayson reached into his pocket and pulled out a black velvet jewelry box, his eyes intense with longing. "I believe this belongs to you."

Sonji stared, breathless, at the object in Grayson's hand. Her lip quivered as she took the box and opened it. Inside was a two-carat diamond set in a harvest gold band. Carved on each side of the band was a tiny scarab swirled in diamond dust.

A smile wider than the Nile consumed Sonji's entire face. Before Grayson could utter the question he'd wanted to ask for so long, she blurted her response. "Yes!"

He stood and hoisted her into his strong arms. Then he kissed her steadily, passionately, possessively—like a man to whom the world had just been delivered.

Sonji's happiness came in a parade on her face, and her eyes lit up like roman candles.

Lord help me, Grayson thought. *This woman and her dimples! Umph, Umph, Umph.*

Sixteen

"Get out!" Jerika and Sonji yelled in unison.

Grayson feigned a long face. "Now see. I was just coming to check on you fine ladies, and this is how you treat me?"

Jerika pointed a stern finger toward the living room. "Grayson Bartholomew, if you don't get out of my kitchen, I'm going to make Klarice come in here with us, and you won't be able to play with her until after dinner."

Grayson stubbed the tip of his shoe into the floor. The sound of his sigh carried heavily across the room. "All right. But you can't prevent me from stealing a kiss from my fiancée every now and then."

Grayson dashed up to where Sonji was sitting, planted a swift love peck on her forehead, and retreated quickly out of the kitchen.

"Aw, y'all oughten't be too hard on the man. He's just got a healthy appetite is all," Nzinga said.

"But Miss Zinga Mae, we haven't even started cooking good yet, and he's up in here. If this keeps on, we won't be finished with Christmas dinner until New Year's."

Sonji sat in front of a large, clear plastic bag full of green beans. She couldn't remember the last time she had snapped fresh green beans. The activity was comforting and familiar. Suddenly, she found herself nearly overwhelmed with a sense of happiness. She was right where she wanted to be—surrounded by a family she loved and who loved her.

She and Grayson had picked up her grandmother and headed to Kyle's house early that day. It had all been arranged. The two families would have dinner together and then she and Grayson would announce both their engagement and the pregnancy. But the ring on her finger was an obvious giveaway. So over coffee and getting-acquainted talk, they had confirmed the obvious.

"That's wonderful!"

"Oh, baby, I'm so glad for you."

"Congratulations, man."

"Why are you in a cage, Uncle Gray?"

"No, Crumbcake. Not *in a cage.* Engaged. That means I'm going to marry Sonji. She's going to be my wife."

"Oh," Klarice said. The implications of what she had just heard played across her face as she considered the meaning of her uncle's words.

The room fell silent, seemingly waiting for the current lady of Grayson's life to react to the statement.

"Will you still come over and play with me?" she asked, eyeing Sonji suspiciously.

"Of course!"

"Then I guess it's okay."

The people in the room breathed a psychic sigh of relief.

Sonji continued snapping green beans and smiled at the memory. She watched the exchange between Jerika and her grandmother. They had not met each other until that evening, but they were falling into sync as if they had been cooking together for years.

At first, Sonji was just their helper. She had peeled potatoes, chopped onions, grated cheese, and handed the two cooks pots, pans, bowls, and utensils. She had cleaned up behind them by rinsing dishes and loading the dishwasher. Then, she had decided that she wanted to help cook, and nothing they said was going to discourage her.

"I want to do the greens," she proclaimed.

"What!" the two women looked up questioningly at Sonji.

"You heard me." Smugness transmitted in Sonji's voice.

Nzinga's shoulders rose and fell. Sonji could tell her grandmother was laughing. She was not discouraged. "Well?"

Jerika folded in her lips for a moment and then spoke. "All right, missy. The greens are in the refrigerator. You might as well wash them now."

"Humph," she muttered, squeezing past her grandmother to get to the refrigerator. Sonji opened the vegetable bins and retrieved several bunches of greens—turnip, mustard, and collard.

Then she began preparing them. "And I don't want any help either," she stated emphatically.

Jerika and Nzinga shared a good-natured laugh between them. Sonji knew that their laughter was not mean-spirited. And she decided right then and there that she was going to make the best greens either of them had ever tasted.

By the time they all sat down to eat, Sonji was famished. Unlike her grandmother and Jerika, who had nibbled and sampled a little while cooking, Sonji was too keyed up to eat. She was excited and elated about her family, old and new, being together, and exhilarated by the news she longed to share with everyone.

Several times, Grayson had offered her a knowing glance. It calmed her and reminded her of their agreement to wait until after the meal to share their wonderful news.

Jerika sat at one end of the dinner table. Kyle spoke at the other. "Shall we join hands and bow our heads?

"Heavenly Father. Lord Almighty. Maker of *all* things. We come before you this day filled with honor and praise-giving. All glory to you who have poured out your generous benevolence upon us. We offer our thanks and songs of hosanna."

"Yes, Lord."

"From she who was first among us to he who is yet to be, we are eternally grateful, for your favors have come without measure. Your grace has given us life. Your mercy has given us love. Your divine nature has given us one another. Your Holy Spirit has given us this day, and we take it humbly to sanctify your name."

"Yes, yes."

"In this harvest home, in this marvelous feasting, we bear witness to your works and your unchanging hand that pushed up the mountains, destroyed armies, created men, brought together families, and healed festering wounds. We know that your blessings outnumber the granules of sand. We give glory to each and every one that has been bestowed upon us."

"Well . . ."

"By your word, we pray that thy perfect will be done."

"Amen."

"Hey-man," Klarice said, attempting to echo the grownups.

The feast before them rivaled that shown in the movie *Soul Food*. There was turkey at one end of the table and ham at the other. In between were generous dishes of stuffing, mashed potatoes, green bean casserole, macaroni and cheese, gravy, cranberry sauce, corn bread, baked beans, potato salad, and of course, greens. Even the dog, Smedley, who usually stayed out-side, was invited in to enjoy the bone from the ham. Sonji imagined Jerika and Kyle having leftovers for weeks.

By the time dinner began, Sonji was ravenous. Dishes were passed, glasses were clinked, and plates were filled. Then the soft murmur of conversation took over the room, and Sonji was happier than she could ever remember being. When something under the table startled her, she tensed for a moment. Then she real-ized that Grayson had removed one of his shoes and was trying to initiate a game of footsie. Sonji giggled, then ignored him—determined to let his silliness make her even more giddy than she already was.

After everyone had settled into their plates, Grayson made a strange sound.

"Oh, oh, oh!" he said, chewing.

Sonji was at once concerned. "What's the matter?" she asked, turning to him.

"Zinga Mae, these greens are heavenly."

"Ooh, I wish I could say I'm the cause of all that happiness on your face."

Grayson turned to his sister-in-law. "Jerika, you've outdone yourself."

She shook her head. "Uh-uh. Wasn't me."

The expression on his face went from confusion to realization. "Sonji?"

"Yep," she said, proudly.

Grayson released a deep roar of laughter. "Well I'll be," he said, smiling warmly at her. "My warrior woman can cook!" He kissed Sonji on the forehead and then laughed again. Sonji's grandmother shook her head.

"He sure tickles me," she said.

Nzinga looked from Grayson to Kyle. "Where's the other Mr. Gilmore?"

Grayson frowned. "What other Mr. Gilmore?"

"You mean our dad?" Kyle asked.

"No, no. I mean your brother. Y'all do have a younger brother."

Grayson and Kyle shook their heads in unison, then Kyle spoke up. "No, ma'am. It's just me and big head, here."

Sonji's grandmother sat back and looked up. "Your folks ever stay on Hawthorne Street?"

"Sure did," Kyle responded.

"Did they go to Mount Zion Baptist Church?" she asked.

Now it was Grayson's turn. "For years."

"Humph. I coulda sworn the Gilmores had three babies."

"Nope, Zinga Mae. The only knuckleheads you have to deal with are me and my brother."

"I see," she said.

When the main course was finished, Sonji, Jerika, and Klarice brought out one dessert each. Peach cobbler, pound cake, and chocolate chip cookies.

Kyle wrapped an arm around his wife and brought her to him. Then he kissed her enlarged abdomen and patted her on the backside. Grayson and Sonji exchanged glances and knowing smiles. She would like nothing more than to blurt out their good news, but she knew that Grayson wanted to be the one to share it, and he was waiting for the right time.

"I can't eat another bite," Grayson said, pushing back from the table.

"Uncle Gray is full," Klarice said, chuckling.

Nzinga sat forward and smiled. "I'll bet you never thought you'd see that day, did you, honey?"

"Nope," she said, putting her hands in front of her mouth, obscuring her wide grin.

"You ladies prepared a wonderful meal," Kyle remarked wiping his hands on his napkin. "Simply wonderful."

Jerika glowed in her husband's compliments. "Well, you just remember that come July. It will be the Kyle and Bart show."

"Deal!" the men said in unison.

Kyle leaned toward his brother. "Speaking of the Kyle and Bart show, are you going fishing with me next year or what?"

"I think I'm going to have to pass on that, little brother."

"Man, you been putting me off for too long. What gives?"

Grayson's face lit up the room and he turned his attention to Sonji. "I may be needed at my wife's side to deliver our baby."

Sonji and Grayson held hands and stared wistfully into each other's eyes.

"What?" Kyle responded.

"Sonji's pregnant." Grayson said, proudly.

"Wow!"

"Congratulations, Bart."

Nzinga leaned over toward Kyle and opened her hand. "Cash only please. I don't trust that plastic stuff."

Kyle reached into his pocket and retrieved his billfold. He took out ten dollars and handed it to the older woman sitting like a wise sage at the end of the table.

Sonji was astonished. "Grandma! You made a bet?"

Nzinga smiled her old-lady smile. "As bright as you've been shining all day? I tried to tell Mr. Kyle here that you were in the family way. He didn't believe me, so I told him to put his currency where his conviction is." She looked smugly at them all and stuffed the bill down her bosom. "Congratulations, baby."

Klarice looked at Sonji with serious eyes. "My mom is preger-nint. That means a brother or a sister."

Just then, baby Kya picked the perfect time to chime in. "Daa-baa!" she added.

After dinner, Grayson and Kyle put up the food with the help of Klarice. Kya napped quietly in Nzinga's arms, while Sonji and Jerika sat in the den drinking coffee. Jerika pulled out a photo album and leafed through the pages with Sonji.

She pointed out pictures of Grayson looking like a Mack Daddy in purple suit, matching brim, Florshiem shoes, and gold chain.

"Bart must have been about twenty then."

"I don't get it, Jerika. How can he be so different sometimes?"

"The man you're seeing now, that's the *real* Grayson Gilmore. But marrying Veranda changed him."

Sonji winced. She was hoping she wouldn't have to hear that name anytime soon.

"The fact is that he and Veranda have a history. There's no denying that. Acknowledge it. Deal with it. Just don't let it grip you. Trust me, I know. When you let a man's past hold you like a vice, can't no man break through all that metal." Jerika smiled at Sonji. "Not even those beautiful, black men of ours!"

Sonji listened raptly as Jerika went on with her story.

"She convinced him that status and social standing were the only important things in life. He wasn't even going to pursue a Ph.D. until Veranda dang near threw a tantrum."

"She sounds awful."

"Veranda was a spoiled vixen. Made Bart pretend to be a bourgeois Negro with a chip on his shoulder instead of the man he is—the man you love. After a while, it just stuck."

Sonji sighed. "I like this Grayson much better."

"Well just remember, he's in there somewhere. If anyone can bring it out of him, you can."

"I hope so."

Just then Grayson cleared his throat behind them.

"I better go see what Klarice and her dad are up to." Jerika left the den, touching Grayson's shoulder as she passed. "Congratulations again, Bart."

He nodded. It was obvious that he had been standing there for more than a few moments.

Grayson sat down next to Sonji and stared straight ahead.

"I used to have the most dreadful nightmares that Veranda was dead and not Gray, Jr."

"Oh, Grayson."

"I would wake up cold and sweaty. And damn near frantic. That's when I took up running."

He took her hand in his. "But now I think that my physical running may have been a symbol of what I was doing emotionally, spiritually. Somewhere in my bitter memories, I had lost the ability to forgive. And I've been running away from that."

He turned to her.

"But finding you . . . loving you . . . makes it possible to do what I couldn't—stop blaming Veranda for Gray Jr.'s death. And to absolve myself of the guilt I've felt since she's been ill. Wanting a future with you has compelled me to be a better person today. Right now."

He brought her hand to his lips and kissed it. Sonji's skin warmed to his touch.

"I'm sorry I didn't tell you about all of this. I was an imbecile."

Sonji ran her free hand through the tufts of Grayson's thick hair. "You're not the imbecile, I am. I should have known that you wouldn't betray me. I should have trusted you. But like so many other things in my life, I let it go. I lacked follow-through."

"You sure showed follow-through when you wrote that letter to the dean on my behalf."

"Yeah, I guess so. I guess we've both grown some, huh?"

Grayson grinned and placed a hand on her abdomen. "With more growing to do."

"Well," Sonji said, placing her hand on top of Grayson's, "I had better go check on my grandmother. When I last saw her, she and Kya were joined at the belly."

"Wait. Before you go, I have something for you."

Sonji's eyebrows and nose wrinkled with curiosity. Grayson withdrew a university envelope from his jacket pocket.

"The department secretary was supposed to mail this, but I wanted to deliver it in person."

Sonji's heart thudded like a jackhammer. She took the envelope and quickly opened it. The document inside was nine pages long. Nine pages of initiative, dogged determination, and a deep desire to see the toughest class she had ever taken through to completion.

She closed her eyes and unfolded the paper. Then slowly she opened her eyes. The large letter grade written in bold red on the page was *A+*. Sonji threw her arms around Grayson and squealed her delight.

"Thank you! Thank you!"

"Thanks aren't necessary. You wrote the best paper in the class."

Sonji gently touched the side of Grayson's face. He tenderly touched hers.

"I love you," they said with one spirit, with one heart.

Epilogue

By the time Grayson and Sonji arrived at Sebastian's apartment the next night, the place was already packed with people. Most of them were students from Barnett, but some were faculty, family, and other friends.

"Habari Gani," Grayson heard over the music he recognized from one of the CDs he borrowed from Kyle as Boney James.

"Umoja," he responded in the correct greeting for the day. He placed a hand in the small of Sonji's back and attempted as best he could to guide her through the throng of people.

There was a daring mixture of burning incense and candles in the air. Folding into the atmosphere were the decorations appropriate for the celebration—gourds, fruit, a bandera, and various zawadi. Topping off the comfortable ambiance were sounds of generous laughter and hearty conversation.

As they made their way into the living room, there was still no sign of the hosts.

"Professor, Sonji, Habari Gani!" Capiz said.

"Umoja!" Sonji replied. "How are you?"

"I'm great. Hey, I heard the news. I just wanted to wish you two congratulations."

"Thanks," they responded together.

"Oh, my gosh," Sonji said, looking concerned.

"What?" Grayson asked.

"We are starting to sound like Andi and Sebastian."

Grayson's left eyebrow rose above the rim of his glasses. "Is that such a bad thing?" he asked.

Sonji didn't have to think about the answer to that at all. "No. As a matter of fact, it's a wonderful th—"

Before she could finish her sentence, Andi came barreling around the corner with Sebastian in hot pursuit. The couples narrowly escaped collision.

"Miss Sonji," Andi said, beaming.

"Soon to be Mrs. Gilmore," Sebastian added.

Sonji's first inclination was to shake her head. But she could only hope that her relationship with Grayson be as buoyant and lively as the couple standing before her. "Hi, you two."

Grayson tipped his head. "Miss Simmons. Mr. Dupree."

"We brought some sparkling cider," Sonji said, offering them the bottle she was carrying. "But we didn't know that there would be so many people here."

"Usually there aren't," Andi said, taking the cider. "But a lot of the students you see are from the group of us that banded together to voice our support of the professor. That one incident created a bond between many of us."

Grayson looked around. He did recognize many of the faces from those who had been with him in the dean's office. The thought of all those students coming to his aid still gave him a tremendous sense of pride and gratefulness.

"We'll go put this cider in a cooler. Why don't you join the others in the living room?"

Soon after their arrival, the official celebration began. They started by singing "Lift Every Voice and

Sing." Then Andi recited a Kwanzaa prayer that she had written. Sebastian poured libations to honor the ancestors and then he asked permission from Grayson, who just so happened to be the oldest person in the room, if he would give the elder's permission to continue with the ceremony.

Then Andi, who was the youngest person in the room, lit the Unity candle on the kinara, and each person, irrespective of race or ethnicity, stated the ways in which he or she had practiced the principle of Unity over the past year.

Byron Moore, who had been relatively quiet that evening, gave a touching testament to his practice of the principle by recounting the incident with Grayson, the dean of the arts and sciences school and the angry students. He finished his talk by mentioning what he thought was the most important union—the union between man and wife. Then he congratulated Grayson and Sonji on their engagement.

When everyone had a chance to share something about Unity, they all formed a line into the dining room to partake of the potluck dinner.

By eleven P.M., most everyone had gone. Grayson, Sonji, and Byron were the only stragglers.

"One of these days I hope to be as happy as you brothers are," Byron said, looking at the two men then motioning to Sonji and Andi.

Andi's eyes widened with curiosity. "Aren't you seeing anyone, Byron?"

"No, Andi. I'm not," he said, shaking his head in exaggerated disappointment.

"Baby?" Sebastian said, sitting up. He reached out for her, but it was too late. Andi was already up and had crossed the room to his desk.

"I can fix that," she said, turning on the PC.

"Baby, stay out of the man's business."

But everyone in the room knew it was too late. In a flourish, Andi's hands moved across the keyboard and moments later the red, green, and black homepage for BlackLuv appeared on her computer screen. Sonji and Grayson smiled knowingly and held hands.

"What's that?" Byron asked.

"It's the gateway to your soul mate," Andi responded, glowing like a celestial spirit. She combed her fingers through her untamable hair and turned to Byron. "First, you'll need a profile."

A NOTE FROM THE AUTHOR

Thanks for going on Grayson and Sonji's journey with me. I hope you found it to be a fulfilling one. I know I did.

Many people say that mental illness is one of the best kept secrets in the African-American community. Many of us know at least one family who has, under the best intentions, attempted to "mainstream" someone who might very well benefit from professional therapy and treatment. As this issue gains more and more media attention, I hope you are reminded that the healing process can begin anytime, anywhere—if we let it.

ABOUT THE AUTHOR

Kim Louise is a resident of Omaha, Nebraska, where she lives with her son, Steve. She has a bachelor's degree in journalism from the University of Nebraska at Omaha, and a master's degree in Adult Learning and Development from Drake University. Kim's articles and poetry have been published in numerous regional and national publications. She is also the winner of several writing contests, slogan contests, and a poetry slam.

In her "spare" time, Kim enjoys card making, calligraphy, surfing the Net, writing poetry, and public speaking.